UNDER THE

scarlet tree

UNDER THE

scarlet tree

To Leslie and Luanne,

I hope that you
enjoy this book!

Danielle R. Wilson

DANIELLE R. WILSON

Formatting by Daniel J. Mawhinney
www.40DayPublishing.com

Cover design by Jonna Feavel Thames
www.40DayGraphics.com

Printed in the United States of America

introduction

I knew what they were. I suspected it would eventually happen. I just didn't expect it to spiral out of control this quickly.

From my understanding, it started in a laboratory in the middle of Nowhere, North Dakota. There was a local doctor named Landon Kovich, who was widely known within his community for his uncanny ability to cure the incurable. Locals said he had the hands of God. Still, the good doctor wasn't immune to hardships. According to local newsletters (later released to the public), his young wife had died from a brain tumor. The man who cures the incurable, couldn't save his own wife. Once the news of her death was made public, the locals lost faith in the doctor. Driven mad by his desire to solve this mystery, the good doctor dove back into his work. Dr. Kovich was determined to find a cure for brain cancer—he needed to avenge the death of his wife and restore his good name. He made it his life's mission to find a cure, and for a while, everyone thought he had.

Reports started showing up in different places—the news, social media, and the ever-present gossip grapevine. The locally known doctor's name became known statewide, nationwide, and eventually worldwide. There were a lot of different rumors milling around about the progress that Dr. Kovich had made. It was reported he created a drug called Charanil, named after his late wife Charlene. He began experimenting with lab rats and tracked his results. When promising results began to show, Dr. Kovich took his results to the medical community to get it approved for human trials. The medical community exploded with chatter revolving around Dr. Kovich and Charanil. Some people were skeptical, but the CDC was hopeful and approved experimentation with chimpanzees. Another eight months went by and Dr. Kovich released news that the chimpanzees were beginning to show positive results. Against medical approval, Dr. Kovich allegedly began testing Charanil on a volunteer terminally ill brain cancer patient, Jason Farren. He was illegally testing the drug on humans, against all medical ethics. He managed to stay under the radar while doing these trials. It wasn't until Jason Farren had been cured from his brain cancer that Dr. Kovich shared his findings with the medical community.

The story blew up and spread across America like wildfire. Although Dr. Kovich conducted the tests illegally, no one seemed to care. Everyone was thrilled with his amazing discovery. He had done the impossible—he had created a cure for brain cancer. Terminally ill patients flocked to North Dakota for their chance to receive the lifesaving Charanil. Patients' tumors began to shrink, and within weeks they were cured of their brain cancers. Dr. Kovich became the most popular man in America. Everyone wanted a chance to try Charanil.

What America did not know was, Dr. Kovich made the mistake of not keeping track of the experimental animals. He had accomplished what he wanted—his life's mission was fulfilled. He had cured an incurable disease with Charanil and became wealthy and famous as a result. He didn't give his experimental animals a second thought. Had Dr. Kovich kept tabs on them, he might have foreseen what was about to happen.

Jason Farren lived a healthy, cancer-free life for about five months. He was on all the day-time talk shows and news stations. America got pleasure from following his miraculous story. Then, he went missing. Once officials were finally able to find him, it was too late. His body was discovered. Apparently, he had a heart attack—his heart just stopped working. It didn't make sense—he had been healthy as a horse since completing his treatment of Charanil. They kept his body locked up at the morgue to investigate what had happened to him.

Within the next few days, the same thing happened to another brain cancer patient who was also cured by Charanil. Then, more patients died. The media kept the public as up to date as possible, but it wasn't enough, there were too many people dying to keep up with. The treatment Dr. Kovich created was beginning to backfire. It was causing distress to the patient's heart, resulting in heart failure. No one could have predicted what the scientists weren't telling us. The deceased patients had no heartbeat—but they had brain activity.

What happened next was shocking. Jason Farren came back to life and was biting people. When I heard the news, I knew what it was. With the zombie phenomenon so popular, how could I not guess what was happening? Some people thought it was a hoax. Jason Farren had taken a bite out of the coroner's cheek after coming back to life. The only explanation was the dead were coming back to life. They became the undead. Society didn't seem worried about it, there were hardly any cases and the military would contain the issue. I went about my routine as normal, as did the rest of the world. No one believed it would turn out to be this way. No one was prepared for the heights to which this would escalate to.

The word zombie was such a cliché. I called them the undead because that's what they were. When I thought of zombies, I thought of people who looked unrested, slow moving, and out of it. This was not how the undead were. The undead were just that, dead but not dead. Dead because they had no beating heart or emotions, undead because they could do pretty much anything else. They still functioned like humans; they were just as fast as we are, and their bodies operated like ours. They could figure out how to get in and out of places. They were smart. They had advantages on us. They were hard to kill and their senses were excellent, they could hear and smell everything.

The undead were practically unbeatable, which is why the situation spiraled out of control. I say practically because there was hope. There was a way to stop them. The alive just needed to gain control and take the world back.

prologue

Silence filled the car. I glanced back at Logan; his heavy, ragged breathing had leveled out and returned to normal. His body posture was loosening up and he relaxed against the seat. He rubbed his eyes with his dirty hands and sighed, relieved to be alive. June and Blake sat next to Logan, looking at Logan with wide eyes.

"Do you mind switching spots with Elana? You're covered in blood and scaring Blake," June asked Logan, oblivious to the fact that her son almost got us all killed.

"I'm not pulling over for them to play musical chairs," I replied to June. I glanced in the rearview mirror and didn't see any undead, but I still didn't want to chance it by pulling over.

"It's fine Mya, pull over. I would like to grab a water out of the back anyway. I want to try to wash some of this blood off. It smelled like their bodies had been rotting for days, not a few hours," I pulled the car over.

Logan grabbed a water from the back, washed his face off and took a sip and then passed the bottle around to everyone in the car. Elana moved to the backseat—Logan moved to the front. I put the SUV back in drive and continued down the road.

There were no undead aimlessly wandering around, looking for humans to feed on. There were no signs of human life either. The leaves revealed fall had arrived—bright vibrant reds, yellows, greens, and oranges. All the colors blended, creating perfect harmony. The world was ironically beautiful and hideous at the same time. I felt hopeful that even in the betrayal of our universe that the beautiful things in the world will conquer.

I relaxed, confident that we were safe for the moment. I let my thoughts drift back to my childhood. When our parents passed away, I was only eighteen years old. It was the most difficult time of my life. My parents were out on a date to a club in the city. The club caught on fire, and the roof collapsed. My parents and seventeen other people died that night.

Ally, my older sister, was out partying while I stayed home watching after our younger brother, Logan, and our baby sister, Lilianna. When our parents didn't come home in the early morning hours, I began to panic. I hoped they had too much to drink and got a hotel room for the night.

The next morning, a couple of police officers arrived at our front door. They informed us our parents had been killed in a tragic accident. The fire broke me—leaving a hole in my heart and my life. The devastation shattered our lives, changing them forever. I couldn't contain my grief. Neither could my sisters. Logan, being the only son, had been brought up following typical gender roles. He was expected to be a man and control his emotions. He treated this situation like he was raised to do. So, he checked his emotions and took care of us. Logan was the reason we were able to move past it and continue with our lives. All but one of us.

Even though Ally was the oldest, she always struggled emotionally. When we were growing up, my parents continually stated she was sensitive. It would take almost nothing to set her off in a crying fit. According to my mom, she had cried a lot as a baby—she was never satisfied. Growing up, Ally was a loose cannon—a wild child. She was constantly out partying, taking drugs, and sleeping with random guys. After our parents died, Ally had the hardest time. She struggled with their death more than our fourteen-year-old sister. She barely got out of bed. She wouldn't talk to anyone. Logan tried his hardest to get her back up on her feet, but nothing worked.

Two weeks later, at the age of 21, she killed herself. She had taken too many pills and overdosed. She killed herself in our parents' bedroom, on their bed. She had written a suicide note saying she couldn't go on anymore. She apologized in her note. I remember thinking, *how ridiculous. Why are you sorry, Ally? Because you left us?* We didn't want her apology, we wanted her to live. The whole situation ticked me off. I resented her for leaving us behind to struggle. I resented her for being selfish and not thinking about the rest of us, especially Lilianna.

Lilianna found Ally dead in our parent's room later that day after school. It broke my heart that she was the one who found our sister. She attended therapy for a long time and suffered from horrible nightmares. She would wake up in the middle of the night screaming, hot tears streaming down her face. The nightmares subsided the older she got, but she still got them occasionally. The last time she came home, I heard her screaming. Instead of instinctively running for her, I let her cope on her own. She could handle them. She had to.

After Ally committed suicide, I became the big sister. Even though I was only eighteen, I had taken on the responsibility of caring for Logan, who was sixteen, and Lilianna, who was fourteen. We did have extended family around that offered to take them in, but I said no. We needed to stay together to keep our lives as normal as possible. We had inherited a decent amount of money from the deaths of our parents. Enough money for us to survive and for me to go to college. Logan was older and he didn't need a lot of parenting. Lilianna, however, needed an adult around. She was still so young. There was so much she needed help with. I took on the role of a mother in all facets; I packed her lunches, did her laundry, helped with homework, chauffeured her around, taught her right from wrong, and helped her grow up. Logan combined the big brother and dad roles. She never wanted to disappoint him. With all the bad that happened in our lives, Lilianna was still able to overcome everything and grow into a beautiful young woman.

Two years later, when Logan turned eighteen, he joined the marines. Losing him was a hard pill to swallow. I didn't realize how much I relied on him until he left us. I didn't want him to go, I wanted him to go to college and make a career for himself. He was determined to do this though. I gave in and accepted that this was his decision. I couldn't deprive him of that. He deserved to do what made him happy. Plus, he swore when his tour was over, he would go to school and have it paid for by the marines. When it came down to it, I was happy for him. Even though I didn't agree with his career choice at the time, I was proud of the man he had become. The night before he left, Lilianna and I made him his favorite dinner, homemade macaroni and cheese. We had a mini celebration for him. The next day we saw him off at the airport. With tears in our eyes and pride in our hearts, we waved goodbye as he disappeared into the terminal.

Once Logan left, it was just Lilianna and me. We missed Logan terribly. It was weird to not have a male presence in our life. Two months later, I met Scott. He quickly became a part of the family. He was always around. He helped us out a lot with things Lilianna and I weren't able to do. He was also great with Lilianna, always joking around with her and giving her advice. It was in those moments I knew I was going to marry him.

When Lilianna graduated from high school, she wanted to go to school at Indiana State University. I didn't like the idea of her being that far away. As nervous as I was to let her go, I knew she deserved to follow her dreams, just as Logan had. I couldn't hold her back for my own selfish reasons.

In the four years that she was at school, I didn't see her much. She would come home over Christmas, summer break, and other random special occasions. It was hard to deal with at first, but Scott helped to distract me. Our relationship continued to blossom. Lilianna graduated early, earning her Bachelor's in Psychology. Next, she enrolled in the master's program at Indiana State University.

A year after Lilianna left for college, Logan was released from the marines on medical discharge. Having him home again was wonderful but challenging. His deployment changed him. He was harder—more serious. He would react in the most extreme ways to the simplest of things. Someone would ring our doorbell and he would drop to the floor and take cover. When Logan began attending therapy, his mental state started to improve. He met his girlfriend Elana and started a new life of his own.

Our odd little family often engaged in conversation about the current entertainment phenomenon—zombies—and had discussed the 'what-ifs' when imagining zombies being real. The idea of the dead becoming undead was mesmerizing. We all talked about how we wouldn't be dumb like everyone in the movies. We were positive we would survive.

It was silly to be so naïve—so foolish to fantasize about something like that, something that could destroy the world and everyone we cared about. I was reckless to think we would make it and be okay—that I wouldn't experience the pain and despair portrayed in so many story lines. I was about to learn how wrong I was.

chapter one

The first day of the end of the world, Wednesday October 21st, started slow. I had worked every day that week except Wednesday. I didn't take the day off because of "the cure of doom" (a term the media coined for what had been going on), I decided to take it off because I was not feeling well. I wretched one last time into the toilet, leaned back, and took a deep breath of fresh air. I flushed the toilet, stood up, and turned toward the sink. I leaned down and washed my face and mouth with water. I looked up into the mirror, staring into my blue eyes. My blonde hair was tossed up into a messy bun and my face glistened from being flushed. I brushed the necklace around my neck, fingering the letters of my name, *Mya*. It was a Christmas gift from my husband, Scott. I took another deep breath, certain I was done being sick and started the shower.

As I washed the illness away, I thought of recent events. The media had only released pieces of information, never the full story. It was hard to tell the difference between reality and media-spun bullshit. I believed in the cure of doom. I knew something wasn't right about that Charanil drug. I wasn't worried about what was happening out in North Dakota—in the middle of the country—I lived on the east coast in Pennsylvania. Rumors did begin to surface of cases in Philadelphia, but they were just rumors.

I turned the shower off and got out before I let the rumors fill my head with worry. Things were going to be fine. In my towel, I sat on the chest at the end of the bed, scrolling through social media. Most of the posts were related to the cure of doom patients who were dead and coming back to life. *Maybe this is serious,* I briefly thought. I shook my head and put the phone on the bed and proceeded to get dressed.

Over the course of the morning, I folded laundry, did dishes, and dusted the house, trying to keep myself busy. I had the news channel on and would check in periodically. Occasionally there would be an announcement at the bottom of the screen with another new victim of the cure of doom, this time it was in Philadelphia. I slowly sat on the sofa surprised by this. The cases were getting closer to where I lived in Springfield, Pennsylvania. I started to panic on the inside, my heart racing. This whole thing was really turning out to be a pandemic.

The television then displayed a female news reporter standing outside of a hospital. The scene behind her looked chaotic—ambulances loading people in and out, family members rushing their loved ones into the ER. In a catatonic state from the scene playing out before me, I nearly didn't hear my phone ring.

A jingle brought me back to reality. I looked at the caller ID, it was my brother Logan. I answered the call and Logan immediately dashed into a rant about the cost of cigarettes. Still distracted by the news, I was only half-listening to my brother whine about his disgusting habit.

"Mya, are you listening to me?" Logan asked on the other end of the call. Logan and I talked two to three times a week.

At the bottom of the television screen in big bold red letters, it said, THE DEAD ARE RISING. My jaw hung open in disbelief as I watched people on the television running around screaming for their lives. There was a small cluster of people surrounding another person who was laying on the ground, it looked like they were helping him. I quickly realized they were eating him. Blood was everywhere, all over the sides of buildings, the ground, on people. Everyone was frantic. It looked as if I had a movie on. The entire scene had drastically changed in a matter of minutes. I scanned the screen to see where the location was, praying it wasn't anywhere near here. It read South Philadelphia.

I was in shock—I couldn't catch my breath. It was the most graphic news report I'd ever seen. Every report up until then had only discussed the death of the patients. It was showing the dead patients—except they weren't dead—they were alive and running around in their hospital gowns with blood smeared all over them. The patients were up and out of the hospital feasting on people in the streets. Only an hour from where I live.

"Logan, you need to turn on the news, now." He scrambled on the other end to find the remote and then the screams in the background mirrored mine. We both watched in silence as the chaos unfolded in front of us. The female news reporter was still standing there like an idiot and she became the meal of two middle aged women. The camera continued to roll as her flesh was being consumed by the undead women. Two minutes later the channel went static-gray.

"Mya, what is going on? There's no way that was real. What is happening?" The panic was evident in Logan's voice. My brain couldn't process his persistent questions.

"Go get Elana and come to my house. We need to go get Lilianna in Indiana." Logan and I both hung up.

The phone rang three and a half times before Scott finally answered. "Scott, Scott, where are you? You need to come home. It's happening, it's actually happening." I sounded frantic, but hell, I was frantic. I didn't want to be next. I wanted to live and get out of there.

"Baby, calm down. What's happening? I'm on my way but traffic is bad today, I won't be there for a while."

I sighed before I began my explanation. "It's happening, here in Philadelphia, the cure of doom. One died at a Philly hospital and on the news…there were people running around screaming. Some of them covered in blood being chased, other people were chasing them. All those rumors, it's happening. Scott, you need to get home now!"

Scott and I met when we were in college. We both attended Widener University. We met in statistics class our sophomore year. He tutored me one day after class and I became infatuated with him. As he helped me, I would study him more than the equations. His forehead creased when he concentrated hard on a solution. His green eyes would sparkle, and his grin would reach from ear to ear when I finally got an answer right. He made me feel good about myself. During our tutoring sessions, Scott decided he wanted to become a math teacher. Once the semester was over, our tutoring sessions came to an end. I was worried I wouldn't see him anymore. Little did I know, Scott felt the same way I did.

After our class final, he walked up to me and asked me out to dinner. I could tell he was extremely nervous, he stuttered over the word date at least three times before he was finally able to get it out. Scott picked me up at exactly seven o'clock. He brought flowers and held the door open. He was a true gentleman. He dressed to perfection—he even ironed his shirt. I knew he was exceptional, and I couldn't wait to get to know him better. Over dinner we laughed and flirted, we even held hands. The rest, as they say, was history. We fell in love and had been happily together ever since.

We married the year after graduation. Scott took a job at Ridley High School in Folsom as a math teacher. I pursued my dreams of becoming a physical therapist and landed a job at Springfield Hospital. Just a year prior, we bought our first house. We were the picture-perfect couple. We sent out change of address cards and took a picture while standing in front of our new house on Harwicke Road.

Earlier that morning, after losing my breakfast for the third day in a row, I found out that our lives were about to change for the better. The stick showed a plus sign. I could not wait to tell Scott the news. It wasn't exactly our plan, but it was something we had talked about. The news would have to hold off until we got to safety.

UNDER THE SCARLET TREE

Waiting for Scott and Logan to arrive, I nervously chewed off my fingernails as I paced the floor. Peering out the window, I could see my neighbors rushing around to get out of town. Far off into the distance, toward the city, the sky was filled with thick black smoke.

I watched my neighbors load their cars with suitcases and boxes and hastily shuffle their kids into their cars. I left the track I had created in the floorboards to pack the essentials.

In the cellar, I grabbed a bin labeled 'Mya's summer clothes' and dumped the contents. I loaded the canned soups, canned vegetables, beans, and bags of ramen into the bin. Upstairs, I rummaged through the kitchen. I filled the bin with crackers, granola bars, band-aids, and medicine. Everything that was nonperishable went into the bin—my cupboards left bare. I put all the kitchen knives into the bin, in hopes all I learned through zombie movies about puncturing the brain was true.

I put the bin down next to my maple wood front door and went upstairs. I collected the biggest suitcase I owned and threw it on the bed. I packed several pairs of socks, underwear, two comfortable outfits, our warmest jackets, and blankets for Scott and myself. I stuffed everything into the suitcase, sitting on it to zipper it shut. I went to my closet and grabbed my running shoes, a pair of my comfiest yoga pants and hoodie, and put them on. I lugged the suitcase down the steps and put it next to the bin. Back upstairs, in the hall closet was where I stored extra toiletries. I held my hoodie out creating a makeshift basket, and put all the toothpaste, toothbrushes, deodorant, and medicines into it. I carefully ran back down the steps and dumped the contents into the bin. I hurried back up my carpeted steps for what could be the last time ever. I snatched the big bag of toilet paper, tissues, and paper towels and put them by the front door as well.

Back at the window, I checked for any signs of either my brother or husband—nothing. I glanced around the room, scanning for anything else I might need. As my eyes surveyed the room, they landed on my wedding photo. My heart lurched—how could I possibly leave that behind? I started thinking of all the family photos that were up around the house. I began running around, taking all of them down to bring with me. I ended up with more than I could carry. *I am being ridiculous.* I took a deep breath and spread the pictures out around me. I pulled my favorites out from their frames—my wedding picture, one of my siblings and myself, an old picture of my parents, my college graduation picture, and my favorite picture of Scott and I goofing around. I found a safe pocket in my suitcase and tucked the photos safely away.

I flipped through the television for any news updates. All the stations were static. I returned to pacing a track into the floorboards, periodically looking out the window. *What is taking them so long?*

I did another pace and checked the window again. My brother's blue Subaru was drifting around the street-corner. He swerved to gain control of it and slammed the brakes as he parked in the middle of my front lawn.

Logan and Elana rushed out of the car, tripping over themselves, not bothering to shut the doors. They were accompanied by a round-faced, middle-aged woman and a little boy, presumably her son. In my brother's hands was a Louisville Slugger baseball bat smeared in blood. My brother was six feet tall and built like a marine. His white sweatshirt was splattered with blood. Elana, his girlfriend, was significantly shorter. Elana's clothes were torn and blood-stained. I opened the door and they rushed by me, as if they were being chased by the undead.

My brother embraced me and said, "Mya, I'm happy that you're okay. It's a different world out there. These dead people are taking over everything. I'm surprised to see your neighborhood is untouched. It won't be that way for long, we need to get out of here. They're just a few blocks away." Logan was operating with a sense of urgency. He picked up my packed bin and suitcase and reached for the doorknob.

"Logan wait, we can't go. Scott isn't here yet. He should be here soon. Please, let's wait a couple more minutes," I pleaded to my brother, the desperation clear in my voice. Logan hung his head in frustration but knew there was no convincing me to leave behind my husband.

"I'm going to pack up your SUV." Logan picked up the bin and suitcase that I had placed next to the front door and headed toward the garage. I knew his patience wouldn't last long.

Elana was slowly rocking in her seat at my kitchen table, her brown, blood-soaked hair swaying back and forth. Her usually green eyes were a dim gray and were fixated on a crack in the floor. I gently placed my hand on her shoulder. She jumped and almost fell from the chair. "Elana it's okay, it's Mya. What happened?" I asked. When no answer came, I asked again.

"She was attacked, at our apartment complex," said the round-faced woman. "I'm June. I live in the apartment underneath hers. This is my son Blake. When we saw Elana and her boyfriend running down the steps, we begged for them to take us with. I'm a single mom and I don't know anything about protecting us from this. The apartment complex was quiet and then we heard screams coming from Elana's apartment. Next, I heard Logan's footsteps and saw him rushing up the stairs. A few minutes later they came down, all covered in blood. I didn't ask any questions, I just begged for them to take us." I could tell she was nervous about being there. She kept playing with a string hanging off the bottom of her sweater. "I know that we're just strangers, but please don't make us leave. We don't have anywhere to go."

"No June, of course you can stay." I gave her shoulder a soft squeeze and went to the sink. I grabbed a wet paper towel to tend to Elana's abrasions. I stroked Elana's long caramel-colored brown hair out of her face and began cleaning the cuts on her arms. When I first reached for her hand, she quickly pulled it away and backed up a little. "It's okay, you're safe now." She looked up at me with her big green eyes and I could see the tears filling in them. A tear escaped and slid down her cheek, I brushed it away and cleaned her cuts on her left arm.

After a few moments, she finally spoke, "My roommate, Casey, she attacked me. She came home from work—she's a nurse—and said that a child had bit her that morning. I didn't think anything of it. She went to her room to lie down." She looked down at her hands, her fingers twisted together in anxiety regarding what she said next. "About an hour later, I heard this weird noise come from her room and then a crash. I went to check on her. She was lying on the floor; her lamp was knocked over." She paused, taking a deep breath. "Her skin looked weird—not normal. It was dull, gray, it looked lifeless. I almost touched her but stopped myself. When she turned her body, I finally saw her face. I didn't recognize her. Her face was sunken in. Her eyes sat in hollow pockets and were filled with hatred. Her eyeballs were jet-black, like the devil was in her." Elana shuddered at the thought. I nodded, urging her to go on. "Casey growled at me and scared me. I tried to back away from her, but she lunged at me, knocking me into a mirror. She tried to claw at my face, but I ducked, and she scratched the wall. I ran from the room, but she just kept coming. Her jaw chomped down repeatedly, hungry for my flesh. I was so frightened that I backed into my glass table and fell right through, that's how I cut myself up. Casey chased after me and fell on top of me. That's when Logan came in the room. He grabbed her, threw her against the wall and shoved a pencil into the middle of her forehead." Elana muffled a sob and put her shaking hand over her mouth. My mind swarmed with a million questions, instead I said, "You are safe now."

I turned to June. "Can you keep cleaning these cuts? I'm going to go grab some bandages and clothes for her."

"Yes, of course." June switched places with me and tended to Elana's wounds while I raced upstairs. I grabbed a pair of yoga pants and a hoodie. I also grabbed some socks to use as bandages since all the actual bandages were already in the car. I made my way back downstairs. The knob to the front door began to turn as I reached the landing at the bottom of the steps. My heart skipped a beat, hoping it was Scott.

To my disappointment, Logan walked through the door instead of Scott. "The car is packed. Where is Scott? When is he supposed to be here?" Logan asked me, the annoyance clear in his voice. I felt irritated both with Scott for his tardiness and Logan for his impatience. Everyone was on edge.

"He said he would be here. Please let's wait a few more minutes. We can't leave without him, he's my husband!" I pleaded with my brother. I couldn't imagine leaving Scott behind. "Fine," he muttered in response. We sat in total silence around my kitchen table. Elana had changed and continued to stare at her hands while Logan rubbed her back. June continued to play with the unraveling string of her sweater while Blake played with a toy car on the floor. The longer Scott took, the more anxious I grew. My mind was overrun with dismal thoughts of what might have happened to Scott. *Where is he? Why is he taking so long?*

The silence was interrupted by screeching sirens going off in the background and then a loud explosion. The only building in the vicinity I thought could explode was a gas station about a half a mile from my house. The outbreak, those things, the zombies, the undead, they were getting closer. I glanced around the table pausing on each person, trying to read their expressions. *Are they thinking what I'm thinking? The undead are coming.*

Blake broke the silence, "Mommy, what was that?"

"It was nothing, baby," June quickly dismissed his question, unsure of what to say to her child.

The next thing I knew, Logan threw me over his shoulder and walked out the front door. I kicked and smacked at him to put me down. He was going to make me leave without Scott. I begged. I cried. But he wasn't listening to me. Elana, June, and Blake had all climbed into my SUV. My brother threw me into the car and slammed the door. He ran around to the driver's side and climbed in. As he was about to put the car in drive, I saw Scott's car round the corner.

chapter two

"Look!" I shouted at my brother, pointing toward Scott's car. My demeanor changed once I saw that my husband was safe. Across the neighborhood, there was evidence that the cure of doom had made its way to Harwicke road. Neighbors' belongings littered their yards, doors to houses and cars hung ajar.

As Scott rounded the corner, there was movement coming from the yard of the corner house on the right. Our neighbor, Missy Samuels, fled from her yard, outrunning her undead husband, Bob Samuels. Missy stepped out into the street, directly into Scott's path. He frantically pressed on his brakes, the noise halting Missy in her tracks. She had just enough time to turn and face Scott before he hit her straight on with his car. The car pummeled her, tossing her body high into the air. Her body plopped onto the ground. Lying in an awkward position and blood pouring out of several orifices, there was no doubt she was dead. Scott clambered out of his car and knelt next to her body examining her for signs of life.

Logan sped the car up to the scene. Before he even had a chance to put the car in park, I climbed out. Logan threw the SUV into park, jumped out, and took down Bob Samuels. I approached Scott, he had tears streaming down his face. He looked up at me, "She's dead. I killed her." Scott began to sob. I leaned down and swung my arms around his neck to comfort him.

"I don't mean to interrupt this little moment, but we really do need to leave," Logan shouted at us. At first, we ignored him, then he shouted at us again, "Mya hurry, look!" I saw a limping man, covered with blood coming out of the Samuels house. He was one of the undead. He must have infected Bob Samuels. I tried to urge Scott to get up, but he wouldn't budge. With each passing second the man moved closer and closer to where we were sitting in the middle of the street. Logan went toward the Samuels' house to put down the limping man.

"Scott, come on, we need to leave!" I begged, tugging on his shirt. He wasn't thinking rationally, he was in shock.

"I can't leave her here like this. I killed her. We knew her, she isn't just some random person, she's our neighbor. I need to make this right." Scott stood up and went to his trunk. He came back carrying a blanket. As Scott folded Missy's arms over her chest, I noticed a strange mark on her wrist. Before I could comment on it, Scott had covered her with the blanket. His head hung low with despair. He was mumbling a prayer.

Unexpectedly, Missy sat up. Scott, taken aback, placed his hands on her shoulders. She jerked forward and sunk her teeth into Scott's neck. Scott's reflexes kicked in and he shoved her off him. Her body flung backward, and her teeth took a huge chunk of his throat. Scott screamed out in agony and desperately grasped at his neck to stop the blood from sputtering out of his arteries. His blood soaked my hair and clothes. I panicked and placed my hands over his, trying to help stop the rush of blood. Missy was back on her feet in seconds and coming back for us. Scott pushed me aside, his body landing on top of mine to protect me as Missy clawed at his back. Scott was unable to apply pressure to his neck wound which bled out all over me. I sobbed, choking on his blood. His blood filled my eyes, impairing my vision. I blinked through the blood, and when my vision cleared, I was face to face with Scott. His face was pale and lifeless. He was dead.

Logan had pulled Missy off Scott and bashed her brains in, but it was too late. My husband was dead. I lied on the street, his dead weight crushing my body. I struggled to breathe through the pressure and sobs. Logan pulled Scott's lifeless body off mine. I lay there stunned, unable to move. "Mya, are you hurt?" Logan gently asked me, helping me to sit up. I looked to my left at Scott. I held his lifeless body and cradled his head in my lap. I rocked back and forth sobbing over the loss of my husband. *I didn't get a chance to say goodbye or tell him that I love him. I should have said something about the mark on her wrist. I could have saved him. Is he going to turn into one of those things now?* A million thoughts flooded my brain.

I needed to act fast. I gently placed my husband's head on the pavement and went to the trunk of my SUV. I pulled out a knife from the survival bin of random contents that I put together.

In zombie movies, they kill the dead before they become the undead. A sign of respect for their loved one so they don't end up lost and roaming the world looking for food. It was the only option I felt like I had.

I knelt next to my husband's body, kissed his forehead, and shoved the kitchen knife into the back of his brain. I could not let him turn into the undead.

I didn't expect the knife to sink in, getting stuck in the brain matter. His skull sucked it in and held on tight. I shrieked when I tried to pull the knife out and it wouldn't budge. *Did I actually just stab my husband in the head?* Logan and Elana watched from the side with pity in their eyes. June watched, horrified that I did this to my husband, the judgment clear in her eyes. June shielded Blake's eyes from the disturbing scene. I folded Scott's hands over his chest and removed his wedding band. I clutched the ring close to my chest and sobbed. Logan came over and placed his hand on my shoulder, "I'm sorry, Mya, but we have to go. It's not safe here." I crawled over to where the blanket was and snatched it. With hot tears streaming down my face, I laid the blanket over my husband's mangled body. I placed a hand over his heart, *"I'll love you, forever."*

24

I looked up at Logan through my tears, not able to make out his face. Logan helped me off the ground—I could barely stand. My legs were weak from shock. Logan helped me into the SUV. I leaned my head against the window, unable to process. Turning off Harwicke road, I looked out the window at the end of my life as I knew it. I *will never see my husband, my house, or Harwicke road again.*

Pausing at end of the neighborhood, Logan couldn't decide which direction to take. "Which way, Mya?" Logan asked. He sat there staring at me, demanding an answer. My brain felt like mush, I couldn't think. "Mya, I need an answer!"

"Just pick one." I was uninterested.

"Let's weigh the options, what is to the left and what is to the right?" Logan asked, trying to get me focused on the task at hand.

"Right is toward the city. Left is where the explosion likely came from," I mumbled. He nodded and turned left.

I looked down at my hands, I was still clutching Scott's bloody wedding band. I cleaned it off on the inside of my shirt. I examined the ring, thinking back to the day we had exchanged our wedding rings and vows and pictured Scott's handsome grin as he mouthed the words "I do." The magical feeling when our lips touched for our first kiss as husband and wife was the best day of my life.

I sighed heavily, unlatched my necklace, and slipped the ring on the chain then clasped it back on. The ring fell perfectly into the dead center of my chest. At twenty-seven years old, I was already a widow. Another set of tears rolled down my face.

Glancing down, I realized my clothes were filthy and blood-stained. My long blonde hair was matted with blood. My hands and clothes were stained red with my husband's blood. I looked at myself in the mirror and realized the sticky red substance covered my entire face. I licked my fingers and scrubbed at my face—it remained the same. My body was consumed with grief, I felt numb. I struggled to focus on what was happening around me while Logan weaved in and out of the random cars that littered the road.

We had a long trip ahead of us to get to Indiana and I needed to stop and get my head out of the grave. I did some deep breathing exercises, sat up in my seat, and willed myself to become more aware of my surroundings. We were nearing the gas station. The shops leading up to it were deserted—it was a ghost town. As we approached the gas station, the air grew thick with smoke, obstructing our view.

In front of us an undead woman crawled what was left of her body across the ground toward the smoke. She was missing her lower torso and her insides were dragging along behind her. Logan ruthlessly swerved to run over her head. As the SUV tire made contact with her skull, we felt a thud. I looked over at him and he shrugged, then responded, "One less to kill later."

My brother always had a strong survival instinct. He was strong growing up in a house of girls. He was strong when he enrolled in the marines. He was deployed to Iraq and released three years later on a medical discharge. His group was attacked. Of twenty men, only my brother and the two marines he saved survived. He doesn't like to talk about it, but he did seek counseling. He met Elana in counseling, and they have been together since. Lately he has mentioned proposing to her. Logan is a survivor. He will survive this even if the rest of us don't.

chapter three

The air around the gas station was foul. With the windows up, the car was still overpowered by the stench of burning flesh and gasoline. The gas station was completely engulfed in flames. The area was littered with people—well, the undead—in flames. The explosion drew the undead and there were dozens engulfed. Some were dead on the ground, while others were walking around unaffected by their burning flesh. The searing undead were blocking the road. There was no way around, we needed to stay on this road to get out of town. At a safe distance from the gas station, Logan stopped the SUV.

"What should we do?" Elana asked, it appeared her earlier shock had worn off. I, on the other hand, still struggled. My hands shook and my heart pounded. I had just watched my husband get eaten alive. I couldn't get the image of his lifeless body spewing blood all over me, out of my mind. My sweet, caring husband was gone and not coming back, and I was not ready to accept that.

"They are already distracted. Don't you think we can slip by without them noticing?" I asked my brother. Logan processed the scene in front of him. I pictured the wheels spinning in his mind.

"No, the SUV is too loud, and they would hear us. We need to create another big distraction. The explosion initially distracted them, but they are losing interest in the fire. The undead know there is no food there anymore. Look at them, they are aimlessly wandering around, waiting for something to catch their attention. I have an idea.

I'm going to park the SUV here. Mya, you get in the driver's seat. I'm going to double back and create a distraction to drive them away from our path." Logan's eyes beamed with excitement.

"No, Logan. It's too dangerous. You can't go out there alone. It's too risky, you won't have anyone to watch your back. What if something happens to you? We need you." I started to protest.

"Mya, I'm not going to argue with you. I'm going to start a fire in the cars behind us. The undead are going to pass by the SUV. You need to stay silent and remain still. Keep the doors unlocked so I can get back in quick. I'll cut through the trees and come back to you. Be prepared to drive away, and if you have to, you must leave me behind. Promise me that you won't hesitate?" I nodded at him reluctantly. He squeezed my hand, grabbed his baseball bat, then turned around and gave Elana a kiss. Before either of us could make the argument for him to stay, he was gone.

"This is stupid, an unnecessary risk. Not only is he risking his life and possibly leaving us stranded, he's also risking our lives by driving those things near us. So idiotic." June complained about my brother. Her negative attitude annoyed me.

"He's being the hero that he was born to be. He likes to be needed. I give him credit for being so brave. Sometimes though, men are, in fact, idiots." Using her therapeutic skills, Elana defended him and made June feel at ease at the same time. I took Logan's place in the driver's seat and Elana crawled from the backseat into the passenger seat beside me.

I watched Logan from the rear-view mirror. He was brisk and silent on his feet, moving about unnoticed. He was skilled, gifted by years of serving in the marines.

Logan moved swiftly around the SUV and opened the trunk. He pulled out three t-shirts from one of his bags. He walked to the last three cars on the road, a minivan, a station wagon, and a fancy sports car. He opened each of their gas tanks and dipped each end of the shirts into the gasoline. He flipped the shirts around, leaving the saturated side hanging out of the tank, dripping gasoline down the sides of the vehicles. Logan pulled a lighter from his pocket and lit the end of the shirt in the minivan. He proceeded to light the end of the shirts hanging out of the station wagon and sports car. While lighting the shirt in the sports car, the minivan erupted into flames.

I flickered my eyes to the road in front of me and watched in anticipation as the undead turned their heads. Quickly, one by one, they started walking, limping, and dragging their bodies toward the flames of the burning car. The next two cars exploded and all the undead rushed toward the blast—toward the SUV. Logan's plan was working.

I glanced in the rearview mirror again searching for my brother. I couldn't find him. My heart rate increased, and my palms were slick from nerves. I didn't want to upset Elana, so I kept quiet. I prayed to God that my brother was okay. On the inside I was panicking, on the outside I was calm. I glanced back and forth between what was in front of and behind us, searching for Logan. *Where is he?*

Elana must have caught onto my nervous energy and turned around, searching for her boyfriend. "I don't see him. Mya, do you see him? Can you see anything? The smoke is too thick, where is he? Oh my god what if something happened to him? What if he blew himself up?" She began rocking in her seat, making the SUV slightly sway.

"Elana, relax and take a deep breath. Logan is too methodical to make the mistake of blowing himself up. I need you to sit still so the undead don't realize we're in here."

"Okay. Jesus, I'm ridiculous, you're right." She took my advice and relaxed her body, putting her nervous energy into twisting her fingers.

I put my finger to my lips, signaling the car to be quiet. Outside the car, the undead passed by. Some of them moved quickly—at a slow jog, eager to get to the fires. Others, the injured ones, moved slower, dragging their mangled body parts behind them. I counted forty-six undead before I lost track and refused to count anymore. Knowing how many there were felt intimidating. Logan was right, we wouldn't have been able to go around them. They would have easily overpowered the SUV.

The undead walking by the SUV had me on edge. I was paranoid that they would catch our scent considering they were less than three feet from us. I sunk a little lower into my seat, trying to conceal myself even more, Elana, June and Blake followed suit. Time moved at a snail's pace as the undead made their way past the car.

The last few stragglers walked by the car, and my body began to relax. The tension eased in my shoulders and my heart rate returned to normal. The screams in my mind had subsided. Everyone let out a big sigh of relief.

Unexpectedly, Blake sneezed. The sneeze caught the attention of three of the undead closest to the SUV. They turned their bodies and shuffled up to the car. They began bashing their heads, bodies, and hands on the window where Blake was sitting. He instantly began to scream. "Shhh, baby you need to be quiet," June said as she tried to get her child to quiet down. June quickly switched places and put Blake on the ground and covered him up so he would relax. She told him to put his iPod on. Within seconds the child quieted. It was too late though.

The undead outside the car doubled, and then quickly tripled in numbers. They violently banged on the windows, starved for our flesh and eager to get inside the vehicle. One of the undead managed to crack the back-passenger side window where June was sitting. Tears were streaming down her face. Her eyes filled with panic.

"What do we do?" June shrieked out, scared for her life.

As much as it pained me to leave behind my brother, I knew I had to. I put the SUV in drive and slowly urged the vehicle on. Elana noticed what I was doing and immediately protested. She grabbed my arm away from the steering wheel causing the car to jerk left, running over an undead. "Mya, you can't leave without him!"

"I'm sorry I don't want to, but I don't have a choice. If I don't drive now, we will all die. He told me to do this!" I hollered back at Elana, as she tried to stop the SUV. "Elana, stop! Let go!" She continued, ignoring my pleas, risking all our lives. "ENOUGH!" I finally screamed at her. She paused and sat back in her seat, I glanced at her and noticed the fresh tears streaming down her face. I touched my face and pulled away my wet fingers, I was crying too. I blinked away the tears and continued to move the car forward at a slow pace. It was difficult to drive through the mob of the undead who were determined to get inside the car. The windows were splintered and covered in blood. I moved forward at an impossibly slow rate. The undead walked beside the car, I wasn't gaining any ground on them. I dreaded having to leave Logan behind, but I had to.

I fluttered my eye lids to clear the tears blurring my vision. Up ahead, I saw movement in the bushes. I squinted my eyes, hoping to get a better look. I recognized by the height; the movement was caused by a person. The real question was, were they alive or undead?

Nervous at who or what it was, I hesitated with the gas for a moment. When the figure came all the way out, I realized it was Logan. I slammed my foot onto the accelerator, my tires spun on the bodies of the fallen undead. The car finally jerked forward, and I was able to gain a small head start on the mob. I pulled up to where my brother was, and June swung the door open for him. He was covered from head to toe in mud and blood—his baseball bat permanently stained red. He dove into the open door and landed awkwardly in the backseat, "Go! Go! They're right behind me," Logan shouted. I pressed the pedal to the metal and propelled the SUV forward. I glanced in the rear-view mirror and saw at least fifty undead quickly following behind us. The mob had dramatically grown. The faster I drove the further behind they fell. Soon enough, they would be a distant memory, or more likely, a nightmare.

chapter four

Our family made a pact. In the event of an apocalypse, we would be with each other, no matter what. The second this started, there was no doubt in my mind where we were going. I continued toward Indiana.

The drive started out smooth. I had been driving for about forty-five minutes and knew the immediate area well enough we didn't get lost. I took the long way, taking the necessary turns to keep us on the back roads for as long as possible. During that time, we only saw a few of the undead wandering around. They didn't pose any real threat to us. They hadn't even realized we were there until we were unreachable.

"Logan, I'm not sure where to go now. I don't know any of these back roads anymore. I only know the way by highway." I had pulled over and stopped the SUV, I didn't want to waste any gas wandering around. "Why don't we see if any of our GPS's work on our phones?" I asked everyone.

I pulled my phone out and tried for a signal. Almost in unison, we raised our phones up trying to get some type of signal. There was no signal to retrieve though. Technology had failed.

"The cell phone towers must be out somehow. Maybe they had been one of the places with all the smoke," Elana suggested. During the drive, there had been several different smoke clouds coming from all over the place. I had avoided those areas, assuming it would be overrun with the undead.

June began firing questions off at me, "Where are you planning on taking us? We should keep moving. They can come from anywhere. Sitting here is putting us at risk. You need to make some sort of decision."

Logan looked at her and said, "We're going to Indiana. Our sister goes to school there. We have to go get her. We made a promise that if something like this ever happened, we would go and get her. We will not break that promise."

"Well then why don't you just go onto the highway? Isn't it somewhere around here?" June suggested.

"We can't do that. It's probably crawling with them. It's too soon, the outbreak just happened. We should wait at least a day before trying to travel on the highway. It would be a suicide mission to go there now. They will be everywhere. We need to give them some time to move on." Logan always knew the answer for everything.

"What should we do in the meantime?" asked Elana.

I looked around at everyone. Logan, Elana, and I were filthy and covered in dried blood. I looked down at my own attire, and my heart dropped. Scott's blood was everywhere—I needed to get cleaned up.

"Why don't we go find a house and spend the night there? We will just pick out whichever one looks most abandoned." I watched them all think over my proposal.

Blake tugged on my sleeve. "Can we go somewhere to get toys?"

I smiled warmly back at him. I was amused by his innocence. At his age, there wasn't a care in the world. "Sure kiddo, we'll find you some toys," I answered Blake. I looked at everyone else. "Any objections?" They all shook their heads.

"We'll just have to be careful. We don't want to pick a house that already has people in it, they could be armed. We also don't want to pick a house that is overrun on the inside with the undead." Logan said thinking out loud.

"Yes, I agree. We'll have to stalk out the house or maybe a few of us can check it out while the rest wait," I suggested, trying to come up with a solution.

"That works for me, let's go."

We drove on the back roads in search for the perfect house to occupy for the night. It took a while before we picked one. By the time we finally found the perfect place, the sun was getting ready to set. The house we finally settled on was several roads away from the highway. It was far enough from the road, but not so far that you couldn't see it. It was a small place made of bricks. It looked aged, as if the caretakers didn't care for it at all. There was a tire swing out front, which meant that, maybe, it had toys inside. It was important to me that I kept my promise to Blake. He deserved it for being such a brave boy.

I pulled up in front of the driveway, not down it. I was worried that the owners were still there. If they were, there was no telling if they were alive or undead. From the outside of the house, it seemed lifeless. There were no lights, no movements, no smoke in the chimney—no signs that anyone was home at all. But still, we didn't want to take any chances.

"What are you doing now? The house is right there, let's go. I need to get out of this car," June whined at us.

"I don't want to just drive up there and go in. We don't know what's in there. People could live there. There could be undead inside. Is that really a risk you're willing to take with your son's life?" I argued at her.

"Well, no."

"Okay then. Logan what do you think?"

"I'll go assess the situation," Logan said insisting on checking it out before we walked into a potentially deadly situation. We decided that he was going to go snoop around the outside of the house and peer in through the windows. If it was all clear, he was going to wave us up.

Logan jumped out of the car and went around to the trunk. He grabbed a kitchen knife and began to make his way up the driveway. He walked behind trees to avoid being seen. The SUV was hidden well with nature. We watched Logan from the car as he made his way around the house checking all the windows. I rolled down the windows so we could hear any possible disturbance. When he went around to the back of the house, I held my breath hoping that he would quickly return.

About a minute later Logan emerged from the back of the house. He shrugged at us and waved us up. As we approached him, I noticed there was fresh blood on him and on the knife.

Elana hopped out of the car before it was in park, "Logan, what happened to you?" Elana asked as she rushed to his side, enclosing him in a hug, not caring about the blood. The rest of us got out of the car and joined them in standing on the front lawn.

"There was a loner out back," Logan replied to Elana. We began to create nicknames for the undead during our drive, it helped make things less stressful. We referred to the undead that were alone as loners. "She was caught in a bear trap. I put her out of her misery. Other than her, I didn't find anyone else. I saw some scratch marks on the shutters on the back of the house but whoever did that is gone. Everything else looks good from what I can see."

"How can you say everything looks good? You didn't even go into the house and check that out yet?" June questioned Logan. Her whining rubbed me the wrong way. I didn't like that she was questioning Logan's abilities—again.

"Take a deep breath, June, I'm not going to let everyone just walk inside. We should make sure it is safe first, but that's not something I can do alone. I can't get trapped in there with a cluster of them," Logan responded to June. A cluster of them was our slang for four to eight. Any more than that, became a mob.

"Mya, are you up to coming into the house with me to help me clear it?" Logan asked, his tone incredibly soft as if he was talking to a child. *Why is he coddling me?* I then realized he was trying to be gentle because I might have to kill again. The thought of killing again brought flashes of when I killed my husband earlier that day. My heart throbbed thinking of his mangled body lying in the street.

I didn't know if I was mentally ready to go into the house and potentially have to kill again. I wasn't naïve, I knew that I would eventually have to take another life. I closed my eyes and sighed. *Logan picked me because he believes in me and I need to believe in myself. I can do this.*

"Alright, Logan. I'll go. Let me just grab a weapon." I agreed. I walked around to the trunk and looked at my options of weapons. There were several knives, Logan's baseball bat, and a tire iron. I opted for the baseball bat, hoping Logan wouldn't mind. As a kid, I loved to play t-ball, I loved the weight of the bat and the feel of the connection when you finally hit the ball. I held it toward him, asking if it was okay. He smiled, nodded, and grabbed for a second knife.

We headed for the front door. The closer we got the faster my heart raced. I was not ready for this. My palms grew slick from the nervousness coursing through my body. I struggled to get a decent grip on the bat. Logan placed his hand on the door handle and turned—it was locked.

"Ha, I didn't even consider this to be an option. Let's look for a different way in. Girls, stay here and keep guard. If you see anything suspicious, ring the doorbell," Logan said then chuckled a little and walked away.

Logan and I traveled around to the back and, of course, that door was locked too. The back door had a small window. Logan took the baseball bat, wrapped his shirt around it, and smashed it into the glass, attempting to break it quietly. Logan reached inside and unlocked the door. His movements were calculated and precise.

The door swung open and the room was still. The musty smell from the house smacked us in the face as we entered. The door opened into the kitchen—which was filthy. Whoever lived there left in a hurry. The kitchen's stench of dirty dishes and old food. Logan walked over to the cabinets and began opening and closing them.

"What are you looking for?" I whispered at him.

"Pots and pans. No need to whisper, I'm about to make a lot of noise." Logan smiled as he found two pots and then began banging them together. The sound startled me. He stopped the banging and shushed me before I could say anything. He stood there quietly, waiting for something.

After about a minute, he finally spoke, "Noise seems to attract them, so I wanted to draw them to us, if they were in here. I don't hear anything, so it seems as if the house is empty. I still want to check the rooms though just to be sure, in case one of them is stuck somewhere."

We moved around the house checking each room, one at a time. The longer we stayed in the house the more my body began to relax. There was clearly nobody there, if there was, we would have seen or heard them by now.

Logan went to the foyer of the house, where the steps to the upstairs were and shouted, "HELLOO!"

"What are you doing, goofball?"

"Just wanted to make sure there was no one in here before everyone comes in. You know, covering all my bases, you can never be too careful. The noise in the kitchen was for the undead, the hello is for the alive. If there is anyone alive in here, they could think that we're the undead and be afraid of us."

"Oh, clever idea." We stood there for a moment and listened. There was only silence.

I looked over at Logan and he nodded at me. I went to the front of the house and unlocked the door so the others could come inside. He went upstairs—he insisted on checking the entire second floor.

"What's going on? What was all that noise? Are you guys okay? Where's Logan?" Elana's face filled with worry.

"Everything's fine, we were just creating noise to lure anything out that might be here, undead or alive. We are almost positive that there is no one in the house. Logan is fine, he is checking the upstairs to be sure, you know how he is," I reassured Elana and led them into the dining room. Logan finished his rounds and confirmed that the house was empty. He and I took a seat at the table, June followed, holding Blake's hand. Elana stood in the doorway looking at all of us. We were finally relieved to have reached safety, even if it was temporary. The moment was pure bliss.

As we sat around the table lost in thought and taking a quick mental break, Elana was doing some detective work. As a therapist, she was interested in who the homeowners could have been. She was studying all the pictures on the walls and looking through their book collection. She went to look through their pile of mail when she found a torn piece of paper.

"Hey, guys look at this," Elana grabbed our attention.

To whom it may concern,

I have left my house in fear of this epidemic. I hope whoever takes sanctum here gets what they need. There is some water in the basement. I had to try to make it out in the world to be with the only family I have left. You may stay here for however long you want as I will likely not be returning. My home is now yours. All I ask in return is that you leave my shed untouched. It holds something very near and dear to my heart.

Xx Martha

The instant that Elana was done reading that note my curiosity took over and I wanted to see inside the shed. I hadn't noticed a shed. By the look on Logan's face, he hadn't either. We both got up from the table at the same time and walked over to the window to look for the shed. Sure enough, it was out there, slightly covered by tree branches.

We sat around the table brainstorming about what might be inside that secretive, grungy shed.

"We should just leave it alone like the letter says," pleaded June.

"No, I think we should look. The letter said she won't be coming back. We should just see what's inside. It could be anything." I made my case. But I lied because I knew exactly what was in there. It was an undead—one of her loved ones.

"I agree that we should look, but maybe we should wait until morning. The sun has almost set, it's getting dark out there," Elana said.

"No, I can't wait. It'll drive me crazy all night. I need to know before we can get any sleep. There has to be flashlights around here somewhere," Logan made his argument. Nobody disagreed. We all began to look for flashlights. Once we located three of them, we were ready to venture outside.

"Let's go," Logan sighed and took the baseball bat resting against the wall. Logan walked past us toward the back door.

Logan, Elana, and I stood in front of the shed, while June and Blake stayed in the kitchen. June stood at the door, shining her light toward us. Elana and I shined our flashlights on the shed while the three of us stood there contemplating what to do next. Clearly, we wanted to open it, but at the same time we wanted to show the homeowners some respect; we were nervous about what was inside. We all stared at the shed contemplating whether we should open it or not. The shed was red but looked rusty. The paint was chipped away, and the roof shingles were coming off. The shed was closed tight—locked.

"Back up girls, keep the lights pointed at the door," Logan said, making the decision for the group. None of us argued. He swung the baseball bat over his head and into the lock, flexing the muscles in his neck and shoulders. He repeated this several times until the lock finally broke. We backed up and stared at the door to the shed, waiting for something to happen.

We heard a low growl and waited for it to surface. After a minute, nothing came out. We weren't sure what to do. None of us wanted to get close enough to open the door. No one wanted to risk getting bit. We expected whatever was in there to make their presence known, loud and clear.

Elana put her hand on the door handle. Logan positioned himself in front of the door, prepared for what was about to happen. Elana pulled the handle, opened the door, and stepped back quickly to get out of the way.

None of us were prepared for what we were about to see. We gasped in shock as we shined our lights inside of the shed. There were two young children, a boy and a girl, hands tied behind their back and tied together. Logan went to step inside, but I quickly grabbed his arm.

"Wait, Logan, I don't think that it's what it looks like. I think they are undead. If they were alive, they would be crying or something." Logan stopped and looked at me. I could see the desperation in his eyes, he really wanted them to be alive, but he knew just as well as I did, they were undead.

Logan wearily walked up to them and took a knife from his back pocket. The closer he got to the children, the louder their growls became. The two children struggled to grasp Logan. They tried to claw at his flesh—taste the blood running through his veins. It was clear, they were undead.

Logan came back out of the shed. There was a sheen of sweat across his forehead, and tears in his eyes.

Logan shut the door and secured it as best as he could, considering he broke the lock. He sluggishly walked back to us, never taking his eyes off the ground.

"I can't do it. They are too young. I don't think I can do it. What is everyone else's opinion?" Logan confided in us.

"What is it? What's wrong?" June hollered from the door. Elana waved her over. June took Blake's hand and started towards us, but Elana stopped her.

"No, just you June. He shouldn't see this," Elana responded. June left Blake, told him to stand in the doorway, and walked over to us.

"Okay, what is it?" June asked.

"It's children," was all Logan could say.

"What do you mean, 'it's children'? Get them out of there, poor things." June's facial expression changed as she processed what that meant. "Oh." June looked down at her feet.

No one knew what to do. *Should we just leave them be? Let them stay in that state? Or should we kill them?* They weren't regular undead adults, they were children.

I placed my hand over my abdomen briefly and removed it before anyone else noticed, and said, "I agree with you Logan, I can't kill them either."

"As difficult as this is, I'm not willing to risk Blake's life because of other undead children. I say we finish the job," June pleaded.

"I think that is a horrible idea June. We can't do that. Didn't you read the note, it asked to please leave it be. If we secure it enough things will be fine. How could you say such horrible things?" Elana said.

"So, are we in agreement then?" Logan asked.

Even though we all knew it was wrong, we left them locked in the shed. None of us could bear to kill them. June obviously didn't want to deal with the risk, but when it came down to it, she wouldn't get her hands dirty. No one wanted the experience of shoving a knife into a child's head.

Logan found some planks, nails, and a hammer in the garage and put up a stronger hold on the shed's door. Once the undead children were tightly secured inside the grungy shed, Logan spray painted 'do not open' across the shed. Once that was taken care of, we all went inside and turned in for the night.

Showering was like a little slice of heaven during the endless hell. All day I had been trying to keep Scott's death at the back of my mind.

As the blood washed off my body and down the drain, I finally allowed myself to grieve for my late husband. I sat on the floor of the shower and hugged my legs. I sat there and sobbed into my arms. I'm certain that my cries were loud and ugly sounding, but no one came to check.

After I cried all the tears I had to offer, I picked myself up and turned off the water. I skipped the meal of canned beans and went directly to bed. I laid down clutching my husband's wedding ring, which lay around my neck. I began to think of my life without him, but it was unimaginable. I fell asleep thinking of what horrors the next day might bring.

chapter five

I woke up the next day feeling as if I had slept for days. All my muscles were stiff. I rolled over in bed to see what time it was and realized those weren't my sheets, that wasn't my clock, and that wasn't my bed. At that realization, my eyes grew wide, my heart began to pound, and my ears started to ring.

I was in a stranger's house. I was on the run from cannibals—the undead. My husband was dead—my neighbor took a chunk out of his throat—then I stabbed him in the head with a knife to finish the job.

I put my face back into the strange pillow and let out an angry scream that turned to tears. I laid there for a few more minutes sobbing into the pillow before collecting myself. I knew I couldn't let anyone see me like this. They would act weird. They would tiptoe around me, careful not to upset me. Worst of all, they would be worried I couldn't handle myself, especially Logan. I knew he was counting on me to remain levelheaded.

I sat up in bed and did a nice long stretch releasing tension in my back and shoulders. I got up and headed to the bathroom to shower. Knowing this might be my last shower for a while, I enjoyed every second of it. After my shower, I realized for the first time that my burgundy suitcase was in the room. Logan must have brought it in while I was sleeping.

I opened the suitcase and was instantly faced with all of Scott's clothes. I drew in a sharp breath and willed myself not to cry. I briefly ran my hand over his clothes. I picked up his favorite shirt, a light blue polo, and smelled it searching for the scent of him. The only thing I smelled was our laundry detergent. Unable to look at Scott's clothes anymore, I quickly retrieved my clothes and shut the suitcase. I wasn't ready to look at his things.

After I dressed, I wandered downstairs toward the kitchen. On my way to the kitchen, I stopped in the living room and examined the décor. The atmosphere of the house was very homely. It wasn't too dirty, but it wasn't too clean. It was the perfect balance of what a home should be. Family photos covered every wall in the house. I stopped to examine some and realized that this family looked so happy. I saw a picture of who I assumed was Martha with her two young children and a man I assumed to be her husband. They were all smiling—perfect dentist smiles—and looked happy. I felt sorrow for their family. Looking at their family photos made me long to have Scott again. My heart ached knowing that we would never have a photo like that. I placed a hand over my abdomen briefly and quickly removed it. I could not do this now. I needed to be strong.

I rounded the corner into the kitchen. Blake was coloring at the kitchen table and June was cooking breakfast. I looked around for Logan and Elana, but they were nowhere to be seen.

"'Morning Mya, I'm making some eggs if you want any. I found some in the fridge," June offered, as she stood over the stove. A small, fake smile danced across her face.

My stomach answered for me with a low growl. I smiled at her and said please. As I waited for my breakfast, I sat down at the table with Blake. He was coloring a sesame street coloring book and was doing an excellent job of staying within the lines.

As June served breakfast, Logan walked into the room with Elana. Under his arm, he carried a bundle of papers. He placed them down in front of me and unrolled them. There were several maps of Pennsylvania. He had highlighted different possible routes to Indiana.

The obvious way was to take the highway, but that was also the most dangerous.

"What should we do? The highway is pretty much a straight shot to Ohio. Once we're in Ohio, we can find some more maps and then do the same again for Indiana," Logan said as he rubbed his face. "If we take the highway, we are running the obvious risk of coming across clusters of the undead, probably even mobs of them. If we don't take the highway, we may get lost and still run into clusters or mobs of them. Either way, avoiding the undead is going to be pretty much impossible. I think before we decide on anything, we need to accept that there will always be the danger of the undead."

Logan had made some good points. I sat pondering what our options were. The wheels in my brain turned and I came up with a logical solution.

"I think we should take the highway. It's the most logical." Before I could even finish making my argument, June, instantly began to protest: "No, no no no no. We are not going on that highway, it is suicide. Last night when I suggested it, you said it was a bad idea and I am now agreeing. It's a bad idea. How could you deliberately put all of us, including my son, in danger?" Her tone was harsh, she sounded angry.

"We have weapons. Most highways run alongside woods. We can drive on the highway as long as possible and then, when we can't go any further, we will think of something else. We can hide out in the woods if a mob were to come by. When we run out of gas, which we will, there will be plenty of cars to choose from." Once I finished my speech, I looked at everyone for their thoughts. Logan's face showed pride. June crossed her arms; she was clearly not happy about the plan.

"That's the plan then. If we're careful, then it should work out, and, hopefully, it will get us one step closer to Indiana. We shouldn't go today. We should take the rest of the day to collect whatever we can from here, fill the tank, and rest up before our next journey. We should leave just before sunrise tomorrow to utilize the daylight on the highway while we can still see everything that's going on," Logan said as he started to rise from the table.

"No, we shouldn't do this. This is not a smart decision. Why don't you people ever think?" June stood from the table. She cleared the dishes and heaved them into the sink. They shattered as they landed.

"Listen June, we're going and that's that. If you so earnestly disagree, then don't come. I don't think it's a wise choice, but it is your choice. Stay if you want. You may survive this out here, it's possible, but it will only be you two. I am definitely going with Logan and Mya and if you're smart, you will too," Elana bluntly expressed herself. As soon as she made her point, she turned on her heel, and went with Logan to scavenge supplies.

June said nothing, she stood there looking dumb-founded. The atmosphere felt awkward, I wanted nothing more than to be out of the room. I stood, shrugged at June, and left the room.

I spent the remainder of the day searching the house and collecting items that I thought might be useful in the future on our journey. As I rummaged through the house, I thought back on my life. I already missed my old life. I had a difficult time accepting that everything had completely changed. It would never be the same again.

I would never see my patients again. I would never see my house again. I would never see my husband again. The little bean growing inside of me would never know his or her father. The new life that was forced on me would never compare to my old one. One day's difference separated my old life and my new one. One day I woke up to my husband and just hours later he was dead. This new life was a burden. It was a fresh new start that no one asked for or wanted.

chapter six

The next morning, we rose just before sunrise. Logan went from room to room to wake everyone up. He even went and woke June up, who had reluctantly decided to come along with us. She would rather take the risk of leaving with us than staying on her own with her son.

We dressed and met in the foyer, rubbing our eyes and yawning. No one (except for Logan) wanted to be out of bed. None of us were excited to put ourselves into danger again. If it weren't for Lilianna, I don't think I would have ever left that home. But I had to, for her. I also did not want to live next to undead children for forever.

"Come on girls, pull it together. We are about to leave the safety of this house. I need everyone to be alert." Logan's serious tone made me realize that we were leaving a haven and going into hell.

In minutes, we were back in the SUV. We had reloaded all our items and added the new items that we collected from the house. The SUV was packed to capacity; there was no possible way we could fit anymore items into the trunk. Logan had even strapped a few items onto the roof. He insisted on driving. I let Elana sit shotgun with him and I sat in the back with Blake and June. As we left the driveway, I looked back at the home we were leaving—our safe place. I placed my head against the cool window and tried to keep my emotions in check. Leaving meant we were deliberately putting ourselves in danger. The risk was worth it. I needed to get to Lilianna.

Once we were back on the main road, I gave Logan directions to get us back on the highway. We drove without any interruptions the entire way. When we approached the highway, he slowed the SUV and put it in park on the merging ramp. I looked over at June to see if she had any idea why Logan had stopped the car. She simply raised her eyebrows and looked back out the window.

"Logan, what are you doing? Why are we stopped?" Elana asked him.

"I don't think it's a brilliant idea to drive right onto the highway without knowing what it's like first. What if the undead are all over it where we get on at? It's an unknown area. I don't want to risk it. I'm going to go by foot to investigate first. I'll be quick and quiet, don't worry about me. If I'm not back in half an hour or if the undead start to show up, leave. Go back to the house. I will find my way back to you guys," Logan said. The danger didn't seem to faze him. There was no point in arguing with him.

Logan hopped out of the SUV and headed to the trunk. He took out his baseball bat and a knife. I realized that having a gun would be greatly beneficial. We would have to try and find one. I got out of the car, gave my brother a quick hug and jumped into the driver's seat. He said his goodbyes and began walking up the ramp with an easy yet cautious stride.

We watched until Logan was no longer in sight. I wish I could say I was able to sit and patiently wait, but I couldn't. I constantly looked at the clock, checking to see how long it had been. Time was hardly moving.

"These past five minutes feel like an eternity. When is he coming back?" Elana whined.

"I don't know, soon. Be confident, he's tough. He'll be okay," I affirmed.

"Well, let's hope so, if not, we're screwed." June didn't seem to care if he was in trouble. I became infuriated with June. I could have strangled her.

We peered out the windows, craning our necks to try and see further ahead, searching for Logan.

After fifteen minutes, Logan rounded the corner and came back into view. His clothes were clean and blood free. I let out a sigh of relief. He approached the car with a smile. I got out of the front and let him back into the driver's seat.

"The road is clear. I didn't see any movement at all. There are barely even any cars on the highway. There are a few here and there but that's it. It'll be easy for us to maneuver through. Looks like it's our lucky day." Logan flashed an award-winning smile. "There's nothing stopping us from taking this way. It was meant to be." With that, he put the SUV in drive, and we began our journey down the highway.

For two hours, our drive was carefree. No sign of the undead, not many abandoned cars, no blood spattered on the pavement.

Just as I was beginning to relax and enjoy our uninterrupted ride, I heard screams. I looked at Logan and he immediately stiffened. It seemed as if we were the only two who heard it. Elana was picking at her nails and June was whispering to Blake.

Logan slowed the SUV down, which caught everyone's attention.

"What are you doing now?" June asked, annoyed by the sudden stop.

"I heard something. Everyone stay quiet," Logan whispered to us.

We sat in silence, confused by what we heard. It was eerily quiet outside. Logan decided to move forward little by little to see what was ahead of us.

As we inched our way forward, we could hear the commotion. The screams started up again and got louder. It was an ear-piercing scream coming from what sounded like a baby. I instantly reacted and placed my hand over my abdomen. I looked over at June, her arms were wrapped around her son and she was covering his ears. I searched for the iPod, and quickly gave it to June so she could block out the horrible sounds for Blake.

When we were close enough to see what was happening, it left us speechless. There was a group of people who were frantically trying to fight off the undead. There were not many undead around them, few enough that they could handle themselves. We sat, watching them fight for their lives.

Once the group had slaughtered the undead, they immediately tended to each other and gathered their belongings. Just as they were getting ready to move on, another small cluster of the undead shuffled out from behind a school bus.

One of the undead grabbed a younger man (who was clueless about what was going on) and took a bite out of his shoulder. The young man's screams echoed loud enough that anyone within a two-mile radius would have heard. The rest of the group put their defenses back up, but it was clear they were growing tired.

I knew that we should turn around and let them handle it themselves. We shouldn't risk our own safety for strangers. There was no real debate on what we should do, but I couldn't find it in my heart to just look the other way. While I hastily pondered this, I thought of the baby screaming. My motherly instincts immediately kicked in.

"We have to help them Logan. This isn't right. We are just sitting here watching these people get killed. They have an innocent little baby with them, for God's sake," I pleaded with my group. I could hear more screams from another young woman whose flesh was being torn off her leg. Before I could finish my thought, Logan hopped out of the car and went to the car next to us. I knew he wouldn't be able to walk away from those innocent people who, without us, would likely die. Elana and I got out of the car and joined him outside. As I watched him frantically run around, I realized he was preparing get-away vehicles. He chose cars that were left with the doors open to make as little noise as possible.

"Okay, here is the plan. I'm going to hot wire two cars. With these two cars and our SUV, we will go over and get whoever we can out of here. June will take the SUV and hang back; she'll pick me up after I help out. We know how she is and I'm sure she won't be thrilled with this. Elana, you take this car, and Mya you take the car next to it," Logan informed us of his plan. He finished hotwiring the cars and we took off to save the lives of these strangers.

As we approached the scene, the number of undead took me by surprise. We were outnumbered. They were all over the place— flooding the area. It was a mob of them. We were wrong about how many of them there were.

I knew, in the pit of my stomach, that we should have just turned away, but it was already too late for that. They saw us coming to help. We couldn't crush their hopes.

When we were close enough, we got out of the cars to help fend off the undead. In total, there were eleven people in their group including the two people who were already attacked and the baby.

The group of people had positioned themselves in a semi-circle backed against two minivans. Their weapons consisted of a hammer, an axe, and a fire poker—everyone else had knives. They were ready to take on the undead.

Elana, Logan, and I ran up to the mob of undead and attacked from three different angles. I attacked straight on, Logan came in from the left and Elana from the right. As I approached, an undead child attacked a teenage girl. The undead child was on top of her and clawing at her face. The teenager was struggling to hold the child away from her face. The undead child growled and chomped his teeth down, making a loud noise when they collided. The child continued to swing his arms around and managed to scratch her face. The pinned down teenager screamed. As her screams grew louder her arms appeared to get weaker. Her shrieks caught the attention of straggling undead and they turned towards the commotion.

I quickly ran up and shoved my kitchen knife into the skull of the undead child. As I pulled my knife out of the child's skull, blood shot out, splashing my face. I stood frozen in place, shocked at what I had just done.

I looked down at the child I had killed. Distracted, I didn't see the undead old man approaching me. He ran at me and hit me from the side. He knocked me over and came down on top of me. I fell hard onto the pavement, smashing my shoulder. I instinctively grabbed my abdomen, worried about what might happen to us. In the commotion, I dropped my knife. I was completely vulnerable to the undead man—a free meal. I wanted to give up and let the undead end my life, but I couldn't do that to my unborn child. He or she deserved a fighting chance in the world.

Before the undead old man had a chance to sink his teeth into my throat, I brought my arm up and elbowed him in his eye socket, jerking his head back. When my elbow connected with his eye socket, it sent a sharp numbing sensation up my arm and into my injured shoulder. I repeated the action, hoping to throw him off my body. The third blow to his eye socket was ten times more painful than the first. I knew I couldn't stand to do it again and the old man wasn't letting up. The blows to his face did nothing to disorient him. He continued to reach for my throat. He shrieked at me as he realized he was about to win the battle for my life. He grabbed hold of my shoulders, digging his fingertips into my injured shoulder. The pain momentarily blinded me. I could only see bursts of stars behind my eyelids. I thanked God my sweatshirt was thick, and he wasn't able to break skin. I screamed at the top of my lungs, hoping someone would hear me. *Logan must be listening for me; he will save me, I know he will.*

I held the undead away from my face, stuck in the same position as the teenager. My right arm was growing weaker and started to tremble under the pressure. As my arm was about to give way, a fire poker was shoved into the old man's skull. The fire poker went through the skull and into his eye socket, causing his eyeball to pop out of his skull and fall on my face. I screamed and screamed and screamed. I swatted the eye off my face. The undead's grip released from my shoulders and there was a new set of hands on me. As I was about to attack the person the hands belonged to, I opened my eyes and realized he was alive, not undead.

He extended a hand and pulled me to my feet. I was disoriented from what was going on and hadn't realized we were about to be overrun by the undead and everyone was fleeing the scene. I was frantic to make sure that Elana and Logan were safe. I scanned the highway in search of either of their faces. I spotted Elana running to her car, but I couldn't find Logan.

The man who saved my life started pushing me in the direction of the car I drove over. He opened the door and tried to shove me into the car. I noticed I was mouthing Logan's name over and over. Once I realized I was saying it out loud, I began to shout it at the top of my lungs. "LOGAN! LOGAN!" My eyes darted around the scene searching for Logan. I couldn't find him. Panic started to set in.

I finally spotted him approaching the minivans. *What is he doing?* I shouted at Logan and waved my arms around to get his attention, but he ignored me. In the distance, I heard another man shouting. I located where the shouts were coming from and saw the man, but he did not seem to be in immediate danger. The man frantically waved his arms around and pointed in the direction of the minivans. He was shouting "Help me!" *Help him with what? What could possibly be in the minivan that was this important?*

While that played out in front of me, the man continued to push me in the direction of the car. I shoved him back, "Get off me! Don't touch me! Keep your hands off me!" The man dropped his hands. I looked back in the direction of my brother and the minivans and finally realized what he was doing. On the ground, next to the front tires of the minivan, sat a car seat. The screeching of the baby blended into the shouting and screaming.

Logan bent down to grab the handle of the car seat. As he picked up the car seat and turned to run, a crawler came out from under the minivan and grabbed his ankle. Logan tumbled forward and sent the car seat flying into the air.

53

Out of nowhere, my savior sprinted toward the flying car seat. He reached it in time to catch it in midair, landing hard on his back, with the car seat on top of him. The baby's father immediately rushed over to the hero, snatched his baby up, and began placing kisses all over its face.

Focusing on the baby, I momentarily forgot about Logan. I scanned the area looking for him. At first, I couldn't see him, then I remembered he was on the ground. I shouted his name again. As I was about to run to help my baby brother, the man who saved me wrapped his arms around me, trapping me, preventing me from going to my brother.

While I screamed and smacked at this brave but annoying man, I noticed two younger men who looked exactly like him, heading toward Logan. As they approached him, I watched him bring his leg up and connect his marine boots to the face of the crawler. Its face caved in and he was able to free himself from his grasp. As the two young men approached Logan, they were smashing the faces of the undead that surrounded them. Once the three of them connected, they quickly became surrounded by the undead.

I nervously watched the scene unfold in front of me. I shot a glance in my hero's direction and noticed a worried look across his face. His nervousness only fed my nerves more. I couldn't stand back and watch anymore. While he was distracted, I stomped my foot on top of his, he shrieked and loosened his grip. Before he had the chance to stop me again, I ran towards the mob. I saw Logan's baseball bat lying about ten feet in front of me. As I ran past it, I crouched down, picked it up, and immediately began to swing. The baseball bat connected with several skulls. Each impact sent a ball of fire up my injured arm into my shoulder.

I looked to my side and saw the hero fighting alongside me. He held a crowbar; his actions mirrored my own. The five of us fought our way through. We were able to make a small path for the three men to make it out and move toward safety.

Once the three men were next to us, we sprinted toward the car. As we approached, I realized the SUV was nowhere to be seen. Neither was Elana. I heard a noise to my right and realized Elana picked up the father and his baby.

Even though the car I drove was tiny, the five of us piled into it and took off. Logan insisted on driving. He sped toward Elana and pulled up next to her car then rolled down the window.

"We need to get out of here. There's just too many of them, we'll never be able to pass right now. Where's June? We need to get off the highway. I think we should head back the way we came and get off at the first exit we see," Logan shouted to Elana.

"I have no idea where June went. She got three or four people into her car then left. My guess is she's waiting for us where it's safe. Let's head back to the last exit and see if she's there." With that, Elana rolled up her window and took off in the direction of the last exit.

As we drove away, hell behind us, I let out a big sigh of relief. The sigh shook my body, causing my shoulder and arm to scream in pain. I silently counted my blessings. I was thankful to be alive and thankful that Elana and Logan were okay. As I reflected on everything that happened, I realized both Logan and I would have been eaten back there. We both should have been killed. What were the chances we both survived—that we both were saved? Someone up above must have been looking out for us, multiple people. I glanced at the strange man who risked his life for me twice, he must have been sent to me for a reason. Without him, Logan and I would both likely be dead and then undead.

The stranger had saved us, and we saved him and his group. We needed each other to survive.

chapter seven

As we approached the nearest exit, we saw my SUV idling in the middle of the road. Logan pulled the car up next to the SUV and rolled down the window. June rolled down hers, while Elana pulled her car up on the other side.

"Maybe we should just drive back to where we came from. That house was safe, untouched. We could stay there forever and be happy, I know it," June suggested. Her cowardice was a major flaw in her personality.

"No" Logan said, "We can't go back. We would be back tracking our entire day of progress; the entire day would be wasted then. It wasn't that difficult to find the last place. We can find one again and collect some more supplies as well." Logan turned to the backseat, "Where are you guys from? Around here? Is there any place safe for us to go?"

One of the men spoke up for the three of them, "We're from New Jersey so we're as in the dark as you are. We've been traveling down the highway for some time now."

Another man spoke up from the other car, "I grew up around here as a kid. I might know a place we could go to. It's not too far away from here and if I remember correctly, its location is pretty secluded. It's an old, rundown church."

We discussed the option then agreed to head to the church. One after another, we drove away with Logan in the lead, followed by

Elana's car, and then June driving the SUV. After twenty-five minutes of making several turns and avoiding several clusters of the undead, we pulled up to the church. It had been about ten miles since we had seen an undead. I hoped we would be secluded enough to not see any that night. I needed the rest.

The church sat on a nearly vacated back road. The closer we got to the church, the fewer houses we saw. The gravel beneath our tires crunched as we cautiously approached the dilapidated building. Overgrown brush fought for space with our tires as we drew closer to what I assumed was the church. On a hill just past the structure, stood a beautiful scarlet oak tree.

As soon as we put the cars in park, we climbed out of the cars, ready to check out our new home. Before setting foot in the church, I was dissatisfied with our new living quarters. The glass stood at jagged peaks within each frame and the door, attached to one hinge, barely held on. More brush and tall weeds flanked the front steps. I missed the house we had taken refuge in. Maybe June was right. Maybe we should have gone back. I started walking to the church, fascinated by its age and condition. I needed to change my attitude and be grateful we found somewhere safe. As I approached the building, I was able to make out scratch marks on the wood near the windows. My eyes fixated on the scratches. I recognized what they were. I backed up and went to the group. "Shhh," I said to the now large group, holding my fingers up to my mouth. I was nervous about what or who was inside of the church.

Logan caught on to my nervous demeanor and knew something wasn't right. He instinctively grabbed his baseball bat and slowly began to approach the church. Before he made his way there, I caught his attention and pointed out the scratches to him. The three brothers noticed also and in seconds they were next to Logan holding their weapons. Logan and the brothers signaled to each other and entered the church. The rest of us stood outside, quietly listening.

A minute later, the four boys walked back outside. "Nothing in there," one of the brothers stated. They gave the church an all clear. We emptied out the SUV and brought everything into the church.

Once everyone was settled in, we began introductions. It was strange that I had spent a great amount of time with those strangers and didn't even know their names. We were so concerned about our safety that little customs like exchanging names didn't even matter. The one brave man had risked his life to save Logan and I, and I didn't even know his name. I couldn't even give him a proper thank you.

Logan, Elana, June, Blake, and I introduced ourselves first because there were less of us and more of them. After we finished explaining who we were, the new members began their introductions. When I looked at them, I realized they were also separated into smaller groups within their group. Sitting in small groups in different areas of the room, it was clear who was comfortable with each other.

The father holding the baby spoke first. "My name is Will and this sweet little baby is Rose. Rose is six months old." As he talked about her, she gave a sweet drooling smile. She also had the most adorable, pudgy cheeks. "There were some major complications during Rose's birth and her mother didn't make it, so it's just the two of us." He looked at the ground taking a moment. "We are from the Reading area. We don't have a real destination. I was honestly just hoping to hook up with some decent people to ride this thing out with. Before all this craziness, I was a high school teacher, but I haven't taught since Rose was born. I also want to just take a moment to thank you, Logan, for saving her. And you, Carter, for saving her again and watching out for us."

So, the hero's name was Carter. I decided I liked the single father—Will. He was a teacher, like Scott and he loved his daughter just like Scott would have loved our little bean.

The next to speak was the girl with the scratch across her face I had saved. She was accompanied by another girl who looked like her. The girl with the scratch attempted to speak but stopped and winced.

The sister spoke instead, "My name is Julia, and this is my sister Amy. We are, or I guess were, both students at Kaplan University in Maryland." Her demeanor seemed sad. "The man that was attacked and killed back on the highway was our cousin, Jeremy. We were on our way to find his mom in Ohio." Julia glanced over at Amy, who was clutching Julia's hand so hard that Julia's fingers were turning purple. "Do you guys have anything that we might be able to give her, she's in a lot of pain. Her pain only seems to be getting worse."

Thankful for something to do, I got up to retrieve some Advil for Amy. I had to admit her scratch did look painful. She was cut diagonally across her face. Luckily, it missed her eyeball. The scratch was a deep burgundy color; parts of it were still bleeding, but not heavily. While I rummaged through the boxes of goodies, Logan approached me. As I reached in the box my shoulder burst with pain again and I let out a little yelp.

"Mya, are you okay? You're hurt. Let me see," He insisted.

"Logan, I'm fine, it's not a big deal. I just got a little banged up back there. It's no reason to worry." Ignoring me, he pulled my shirt down revealing my shoulder. It was the first time I had bothered to look at it and it was worse than I thought. My shoulder was turning purple and had scrape marks across it from slamming into the pavement.

"Jesus, Mya. You need to learn to ask for help and tell people when something is wrong. This could become a real problem. I don't think it's broken but there is definitely something wrong with it. Just be careful, stop moving it. What are you looking for? Let me help you."

"You really know how to make a big deal out of things. I'll be fine. You're not a doctor, you can't diagnose me." Logan glared at me. "Fine, I'm looking for the Advil. It should be in either this box or that one over there. Oh, and I think we should bring a couple Band-Aids back for the scratch across her face. Maybe they'll help stop infections." I pointed in the direction of the box. Logan searched through it and found the Advil and Band-Aids.

59

"Mya, can you at least take one of these for the swelling or pain or whatever? I can tell your shoulder is bothering you and I don't like to see you in pain."

I took the container of medicine from him and nodded. I walked away, took an Advil out and showed Logan. I pretended to take the pill to make my brother happy. As soon as he turned his head, I spit it out. I wasn't ready to tell him about the baby and I wasn't sure if it was safe to take the medicine. I returned to the group and handed the container and bandages to Julia and resumed my spot next to Elana.

Next to introduce himself was the oldest person in the group. "I'm Quinn. I'm from Bound Brook, New Jersey, but grew up around here. I was the one who knew about the church. Back then, it was in a little better condition than this. I was traveling with Alyssa and Sophie before we met with the brothers." He nodded to who I assumed was Alyssa, but I didn't know who Sophie was. As if reading my mind, or maybe the puzzled expression on our faces, he answered our silent question. "Oh, my bad. Sophie was the older woman who we lost back on the highway." When he talked of Sophie's demise, he took off his fisherman's hat and placed it over his heart.

Next Alyssa went on to introduce herself. "As Quinn said, I'm Alyssa. Quinn, Sophie, and I all live in the same neighborhood. When all the craziness began, we left to reach my husband who's on a business trip in Pittsburgh area. As we were about to leave our neighborhood, it was starting to get overrun. Quinn and I saw Sophie struggling with one of those treacherous things, so we saved her, and she insisted on coming along…" Alyssa stopped talking and bowed her head. I assumed that she was grieving over her lost friend.

The hero of the day was next in introducing himself. "I'm Carter." That seemed to be all he was willing to offer. I waited for him to offer up more. He sat tight-lipped, with his arms crossed. One of his brothers nudged him hard in the ribs. "Uhm, I don't know what else to say. Why is all this important? The world is over. It doesn't really matter who we all are." His brother hit him again. "Fine, I'm a doctor. Is that better? Is that what you were looking for?

Knowing who we are changes nothing that is going on outside of these walls. The world is still all screwed up and likely won't be changing anytime soon." Carter, clearly frustrated, stood up and stomped his way outside. If there were a door, I'm sure he would have slammed it. The man that I thought so highly of, did not seem to be who I thought he was.

I glanced over at the two unnamed men and gave them a quizzical look. I silently asked them to explain what the hell happened.

"I'm sorry about that. I'm Doug and that's Evan. Carter is our older brother. He gets very, uh, temperamental. He usually isn't like this but whenever he loses someone, he gets that way. I guess it's a doctor thing. Whenever he loses a patient, he doesn't talk for nearly a week. Losing two members of our group today isn't something he's going to easily accept. He thinks he can save everyone." He sighed. "Anyways, we're from New Jersey as well. Evan and I are twins and were both enrolled at Rutgers University. When everything went to hell, we knew we couldn't stay where we were. Although we knew we had to leave, we were unsure of where to go. So, we decided to just kind of go with the flow of things. Take each day as it came." He shrugged, appearing carefree.

After all the introductions had been made, the room filled with silence. Everyone looked exhausted—physically and emotionally. Carter was somewhere outside, blowing off steam. I glanced at Logan, who was staring at me with worry etched into the wrinkles in his forehead.

"So, you all told us where you're from and your names but none of you mentioned how you all ended up together. I'd love to hear that story," Elana said, breaking the silence.

Doug spoke, "Well, our group began with just the three of us, Evan, Carter and me. When we left our neighborhood, the main roads were way too crazy to drive on—they were congested with abandoned cars and people running about frantically. Because of the bad conditions on the major roads we decided to cut through a neighborhood. When we turned into the neighborhood, we saw Quinn, Alyssa, and Sophie battling their way to their van. They were about to be overrun when we stepped in. They told us they were heading toward western Pennsylvania to find Alyssa's husband, so we figured why not join them, it gave us a place and a purpose in the world again. It was a small, attainable task. We ditched our car there and took Alyssa's minivan. For about a half a day it was just us. We were looking for a suitable place to spend the night when we ran into Jeremy, Amy, and Julia. They were scavenging a house for some goods and we were trying to sleep there. At first, we almost went at it, when Amy finally talked some sense into all of us and explained we should be working together. She pointed out the fact that humans aren't the real enemy. They were heading in the direction of Ohio, so we figured we could all go together. They also had a minivan, that's how we got two. We decided to use both in case we came across anyone else that needed help. When we set out on the highway, we saw plenty of deserted cars. As we drove along, we saw a deserted car with a man standing on top of it. He began to flag us down when he saw us coming—it was Will. We took him and Rose in with us. We were only with them for a couple hours when we ran into the massive amounts of brain-dead. We were about to be overrun when you all showed up."

I cut in, "Brain-dead?"

"Yeah that's what we decided to call them. We couldn't really think of a better name and we didn't think that zombies fit well," Evan answered.

"We call them the undead. And we would classify the amount that you came across on the highway as a mob," I explained to him.

"The undead, huh, I think I might actually like that better than brain-dead," Carter said from behind me. He had a hint of a smile playing across his face. His attitude seemed to have improved.

"Well it's settled then—they are the undead," Quinn agreed.

chapter eight

Per the doctor's orders, we decided to stay at the old church for a couple of days. A couple of days turned into a week plus. Once Carter was in better spirits, he examined the nasty scratch on Amy's face. With limited equipment and first aid material, treating her had been difficult. Carter made the decision that she needed to rest. We as a group decided to stay at the church to allow her to heal. As he continued to examine her and treat her wounds, he claimed that her cuts were getting infected. He was hopeful he could stop the infection.

He continued to check on her throughout the day and he took note of the progress and regressions she had made. Watching Carter work was mesmerizing. I could tell by his swift and careful movements that he cherished what he did. He took pride in helping others and it seemed to solidify his place in the world.

To keep us safe, the proper precautions had been put into place. The men had fixed the unhinged front door, so we were shielded from the cold and the dangers that the outside presented. They worked together to retrieve old planks from the basement. Using them, they hammered the broken window frames. The old, rundown church had an ancient brick fireplace built into the back wall. Like the rest of the place, it was dirty—totally covered in soot.

We kept a small fire blazing for a little warmth and to cook food. We rationed the food to make it last as long as we could. Even after the rationing, there wasn't enough to last us for very long. We were eating every day, but we were still going to sleep with growling stomachs every night

Despite our improvements to our living quarters, it was no paradise. We were all filthy with soot, dried blood, and dirt. None of us had the luxury of showering in days and I would have done anything for one. Our small fire was barely enough to light the room, let alone heat it. We were afraid to build a roaring flame because we didn't want to attract any attention. I constantly rubbed my hands together for heat. On the coldest of nights, we lay down and watched our breath warm the air. Outside had been cloudy and dull—the sun didn't shine the entire time we were there. I desperately needed some Vitamin D. The old church had no electricity or plumbing. I realized how much I had taken for granted and how much I craved normalcy.

The days were long, and the nights were longer. My sense of time was lost, I had no idea how long we had been there. There was nothing to do but sit around and stare at each other and wait. We'd had some small side conversation, but for the most part, no one wanted to converse. Everyone seemed to be so depressed by our new life and current situation, that no one felt the need to express anything.

I was growing antsy for a new environment. I began to check on Amy every hour, as did Carter, desperately hoping for some improvement so we could leave that dreadful sanctum. Every time I checked on her, there was, unfortunately, no difference in her health. If anything, she seemed to be growing weaker. She was refusing to eat anything. Julia tried to shove some beans down her throat, and it resulted in her being vomited on. Amy was no longer talking, she solely communicated with moans and groans. She also refused to drink, eat, and take medications. She had given up on life and lost the will to survive. I listened to her moan off and on throughout the night.

My shoulder was still injured and tender. Logan had insisted that Carter examine it. As I suspected, just bruised—not broken or dislocated. His orders were to rest the shoulder. Logan watched over me like a hawk, making sure I rested the shoulder. Due to Logan's over-possessiveness, I'd barely done anything. I spent the days grieving for the loss of Scott, but I slowly came to accept his fate. Part of me wished I had died along with him. I know that's terrible to think but the new world wasn't ideal for anyone, especially a young widowed mother. How could I bring a baby into the world in the middle of an apocalypse? I was thankful I was only in the first trimester instead of the third. I couldn't imagine fighting the undead with a full-blown belly. I really wasn't sure how far along I was. I guessed I was two months—maybe a little more. I still had yet to tell anyone about the baby, and I knew I should, but I didn't want to burden the rest of the group.

I decided to hold a small funeral for Scott so I could have closure. It was difficult for me to accept that his body was still in the street in front of our house. I picked the best-looking tree that I could find—the large vibrant scarlet oak tree I'd seen when we first pulled up. I asked Logan to dig a small hole then I buried Scott's favorite outfit—a ratty, old pair of sweatpants and his Weidner University hoodie. I saved his blue polo shirt for sentimental value. I couldn't bear the thought of anyone else wearing them. As for the rest of his clothes, I let the other men wear them.

I decided I wanted Scott to be buried under the beautiful scarlet oak tree because it was peaceful. The property was rundown and the best part about the place was the tree. Logan crafted a cross out of planks he found in the basement. I carved Scott's name into it and shoved it into the ground.

Everyone had offered to be with me, but I needed to do this alone. I spent the rest of the day under the scarlet oak tree, sitting in front of the cross, talking to Scott about the baby. In that moment, I decided I would fight and do everything in my power to give our baby the best life I could.

Even though I was alone, I knew that I had people spying on me from the front landing of the church, mainly Logan. Once or twice when I looked back, I even saw Carter looking in on me. I sat there with Scott until sunset. At sunset, I placed my hand on the dirt, gave it a good pat, and said my final goodbyes. I vowed to never forget him and promised that our child would know about him. I vowed to let his spirit rest and proceed to heaven where he belonged.

chapter nine

After a week of being stuck inside the old church, the sun had risen for the first time. It peeked its head out to say hello, hung around for about an hour and receded back into the clouds. It was November, I wasn't sure of the exact day. Time didn't matter anymore.

I decided to go through the priest's room to search for anything useful. I wanted to do this the first night, but, for some reason, it felt disrespectful and I resisted. No longer. The world didn't seem to be improving and I thought God would understand we had to do whatever we could to survive.

I walked down the small hallway and opened the creaky door with the big cross on it. The room had been left untouched. I stood in the room and looked around. It was a tiny room with only enough space for a desk, two chairs, and a small table. The table held the appropriate items for mass. Every inch of the room was covered in dust. The dust lay so thick that I couldn't make out the word BIBLE on the religious book.

I walked around the desk and took a seat in front of it, not caring about how dirty it was. I was filthy myself. I briefly paused and debated whether this was the right thing to do. I decided to continue with my plans—to hell with it. I began searching the desk. After opening its drawers, I found nothing worth taking. I sat there, disappointed. For some reason, I had a strong feeling I would find something—something I didn't know I was looking for. Something that was in the office. I stood and made my way toward the closet. There was nothing inside—except cobwebs. Aside from the desk, there was no other place for something else. I began to rummage through the desk again, taking the drawers all the way out. In the last one, on the bottom left, I removed it and shook it upside down, as I had all the other drawers. As I turned it upside down, a fake bottom fell along with a pistol. I knew my instincts were right in searching the place.

As I stared at the gun, I debated on what exactly I should do with it. I didn't trust everyone. I couldn't risk the wrong person finding out about the gun. I quickly concluded that Logan needed to know about the gun. I put the gun back into its hiding place and returned the desk to its previous state. I stood in front of the door, overlooking the office for anything that looked out of place. I left the room, closing the door behind me, in search for Logan.

When I found Logan, he was, surprisingly, sitting at Scott's grave under the tree. He looked deep in thought.

"Hey, what are you doing out here?" I asked Logan, puzzled. I didn't expect to find Logan sitting here. It wasn't like him to show any type of emotion.

"Hey sis, just came here to think. You really did pick the perfect place. I'm sure he's looking down thinking the same thing. It's peaceful here, so different from inside." Logan looked down, played with his boot lace, and sighed, "I can't stand to listen to Amy's moans anymore. It brings back bad memories for me. Sitting here is peaceful and gives me a perfect view of what's around us. I'm more useful here than in there."

Speechless at my brother's straightforward emotional answer, I chose to say nothing and smile instead. I sat down next to him and patted his knee. We sat in silence for a few more moments, looking out into the beautiful lush woods.

"What's up Mya? You came out here for a reason."

"You're the only person I trust to know this. I found a gun in the priest's office. I think you should hold onto it."

Logan grinned at me like a kid on Christmas morning, "Show me!"

I led Logan down the hallway into the priest's room, dismantled the desk and gave him the gun. There was no look of surprise on his face at the gun's secret location.

"That's it? There are no bullets in there? There are only six bullets. That won't do us much good." Logan turned the drawer upside down again and did the same with the right drawer. He turned to look in the closet, "There isn't anything in there, I already looked," I told him so he wouldn't waste his time. Logan opened it anyway and rummaged around. He found a secret hiding space in a ceiling tile that had bullets in it. Logan turned, looked at me, and shook the box. I gave him a thumbs up.

"I agree. We need to keep this information between us—and Elana, of course. June won't condone this, and we barely know these other people. It's best those guys don't know about this either. I don't want them getting any ideas." With that Logan tucked the gun into his pants and pulled his shirt down over it. He rearranged the room back to its previous state then looked at me.

"You okay Mya? You're looking kind of pale lately," Logan's worrying had returned. "How's your shoulder doing?"

I debated whether to tell him the truth about the baby. It wasn't the right time. He didn't need the added burden—no one did. Once we were safe with Lilianna, I would tell them both—a family event, hopefully a happy one.

"I'm fine, really. You need to stop worrying about me. My shoulder is still a little bruised but its healing. I'm just pale from lack of sunlight. It's like the sun is punishing us and is refusing to shine, it's getting really depressing," I said brushing Logan off.

"If you say so, just know that I'm here if you need me." He smiled and turned to leave. I wondered if he caught on that I was dealing with more than a shoulder injury.

I followed him out into the main room. As I walked down the hallway, I saw a scrap of bandage on the floor. I bent down to pick it up and, when I stood, I stood too fast and lost my balance. Luckily, the wall caught me. That was the third dizzy spell over the last two days. I quickly collected myself and regained my composure. I smoothed my shirt down and looked around to make sure no one was watching me. As I glanced around, I caught Carter's emerald green eyes intensely staring at me. I felt like he was diagnosing me. I gave him a quick smile and looked away.

Carter approached me, and I turned and went the opposite way.

He didn't need the distraction, he needed to concentrate on Amy. He needed to make her better. I wanted to get out of there.

chapter ten

"She's not getting any better, she's actually getting worse. I'm not sure what else can be done. We didn't learn this kind of stuff in med school. 'What to do when a zombie scratches you' wasn't exactly in our textbook," Carter explained to us the next morning. I was ready to move on and start our trip to get Lilianna.

"What should we do? How do we help her? Should we run out and get some supplies? Please, Carter tell me what to do so I can get my sister back. I don't understand why she isn't healing. She isn't eating or drinking, it's not healthy. She needs an IV or something. Whatever you're doing isn't working anymore!" Toward the end of her rant, Julia began to raise her voice to a holler, frustrated with him. She turned frantic with worry about her sister. I couldn't blame her. I would be the same way had it been Lilianna or Logan.

"I'm sorry, Julia, I don't know what else to try. We could try and get an IV, but I don't know where the nearest hospital is, and it would be a risky mission. Hospitals are also likely crawling with the undead. They were ground zero for this thing, remember?" Carter hung his head low, his face showing defeat. It seemed everyone understood what Carter was trying to say except for Julia—she was going to die.

"I refuse to accept what you are telling me. If you'll excuse me, I'm going to try and feed Amy again. Someone has to, and it seems that I'm the only one willing." Julia stomped off to where Amy was lying down. Her footsteps were so hard, that dust pranced off the floor and into the air. She was wrong about her being the only one willing to take care of Amy. Several of us had offered her a break and she dismissed us. She would not relinquish control of caring for her sister.

Julia resumed her position at her sister's side. She picked up Amy's hand in hers and kissed it, rocking back and forth. We walked outside before we began to talk again about the serious situation at hand.

"So really doc, what's the deal? No doctor mumbo jumbo BS," Quinn asked Carter.

"Honestly, I don't think she's going to make it. I don't know how much longer she has, she's almost completely unresponsive." Carter hung his head in silence.

June chimed in on the conversation: "Not to change the subject or anything, but we're starting to run low on supplies. We only have enough food to last a day or two—if we're lucky. We need to do something soon, think about the children." I was irritated by June's disruption. We had a serious matter to discuss. Serious scenarios that we needed to consider.

"Jesus, June, have some sympathy. We are quite aware of the situation at hand here. Do you want us to kill her faster so you can move on and grab a can of Pringles? Do you understand how ridiculous that sounds? Have a heart!!" Elana snapped at June. I had never seen Elana react like that before. It was clear that Elana wanted nothing to do with June.

Elana stomped off in one direction and June in another direction. The rest of us looked at each other, not sure what else was left to say. Everyone went their separate ways to waste the day away.

I watched Carter walk to the scarlet oak tree where we buried Scott's memory and followed. I needed to talk to him. Carter took a seat with his back against the tree and put his head in his hands. I stood frozen, confused at why he would sit near my husband's grave. Once my initial shock gave way, I continued up to Carter. I needed to discuss the wild scenario I had going around in my head about Amy. I was going to bring it up to the group but decided against it. No need to create unnecessary worry and chaos. It was better to just sit and talk it through with someone. It was a bonus that someone was a medical professional.

"Hi," I said as I took a seat on the ground, sitting Indian style across from Carter. It felt odd to sit there with another man. It felt like a betrayal to Scott, sitting at his grave with a male stranger.

"Hello, I hope this doesn't offend you. I just find some peace here. The tree seems to be untouched by all the bad. If you look around, the other trees have already lost their leaves, but this tree here is still flourishing with the beautiful red color of fall, not ready to accept winters arrival. It's resilient," Carter said.

"I hadn't taken notice of that before. As much as I hate this place on the inside, the outside is breathtakingly beautiful. If I had it my way, I would knock down this church and build something beautiful. It was always a dream of mine to build my own house one day." I picked at the grass, unsure why I was telling him this. "Anyway, I came out here for a reason."

"Are you finally ready to discuss your dizzy spells? Don't think I haven't noticed, because I have and I'm worried. Are you eating and drinking enough? Sleeping enough? There are many reasons why that could be happening."

"Actually no, I don't need your medical advice. I'm fine. You're as bad as Logan. Yesterday what you saw, I just stood up a little too fast. I'm actually here to talk about Amy." I needed to get his attention off my medical situation quickly before he put two and two together.

"What about her?"

"Well, Doctor Carter, if you quit interrupting me maybe I'll tell you," I teased.

"Okay, I'm sorry, continue," he interrupted me again.

"Do you think there's a possibility she can turn into an undead? She was scratched by an undead and is now, basically, dying," I finally spoke my wild scenario out loud.

"In my professional opinion, I would say no. The undead seem to be turning because of the bites. She wasn't bitten. I would say, from a medical standpoint, it isn't the virus that the undead seem to possess. If it were, I think she would have turned by now. She's doing so poor because of the infection the deep scratches have caused and we don't have the proper antibiotics to treat it. In my opinion, it may be possible because, honestly, I have no idea what this crazy virus does. I haven't seen anyone turn yet from a scratch, but it could be possible. So, all in all, I really have no idea." He sent a sad smirk my way.

"Well that doesn't really answer my question now does it? But what you said about the bites does make sense. Every bite I have witnessed the victim died and turned almost instantly. Their injuries were too severe for them to live longer. In her case, her injury wasn't fatal."

"Part of the reason I came out here to think was because of that. I've been wondering the same thing and it annoys the hell out of me that I can't come up with the answer, I'm a doctor for Christ's sake."

"Not everyone has answers for everything." I patted his hand for comfort. We needed to keep watch though. I remembered my neighbor turning undead and biting my husband after he killed her with his car. The mark on her wrist seemed insignificant too. I shuddered thinking about it.

"What was it like to be in love?" Carter's question caught me off guard. I didn't understand why he was asking me this or how he thought it was appropriate.

"I'm sorry. I'm not trying to be rude or bring up emotionally unwanted feelings. I was just wondering. I've never been in love. My entire life has been devoted to med school and then my career. Now that those things don't really matter, I'm realizing that I missed out on one of the most important experiences a person should go through. When I looked at you during the ceremony, how you reacted to Scott's death, I realized that you must have really loved him. Sometimes I hear you cry at night and I see you constantly clutching the wedding band on your necklace. I've also seen you come out here countless times to just sit with his spirit."

"Wow, you're observant. Uhm, love. It's an interesting thing. There's no real way to describe it other than the best and worst feeling that you could possibly experience." I looked at Carter and saw vulnerability across his face. I stared into his eyes, unable to speak.

Carter cleared his throat and looked away. The moment had been incredibly intimate and completely inappropriate given where we were sitting.

I decided to continue, pretending that the connection didn't happen, "Love can't be described, you have to experience it for yourself…"

AHHHHHHHHHHHHHHH

"Oh my God, what the hell was that?" Carter jumped to his feet. There were loud screams coming from the church. Carter offered me his hand, helped me to my feet, and we set off running in the direction of the church.

As we were running toward the church, I noticed that Logan, Elana, and Quinn were outside and running toward the church. That left Doug, Evan, Alyssa, Will, June and the two kids inside of the church. The frantic screams increased in amount and volume.

Logan was the first to reach the door. He kicked the door in and pulled the gun from his waistband. He took stance as if he were a cop. Carter and I quickly followed behind him.

My fears had come true. Amy was up, showing the most movement she'd done in days, but she wasn't herself. She was kneeling over Julia ripping her flesh apart with her teeth. The scratches on Amy's face affected her in the way I feared. They killed her and then gave her life again—she was undead.

I stopped in my tracks—speechless and motionless—stunned by what was happening. I scanned the room to account for everyone. Out of the corner of my eye, I noticed June running back to the priest's room with both children.

I looked back to the chaos. Doug was pulling Amy off Julia, whose screams had subsided as she passed on. Logan was there but had acquired a different weapon—his baseball bat. Evan pushed Amy into a wall and quickly moved out of the way, making room for Logan. Logan rushed over and heaved the baseball bat into Amy's skull several times. During those movements, I noticed that the gun was tucked back into his waistband.

Distracted by Amy, no one realized Julia had already turned undead and was heaving her body off the floor, preparing to lunge at Alyssa. Julia was shrieking as she knocked Alyssa down to the ground. Alyssa began to scream and scrambled to get away. She pulled herself across the floor to escape. Julia was faster and latched onto Alyssa's foot. Julia tugged Alyssa closer and closer. Before any of us could react, Julia sank her teeth into Alyssa's ankle.

In the same moment, Evan pulled Julia off Alyssa by her feet. The movement caused Julia's teeth to rip through Alyssa's skin and almost removed her entire foot. Julia's bite removed a huge chunk of Alyssa's skin—her entire heel and Achilles' tendon were ripped off. Alyssa frantically grasped at her ankle and sobbed. There was blood squirting out from the wound soaking her hands and the floor. There was so much red thickness all over the place. I knew that, in moments, Alyssa would be gone as well.

I stood there, useless, watching everyone fight for their lives. I couldn't decide what to do. I couldn't decide who was worth saving. I couldn't get my feet to move. I stood there and watched the despair unfold in front of me.

Evan struggled with Julia. They wrestled on the floor competing for dominance. Seconds later, Carter dragged Julia off Evan and put an axe into her brain.

Alyssa was in Quinn's arms sobbing. He was rocking her back and forth, comforting her in her last moments. It was clear that she wasn't going to make it. We all knew it and it seemed that she knew it as well. They grasped hands holding on for strength. As the moments, went on Alyssa face grew paler and her body began to shake. In the craziness, Elana had retrieved a knife from our box of goods and silently passed it to Quinn.

A minute went by and we all stood around watching as Alyssa's life slipped from her body. Her eyes rolled into the back of her head and she let out her last breath. Everyone in the room was silent waiting for the inevitable. We stared at Quinn waiting for him to make his move to put her out of her misery before she turned, but he did nothing.

"Quinn, maybe you should uh, you know, before it happens?" Elana offered up, brave enough to say the words we were all thinking.

"I'll do it when I'm good and ready now don't you tell me my business again, woman," Quinn snapped at her while a single tear streamed down his face.

We all glanced at each other and I raised an eyebrow at Logan, as if to signal to be prepared for the worse: that Alyssa would bite Quinn. He seemed to read my mind and silently grabbed his baseball bat again.

Seconds later, Alyssa shrieked and jolted out of death to the undead state. I couldn't even blink in the time that Quinn reacted and plunged the knife into her skull.

"There, ya happy?" Quinn shot Elana a dirty look and gently laid Alyssa's lifeless body down on the dirty floor. He folded her arms over her chest, stood up, and walked out the door.

Nauseous by all the horrific events I had witnessed, I vomited onto the floor. The sudden loss of my stomach contents earned me many puzzled looks. I shrugged their looks away.

In minutes, we had lost three members of our group. I looked around and reflected on the current state of the church. It was a mess, even worse than when we arrived, which was pretty bad. There were two pools of blood, blood spatter all over the floor and walls, and three battered, shredded, ripped up dead bodies. It looked like a massacre. Hell, it was a massacre, three people were killed in a matter of minutes.

I refused to let these events stun us into an emotional coma, I faced the group, "Where do we go from here?"

chapter eleven

I looked around at everyone, their faces lacked any hope. June emerged from the back room, shielding the eyes of the children, leading them outside. We all followed to talk. Inside was tainted with death that none of us could bear to look at. The November sun was beginning its descent, creating a brisk chill in the air. I craved warm pumpkin pie and hot chocolate.

My body trembled, I wasn't sure if it was the chill outside or the three deaths I couldn't stop thinking about. I wrapped my arms around my body tightly hoping to preserve some heat and stop the shaking.

"We obviously can't stay here anymore. It's just not right, the floor is stained. I can't bear to look at it every single day. I can't let my boy play on the ground next to where someone had died. I say we pack up our things right now and get far away from here," June expressed her opinion. Honestly, it was hard to disagree with that. I couldn't sleep in there again either.

"We can't leave yet, we can't just leave their bodies in there to rot, it's not right. They were part of our group. We smashed in their brains—they deserve a proper burial," Quinn argued.

"It's almost sunset, there is not time to dig holes and bury their bodies. By the time we finished that it'd be dark and too dangerous to travel, we need to leave now!" June argued back.

"No, I agree with Quinn. We need to bury their bodies—it's the right thing to do. I also agree with June that it would take a long time and, by the time we finished, it would be dark. It's not safe to be out here in the dark." Carter was trying to play the role of a peacekeeper. I found his change in character refreshing. I was also surprised at his cool demeanor. The last time he lost someone, he freaked. Now he seemed okay—as okay as you can expect a person to be after witnessing three deaths.

"What's really more important, burying dead people who won't even know it or keeping us safe and finding a new place to stay?" June was becoming pushy. "We need to leave this place NOW!"

"Stop being so self-centered. You're probably the most heartless woman I have ever encountered. Do you see the example that you are setting for your son?" Elana spoke up. "Do you seriously think that in the time it takes us to put these poor deceased people to rest, that we're going to let something happen to any of us? Huh? No of course we won't. So just shut the hell up! If you don't want to help, then so be it, but stay out of our way!"

"You people are so irrational and small minded. I'm not sleeping in that disgusting church where those disgusting rotting bodies are. We will be sleeping in the cars." With that, June stomped off, grabbed Blake by his hand, and dragged him in the direction of the vehicles.

"Thank the heavens she walked away. I've had just about enough of her," Quinn said with a quick wink. "So then, we can count her out for doing pretty much anything, which leaves the rest of us. What should we do?"

"It's not safe to stay out here digging the holes at night, that much is clear, we'll start the digging at sunrise," I offered my opinion on the matter.

"Perfect, but what about the bodies? Not that I didn't respect any of them while they were alive, but I agree with June, I can't sleep in there with the dead bodies and the blood everywhere. It's gut-wrenchingly disgusting," Will entered the conversation. Up until that point he stood off to the side observing quietly. After he stated his opinion, he quickly went to the minivan where Blake and June sat and gave June the baby to care after while he helped.

"Well, we can't just dump them outside for the night. Animals will get to them," Logan wisely stated. "I say that we move them into a corner in the church, preferably by a window, so the smell of death isn't trapped in the room. I personally will still be able to sleep in there, I've dealt with worse. I'll start digging tonight so we can set off tomorrow sooner rather than later, we need as much sunlight on the road as possible." With that he retrieved the shovel and began walking toward the tree. We watched as he attempted to shove the shovel down into the ground. After several attempts, he stopped, looked at us, looked back at the dirt and then looked off into the distance.

"Problem?" Carter hollered.

"I don't think this is the right place to bury the bodies. The holes we need to dig for the others will need to be very deep. I don't think we'll be able to get very far here. Plus, the ground is pretty much frozen." He began his stride back to us as he was talking. "I'm going to walk around the church and find a place that isn't as solid." He set off in search for a nice resting place.

"Wait up, I'll grab a flashlight and help out. You'll need it and you shouldn't be alone out there, even if you are a big, strong, tough man," Elana teased her boyfriend and skipped off behind him.

"Okay, Logan's taking care of that. How about we all go get started with the bodies then?" Carter suggested, he seemed uncomfortable saying those words out loud.

We walked inside and froze in the entry way—absorbing the devastation. No one wanted to enter the blood-splattered church. The smell of harsh, metallic blood flooded my nose, but I held it together, not wanting anyone to suspect anything. I put my head down, as if to smell myself, which didn't smell much better. I preferred the smell of my grime to the smell of death. The blood pools were a deep vibrant red against the wooden floors, but the edges had begun to dry.

We split into pairs to move the bodies. Quinn and Will went to move Alyssa's body. Doug and Evan went to move Amy's body. Carter and I were expected to move Julia's body. The bodies were moved to the far corner of the church under a window.

Carter and I bent down to pick up Julia's body. As I grabbed hold of her ankles, the smell of death hit me, and I began to gag. Carter looked at me and raised his eyebrows. I assured him I was fine, took a deep breath, and reached again for her legs.

My fingers wrapped around her ankles and began to lift. Her body was surprisingly stiff. So stiff that I was having a difficult time managing her legs. One of her legs slipped from my grasp and hit the floor with a thud. "S-sorry, she's heavier than I thought she would be," I said.

I picked her leg up off the ground again. Again, I was suddenly hit with the nasty, vile smell of blood and death. That time I couldn't suppress my reaction. I quickly dropped her legs and lunged into the corner. Only that time I had nothing to come up. I crouched in the corner dry heaving with hot tears streaming down my face. Carter put Julia's body down and came over to comfort me, rubbing my back.

"Stop, I'm fine," I said, wiping the spit from my mouth with my sleeve. I looked up at him through the tears and saw the look of concern register across his face. "I'm sorry Carter, but I don't know if I can stomach moving her. Every time I touch her my stomach gets all riled up. Please forgive me."

"Don't worry about it, Doug will help me. Why don't you go get some fresh air?"

I followed the doctor's orders and went outside. I sat down on the steps, making sure to stay close because it was dark out. I sat with my head between my knees, using my knees to rub my temples. I took several deep breaths, attempting to steady my breathing and heart rate. I could feel how tense my body was and how stressed my mind was.

As I collected myself, Logan and Elana rounded the corner with a flashlight and shovel in hand.

"Mya, what's wrong? You've been crying? Did something happen? Did someone do something to you while we were gone?" Logan questioned. He came over and crouched down to talk to me.

"No, Jesus, relax. You're always ready to fight someone or fix some problem. I'm fine, just got a little sick to my stomach. I couldn't handle moving the bodies," I replied.

"Well, I don't blame you there. Why do you think we went to dig the holes?" He smiled at me teasingly and winked. "I may be a big strong tough man, but I can't handle all of that. Brings back bad memories. Plus, I got us a good head start for tomorrow. I broke the ground in three spots and managed to dig one hole that I think will be deep enough. So tomorrow, we just have to finish digging the last two."

I nodded at him. Both he and Elana sat down on either side of me. They put their heads on my shoulders and sighed.

"We wasted too much time here. We've been here for days. I'm so excited to finally hit the road again tomorrow. I'm just worried that we might be too late for Lilianna." He expressed his concerns as if he read my mind.

"Don't think like that. It'll all work out. We'll get there. I know this might sound bad, but now, there are less people preventing us from getting there. But I do think June will be a problem—she's definitely going to slow us down," I admitted.

"Oh, I definitely agree. But what can we really do about that? Nothing. That's just something that we're going to have to deal with. I'm sure Lilianna is fine, she's a brave girl just like her brother and sister." Elana tried to reassure us as she nudged my shoulder and smiled at me.

Our little family moment was interrupted when Carter opened the door to let us know the bodies were moved and we could come in.

The three of us got up and joined the others in the church. The bodies being moved did nothing for the room. It still looked and reeked of death. I couldn't blame June for sleeping in the cars, it was smart. I didn't want to do that, it would be incredibly uncomfortable, and I needed all the rest I could get before our next journey. My eyes traveled the room, looked at the bodies that lay side by side, and immediately gagged. I had to look away and avoid that area of the room.

"It's truly devastating what happened here tonight. If anyone feels the need to talk about it, I'll be free. Oh yeah, I didn't mention this earlier. I'm a shrink," Elana offered up her professional services to everyone.

"There is no changing what happened here tonight. But let it be a lessoned learned. Now we know that scratches will infect your body to the point of death and then you turn undead. This is life altering and lifesaving information that we didn't have before tonight. Also, we learned that pretty much as soon as their heart stops beating, they turn undead. There is not much time to decide on what needs to be done. These three people will continue to be in our hearts, but let's not let their deaths be in vain, let's learn something from them. Hopefully, learning this will in turn save one of our lives somewhere down the line." Carter wanted everyone to realize that we gained new knowledge. I was glad he brought this to everyone's attention, everyone needed to hear it. I thought back to my neighbor, Missy. The mark on her wrist had been small and not fatal, but the impact of the car impaling her was fatal. She died instantly and turned instantly.

The room grew silent, and the silence began to turn awkward.

"I have no idea what time it is, I'm sure it's still early. Why don't we grab some food and then hit the sack. Tomorrow's going to be a long day. It's going to be a long trip," Quinn offered up.

No one seemed to object to his suggestions. Will retreated to the car to be with his daughter and June. I was beginning to think that they might have some sort of connection. The rest of us dug into the last of our canned goods. We would need to find more supplies soon.

The food was delicious. As nauseous as I was, I was also starved. I couldn't stand to eat inside, so I sat on the stoop eating my food, looking out at the tree. I don't know what it was with that scarlet oak tree, but it had me mesmerized. I often found others sitting at that tree too. My thoughts were interrupted when Carter opened the door and took a seat next to me.

"How are you holding up?" He said to me.

"I'm doing okay, considering the circumstances. I just couldn't stomach to eat inside with that smell." I wrinkled my nose at him, my stomach flip-flopping just thinking about it.

"Can't blame you, that's why I came out to join you." He held up his can of beans. Not knowing what to say in return I nodded and returned my attention to the tree again.

Carter broke into my thoughts again, "Are you sure you're doing okay? You keep saying something about the horrible smell. And I'll admit that it doesn't smell like roses in there, but the smell of death really hasn't sunk into the walls yet. Maybe you're coming down with something? Or do you just have extraordinary senses?" Carter began to tease.

I panicked. He was catching onto my secret—he was a doctor after all. I tried to keep up my poker face. "Oh, yeah I've always had a heightened sense of smell—genetics." I offered up a small fake smile.

"Ah, as I suspected." He followed my gaze. "You're sitting here looking at that tree again? Do you sit here and wonder if it will die this winter along with the rest of the world, and its beauty will be forever lost? I know I wonder that every time I see it. It's quite a miracle that it still has all of its leaves." Carter was basically reading my mind, which I found very unsettling.

"Yes, I actually do wonder that. I was thinking that someday I would like to revisit this tree just to see if it survives, well that's if I survive."

85

"If you don't mind, I'd like to accompany you on that trip and see for myself as well. You know, if we're still alive." He playfully nudged my shoulder with his.

Was he seriously making long-term plans with me? This guy barely even knew me.

"I never really did thank you for saving my life back on the highway. If it weren't for you, I wouldn't be here. From the bottom of my heart I thank you, Doctor Carter…" I was embarrassed, I realized I didn't know his last name. "I'm sorry Carter, what's your last name? I never asked before"

"Brooks, my last name is Brooks"

"Well Doctor Carter Brooks, thank you for saving my life. I don't think I ever offered up my last name either. It's Davis, well that's my married last name. My maiden name is Whitten. It's funny now how last names don't even matter anymore."

"Well, Mrs. Mya Whitten-Davis, it was a pleasure to save you. Now, might I suggest that you turn in for the night soon, you look exhausted. I also suggest that maybe you sleep back in the priest's room, so you don't lose your meal."

"Yes, thank you, I hadn't thought of that. I was starting to worry where I was going to sleep." I stood, preparing myself to enter the reeking building. Carter stood as well. I looked up at him. "Well, Carter, goodnight."

Carter brushed aside a piece of hair that had fallen in front of my eyes, "Goodnight, Mya."

I was stunned at the intimate and bold move he had made. For just a second, I thought he might kiss me. I wasn't ready for that, but I was unable to move my feet, they were cemented to the ground. Carter leaned in and I backed up. I was worried he would brush his lips to mine. Instead, he reached for the handle of the door. He opened the door and gestured for me to go inside.

I nervously laughed and thanked him. I felt stupid and childish that he might try and pull a move on me—a grieving widow. I felt like a horrible person to even have those thoughts. Even though it felt like an eternity, my husband had only been dead a short time. I shook my head and made my way back to the priest's room. Elana and Logan decided to sleep with me.

I was beginning to trust Carter. He seemed trustworthy enough. After all, he was a doctor and he did save my life. I closed my eyes willing sleep to take me to a place where there were no nightmares of the dead and no dreams of the future. I wished to sleep a soundless deep sleep. I drifted off to sleep thinking of the moment outside with Carter. I couldn't get his gentle smile out of my mind nor the butterflies out of my stomach.

chapter twelve

The next morning, we rose as the sun began to shine. Logan, of course, was the first one up, ready, and eager to start the long day. I didn't have the peaceful night's sleep I had hoped for. I woke several times due to my bladder and the voices of everyone out in the main room. I desperately wanted to try to squeeze in a couple more hours before our long journey ahead, but I knew that my body and brother wouldn't allow that. He began to stir when slits of light started to shine through the boarded-up window. He tried to tiptoe around us, in hopes he wouldn't wake us, but it was too late for me. When he began to move, I lifted my head and looked at him.

"I'm sorry Mya, I didn't mean to wake you. Go back to sleep. You girls can sleep while us men do the work. I'll wake you when we're ready," Logan whispered, hoping not to wake Elana.

"No, it's okay. I was already up. Can't sleep. I'll come out and help out, or at least offer some motivational words because I really don't want to shovel." I smiled at him. "Go ahead, I'll be out in a minute."

Logan exited the room and I laid my head back down, enjoying the peace the small room had to offer. I wanted to savor what might have been my last moment alone. I was extremely nervous to start out on the road again. I didn't like the uncertainty of what we might come across or what horrible things might happen next.

I listened carefully and could hear voices coming from outside. The priest's room was located at the back of the church. Elana began to stir next to me, the noise disrupting her sleep.

She turned over and smiled at me, "Good morning. I bet you're happy to finally be leaving this place."

"Good morning. Yes, I am. I can't wait to see Lilianna. I miss her so much and I'm so worried about her. But I kind of like this place. I mean yesterday kind of ruined it for me. But this place has something peaceful to offer, I've never been somewhere so disgusting and so beautiful at the same time. The inside of the church is absolutely awful, but the outside is wonderful, almost magical in a way."

"Yeah, I know what you mean, I guess. The inside of this place is horrendous but the outside—it's like a fairy tale." She yawned and stretched like a cat. "I hope our next place has actual beds—I hate sleeping on this hardwood floor. Let's get a move on so we can get one step closer to Lilianna!"

We both collected all our belongings and exited the priest's room. I looked back around the room before I closed the door, thankful for this little sanctum. As we walked through the main room and out the door, I noticed how strong the smell had become overnight. The undead bodies in the corner of the room had begun to rot. I felt horrible for the people who had slept in the room the night before. The blood pools on the floor had mostly dried and left a rank metallic smell imbedded into the floorboards. I started to gag. Putting my hand over my mouth, I ran past Elana, through the front door, down the steps, and vomited. Just as the contents of my stomach expelled from my body, Carter walked up to me. *Great,* I thought, *as if he weren't suspicious enough, he was now seeing this.* I nervously looked up at him, ashamed and embarrassed at how he had just seen me. I wasn't one to be open about any type of bodily function and I was puking my guts up in front of a man I barely even knew.

I took a deep inhale and breathed. Once I was sure that I was done being sick, I wiped the corner of my mouth with my sleeve and sat on the ground, hoping to get a grip. Carter approached me and handed me a bottle of water and a tube of toothpaste.

"Good morning. I see that your stomach is still queasy from last night. Are you sure you're okay? Any fevers? You could have caught a bug? I found some toothpaste in your SUV, hope that's okay. Might be useful, although there is no toothbrush, so you'll have to use your finger." He gave me a warm, shy smile.

"Thank you, Carter. I'm fine, just the smell of the bodies has intensified overnight and is unbearable. I think I'll avoid going inside the rest of the time we're here. I should have known better and held my breath while I walked through the room." I took the water and toothpaste that he offered. "How's the digging going?"

"It's good. Between all of us guys, we'll be done in no time. We're on the last hole now. Logan is really determined to finish it. Has he always had a pushy personality?"

"Yeah, that sounds like Logan. He's always got to be in control, and he is efficient, he needs to get things done in an orderly fashion. He was in the marines, so I think the behavior is kind of drilled into him for forever now," Elana chimed in answering Carters question, she turned and focused her attention on me. "Mya, are you okay? You rushed past me and then you're on the ground. Should I get Logan?"

"I'm fine, just a weak stomach. I wish you would all stop fussing over me. Please don't mention this to Logan. He always seems to overreact about the smallest things. Let him concentrate on getting his task done, I know he's eager to leave, we all are." I smiled at her, trying to give her some reassurance that I was, in fact, fine. She simply responded with "Okay" and went off to where the holes were being dug. I knew that I was doing a crappy job of sliding under the radar and I knew that people were going to start suspecting things. Luckily, my winter coat was big enough that it could hide the small bump forming in my abdomen. It was surprising to me that I was already forming a bump and it had me questioning just how far along I was?

I turned my attention back to Carter, "Let's go look at these holes." We walked around back, a place I had surprisingly not ventured to yet. The ground was frozen. As we walked, it crunched underneath my shoes. The area was a big clearing of yellow, dying grass. The grassy area extended about two yards back and then the forest began. The forest was luscious. Most of the trees had refused to give up their leaves. But the leaves were clearly losing the battle and were beginning to welter away. The floor of the forest was sprinkled with bright vibrant colors, as were the trees. Where the forest began, a clearance carved out a small semi-circle that looked like someone took an ice cream scooper to it. In the semi-circle was where the remaining members of the group stood looking down at the ground. It took a few minutes before we reached them.

"Good morning, guys. I see that you have been busy. How were you able to penetrate the ground? It's frozen solid."

"Logan is the one who did it. Once he broke ground, we all started to chip in. He's an animal. He just picked up the shovel and shoved it straight into the ground, breaking through the first frozen layer," Doug answered my question, obviously impressed by my brother's abilities. I wasn't surprised. I knew he was determined to leave.

"Alright, enough small talk. Let's keep moving. We need to leave here when the sun is high. We need as much sunlight as possible to travel," Logan said, irritated by our conversation because it put the work on hold.

"Is there anything that I can do?" I offered.

"Yeah why don't you and whoever else get the bodies ready to be carried out here?" He suggested. I nodded in agreement. My stomach was already starting to flip at the thought of having to go anywhere near the bodies. I started to walk back to the church while the men were working out who else would help me. As I was walking, Carter jogged up behind me.

"Mya, you don't have to do that. My brothers and I will handle it. Why don't you take some of the wood and make crosses for the plots?" I was so thankful for the doctor's suggestion.

"Thank you. I appreciate that more than you know…" I was about to continue when I was interrupted by loud screaming and squealing. I instantly thought that someone was being attacked. I immediately became defensive. Carter noticed my demeanor and laughed.

"Relax, Mya. It's just Blake. Will is playing with him to keep him occupied and away from the church. Those are happy screams. Come on, let's go."

How could I have forgotten what the happy screams of children sounded like? It was sad to think about. Anytime I heard a loud noise I assumed that someone was being attacked.

Carter told me to wait outside the church while he collected the wood. He came back and dropped down the planks, as well as a hammer and a few nails. Then, he and his brothers went inside to begin moving the bodies. I worked diligently and swiftly, I wanted to finish before they were done. By the time I finished and approached the graves, the men were tossing the last few shovels full of dirt into the holes.

"Great timing young lady. They aren't perfect, but they'll do. I know that they would have appreciated all of this. Thank you, all of you for helping with this," Quinn said. He removed his hat, placed it over his heart, and looked down at the graves, reminiscing on his lost friends. Logan began to shove the crosses into the ground, working them in through the frozen layer.

"Hey, do you guys see that?" Evan asked us, looking to the south. The clearing in front of the forest went on for miles and miles.

We all turned our heads in the direction he was looking, and we were puzzled by what we saw. We were too far away to notice what it was. While we were all focused on looking the other direction, no one saw or heard the bustling in the trees behind us. Before we knew it, an undead man was lunging at Logan and knocked him down.

"Logan!" Elana shouted, terrified. Logan briefly struggled with the undead man before putting an end to him. Luckily, he still had a cross in his hands and plunged it into the undead man's head.

"Move, now!" Logan stood quickly and demanded that we get away from the forest.

"Logan, it's a mob. We must leave now. They are all coming in through the forest. Blake's screaming must have attracted them. There are too many, we can't fight," I explained to my brother.

"Run, grab what you can and get in the cars," Carter said. We took off in the direction of the vehicles. We ran up to the three cars and began throwing everything we could into the trunks, but the undead were also fast. They were right behind us. We didn't have time to grab our items from inside the church. The undead were easy to maneuver around if they were hurt, but the ones who had full, functioning legs were the ones you had to watch out for. They could run just as fast as when they were alive.

"What's going on?" June asked confused by our rush.

"Undead, now, get in the car," Will told her, as he rushed to put Blake in the car, next to Rose's car seat. June clambered around, trying to get a grip on things and quickly piled into the car. Will hopped in the driver's seat, turned the ignition, and waited for the rest of us to get in our cars.

I jumped into the driver's seat of my SUV. Carter surprisingly took shotgun, while Logan and Elana climbed into the back. Doug, Evan, and Quinn got into the minivan. They turned the key, but it wouldn't rev to life. It just kept turning over and over, telling us that the battery had died. It had been the car June slept in the night before. Of course, she would kill the battery and not mention it to anyone.

"It won't go! It's dead!" Doug shouted from the driver's side window.

"Get out, hurry! Just jump into the SUV" I yelled out

"The stuff, we have some of our supplies back there!" Doug said as he climbed out. At this point the undead were only a few feet from the cars.

"Forget it, just get in the car!" Carter screamed at them for being so idiotic.

Doug swung the back door open and everyone crammed into the back.

"GO! GO! GO! GO!" Doug yelled as an undead woman began pounding her hands onto the side of my SUV. I slammed my foot onto the accelerator and sped away spitting out rocks. Will quickly followed. I began in the direction towards the highway.

"Where are you going?" Evan asked.

"Back to the highway. It should be cleared out by now. It's our best bet. We need to keep going toward Ohio," I answered him while looking into my rearview mirror. I turned my attention back to the road, thankful and scared for my life.

I quickly made my way back toward the highway. There were no undead in sight. I didn't want to waste time making sure it was clear. We were technically being chased by a mob, there was no time to spare. Their hunger drove them mad with the need to feed. They would stop at nothing to get their next meal. I had no doubt in my mind that they were following us. We had a decent head start before them, but the time would come when our pace would slow, giving them a chance to catch up. I wanted to put as much distance between that mob and us as possible. I was afraid that with time their mob would grow and be undefeatable—and unavoidable.

chapter thirteen

Once we were on the highway, it was smooth sailing. There were no interruptions and no one in sight. The car remained silent almost the entire drive, everyone thankful to be alive. Instead of communicating amongst ourselves, we were all lost in our minds as we looked out the windows. When we got on the highway, the sun was high in the sky. Since it was November, the sun was starting to set earlier. We had only a good five hours of driving that we could possibly get in. Add a few bathroom breaks and food scavenging breaks, that left us with only four hours of driving. My brother was good at siphoning off gas from stranded vehicles, so we never ran out of fuel. We drove until the sun began to set.

I looked in the mirror at the others in the car. Everyone was crammed together. After all, I had seven people in the SUV including myself. We had gone through almost all of our supply at the church leaving the trunk of the SUV empty. The twins managed to jam into the trunk which made room in the second row for Quinn, Logan, and Elana.

My mind was stuck back at the church. So many things could have gone wrong, we were so lucky to have made it out in time. I was tense the entire drive. My shoulders started to ache, and my hands were starting to cramp from gripping the steering wheel so hard. More than once Carter had reached over and attempted to get me to relax. His acute doctor skills were tuned into my discomfort.

After looking into the mirror for the hundredth time, I looked forward and noticed that the sun was descending. "What should we do? The sun is setting. It'll be dark soon. I don't think it's good to be on the highway at night. We would be too exposed."

"Maybe we should stop and see what the others are thinking. They might want to keep going. Or, maybe, we could all stop and set up camp on the highway somewhere? I don't know, is anywhere really safe anymore?" Evan inquired.

No one seemed to object. I stopped the car. Seconds later, Will pulled up next to us and rolled down his window. We began to shout back and forth between the cars.

"What should we do?" Will yelled across to us. Before I could even answer, Logan let out a big sigh and opened the door.

"I can't sit in here anymore—I need to stretch my legs. We need a break from this car. Plus, I have to take a piss and I'm starving. I'm going to go off and try and find some food or something. Come on babe, you come with me." My brother's statement made everyone suddenly eager to get out of the car as well. I cut the engine to the SUV and Will cut the engine to the car. Once everyone was out of the car, we began to stretch our sore bodies.

"We've been driving for a decent amount of time. You think we lost them?" Doug asked the group.

"I think they fell behind for now. They are fast, but not as fast as the cars. I've been checking the rearview often and so far, I haven't seen any movement. What about you Will, you see anything?" I asked, knowing he could probably see more than me.

"No, the last time I saw an undead was like ten minutes after we pulled out. It was coming out of the woods, but it looked like a loner. Other than the loner, I haven't seen anything at all." He rubbed his eyes, clearly exhausted. "Look, I can't keep driving on like this for long, plus, there's just a little over a quarter tank left in the car. I think we should find somewhere to sleep for the night."

"Where? The middle of the highway isn't exactly ideal," June complained.

"We'll figure it out, honey. Why don't you check on the kids?"" Will diverted Junes nagging away from the situation. I didn't miss his use of the word 'honey'. My suspicions were correct—they did have a little something going on.

"June is right. It is dangerous to sleep here on the highway. But there are no exits around and I'm not familiar with this highway, so I'm not sure when the next one is. It's going to be dark in a half hour or so, so we've got to act fast," Quinn stated.

"Let's wait for Logan to come back. Maybe he saw something or has an idea about what we can do for shelter for the night. He's resourceful." I offered up a silent prayer that he had some sort of answer to this problem.

The highway was relatively empty. Directly to the side of us was an old truck that had caught fire. A little farther up was a pile-up involving three cars which all appeared to be totaled. A few yards away from us were two cars pushed off the road into a ditch. About a mile back, there were a few cars sitting in the road. There were not many cars on the normally busy road. Logan and Elana went to the two cars in the ditch to scavenge for supplies.

About ten minutes later, they walked up, their arms full of random goodies to eat—a couple tasty cakes, some pretzels, and a few juice boxes. That was the best we could do for dinner. Everyone seemed happy to eat it. It had been awhile since we had eaten junk food. I was sick of eating canned beans.

"What's up guys? Figure out what we're going to do?" Logan asked.

"No, not yet. We were hoping for your input. So, got any ideas?" I asked him. I hoped he wasn't mad that we wasted time and had no solution.

He sighed and turned away, facing the setting sun. More time had passed by and sunset was only minutes away. He turned back around to face us, "We can't stay here, that is for sure. We're like sitting ducks just waiting for someone to come and snatch us. Let's just keep driving until the next exit and we will park on the ramp or something. Anything would be better than just sitting here waiting and not knowing what might happen." He had a point. The middle of the highway was not the best idea.

"Okay, sounds like a plan then. Let's go." I agreed. We all got back into our cars. I started the SUV and looked in my rear view to make sure Will was ready to go. I waited a few seconds, and nothing happened. I looked in the mirror and saw him yelling and slapping the wheel.

"Logan, I think that something is wrong. I don't think Will's car is starting," I said to my brother. I looked out the rearview mirror and hoped I was wrong.

"Okay, everyone stay put. I'll be right back. I'll go see what the problem is." He got out of the car to talk to Will. I watched through the mirror as the two men talked. He popped the hood and Logan began to tinker with it.

"Hey Mya, I'm a mechanic back at home. I know Logan said to stay in the car, but I don't think he knows what the hell he's doing," Quinn revealed information about his past life.

"Well you should have said something earlier. Go ahead, they obviously need you, the two of them look stumped." I encouraged him to go help. Quinn got out of the car and joined the two men. He quickly went to work underneath the hood. We all waited and watched in silence. I watched from the mirror and the others turned in their seats to see what was going on. We waited a few more minutes and Quinn began to shut the hood and shake his head. In that moment, I felt my stomach drop. I knew before they came over and confirmed it— the car wasn't going to start.

Quinn, Logan, and Will walked up to the car. Everyone else decided to get out as well since we all needed to discuss this latest development. We had been watching them mess with the car for too long. We needed to get off the highway before dark, which was quickly approaching.

"So, Quinn, what's wrong with it?" Asked Evan.

"I think it's the timing belt. It looks shot. Typically, in most cars, the belts should be replaced around 50,000 miles. Since we picked this car at random, we had no way of knowing its condition," Quinn explained.

"Well then what should we do?" Elana asked and turned to where the sun had set leaving a burnt-orange sky. The sun was no longer visible and soon it would be completely dark.

"There are too many of us to fit into the SUV. We already have seven people in there. I don't think we can fit another four people let alone sleep. I don't see that many cars around us. Take some flashlights and start looking around for a car that isn't all smashed up. We need to do this quick, though—we need to get off the highway as soon as possible," Carter suggested.

Elana and I searched the SUV for the flashlights. My heart sank the longer we looked.

"Dammit, where the hell are those flashlights?" Elana said with frustration. She tossed things around the back of the car searching for the flashlights.

"I think they got left behind. We had some in the church and out where we were digging. I don't think we grabbed them when we left. We left in such a hurry that they were left behind," I said. Everyone stood around for a minute in silence, each of us thinking of what to do next.

"The way I see it, there is no other choice, we have to stay here tonight. We can't go off on foot- that is way too risky, especially with the two young kids. And we can't see well enough to find a car that even has the potential of running, let alone trying to find keys or hotwire a car. Our only real option is to stay the night and tough it out. The second the sun rises, we'll find another car and be on our way. Tomorrow night, we will make sure to not be on the highway at nighttime. The problem, right now, is that we have no idea where we are or what's around us," Logan said. Everyone began to look over their shoulders into the dark abyss that encircled us.

"Alright, let's get comfortable in the cars then. We should have at least one person who stays awake to keep a look out. Will, do you June and the kids just want to stay in the car you're already in? And as for the seven of us, I figure two to a car will fit comfortably—we can spread out using the cars in that collision. There are seven of us, however, so three would need to go in one. I don't think it's a good idea for anyone to sleep alone. We all need to watch each other's backs tonight, especially since all of the cars are placed lengths apart," Carter suggested.

"Sounds good, man. Mya, Elana, and I will sleep in the SUV. The four of you can sort it out amongst yourselves. We should all make sure that we are quiet tonight just in case any undead pass by, we don't want to attract any unwanted attention. If anything were to go wrong, lay on the horn and flash your lights," Logan explained. He climbed into the SUV, pulling Elana along with him. Evan and Doug went off to a silver car that was involved in the collision. Will went back to his car with June and the kids. Quinn, Carter, and I stood there awkwardly.

"Well, it looks like it's me and you buddy. How does that green car look?" Carter asked Quinn and pointed to one of the other smashed up cars.

"Sounds good," Quinn answered and then turned to me. "Goodnight, little lady."

"Goodnight, Quinn, and goodnight Carter," I replied.

"Goodnight Mya, get some sleep." Carter's eyes lingered when we parted. Before I climbed back into the SUV, I turned and looked over my shoulder. Carter was still looking at me with a small smile. Logan and Elana were sleeping in the back seat, so I decided to sleep in the front. I reclined the seat and found a comfortable position. I closed my eyes for a well-deserved night's sleep.

chapter fourteen

That night I had strange dreams. Dreams of Scott and I sunbathing on a beach while a little human played in the sand by our feet. Just before the child turned to look at me the dream cut out. The next dream was of me and Carter sitting underneath the scarlet oak tree back at the church—we were smiling. Then, the dream cut out again and I was walking through the forest, looking for someone. I didn't know who I was looking for—I couldn't find them. Then, I turned. I heard a noise. There was an undead man walking by. I ducked down and hid from him. He wasn't after me he was after someone else. I heard a baby scream and I looked around. The screams got louder and louder, and then I woke up.

It took a few moments before I adjusted from dream to reality. When I opened my eyes, it was still dark out. The sun wasn't far off. I stared into the darkness and tried to shake my dreams. I heard screaming—a baby screaming. I shot up.

"Logan! Logan!" I whispered to him, waking him up.

"What? What's wrong?" He shot up, instantly alert and ready to solve whatever problem. His sudden jolt also woke Elana.

"The screaming, don't you hear it?" I said and we listened. There was faint, muffled screaming. Logan peered out the window.

"I can't see anything. It's too dark. If something was wrong, they would flash their headlights, like we talked about. Maybe the baby is just having a fit. Kids do that sometimes, don't they? Let's just stay quiet and keep watch for now. If it doesn't stop soon, I'll get out and make sure everyone is okay," Logan instructed. We looked out of the windows, into the darkness, waiting for something to happen. Time passed and the sky was starting to lighten. Not light enough, though. We still couldn't see anything out the windows, at least not in the direction of the other cars.

We continued to stare out at the other cars and then, it happened so quickly we could have missed it if we weren't watching. Will's car flashed their headlights once. We waited a minute to be sure that we didn't just think it, blink, and imagine it. Will hit the lights again and this time left them on. The scene was unimaginable. The undead were surrounding the car. There were about ten of them. The worst part was that there were more coming. They approached from the side of the highway, in the forest, and coming up from behind. There were at least forty of them. It was a huge mob. Logan reached for the door handle to go help.

"Wait, Logan, you can't just go out there. It's too dangerous. You would be killed in seconds. There are too many of them. Don't just react, you need to think this through carefully," Elana said.

"Okay, fine. I'll go get the other guys before I decide to go and help them. You girls stay here. Do not move. I don't need to be worrying about either of you."

"Fine. Go. Hurry and be safe. We'll be right here waiting," Elana said.

"Keep the keys in the ignition in case you guys need to leave quickly. Don't hesitate to leave if it gets bad. Don't be stupid. If we get overrun, just leave, don't worry about any of us. You guys, promise me," Logan demanded.

"We can't just leave you and everyone else here to die," Elana and I objected at the same time.

"Promise me or the three of us just leave now," Logan demanded again.

We couldn't leave everyone. I obliged and promised. Elana promised too. Logan got out of the car and quietly made his way over to the green car where Quinn and Carter were sleeping. The green car was directly next to our SUV, so it was possible to see them. The light coming from Will's headlights helped light the area. He tapped on the window and they opened the door for him. He went into the car briefly and the three of them emerged. They kept low to the ground as they made their way to the silver car. They repeated the tapping of the window and Evan and Doug were already awake. They must have been watching and waiting for something to happen. The five men sat between the cars conversing about what they should do.

Meanwhile, in Will's car, chaos was happening. All four of their screams could be heard. I turned my attention to Will's car. Elana and I both sat with wide eyes and mouths hanging open. The amount of undead that surrounded the car continued to grow. The undead pounded on the car with their hands, arms, and heads. Blake's screams could be heard above everything. "Please help!" he screamed over and over.

Neither Elana nor I could bring ourselves to say anything. I desperately wanted to help but couldn't break my promise to Logan. We were stuck waiting and watching the disaster unfold. June screamed loud. She was yelling Logan's name over and over for help. *If they would be quiet, then maybe they would stop attracting more.* The undead had doubled in numbers. The mob from the church must have caught up with us. That was exactly what I had feared.

The sun was starting to rise. I looked back to where the men had been standing and they weren't there anymore. My stomach dropped. "Elana, did you see where the guys went? They aren't over by the silver car anymore."

The rear car window shattered. They were running out of time. Elana whipped her head around and began scanning the area for any of the men. "I can't see them. What should we do?"

"If any of them are trapped, we can always pick them up," I suggested. Elana climbed into the front seat. I looked up and saw something run in front of the SUV. "Elana, did you see that?

Something just ran by. It couldn't be an undead, could it? I didn't see any pass us and we've been fairly quiet."

"What? I didn't see anything?" We were both whispering. I held my breath. The shape ran by again. I then realized that it was Doug. *What was he doing?*

"Look, that was Doug. I can tell by the shirt. What's he doing?" I was staring straight ahead. Even though the sun was rising, it still wasn't bright enough to see well.

Out of the corner of my eye, I saw something bright red. "Elana, look! Do you see that? What is it? Do you think it's help?"

"No, I think that might be a flare. Where did it come from? We don't have one of those!" We both sat and stared at the bright red flickering. Suddenly, there was loud screaming coming from the direction that the red light was coming from.

"It has to be one of the guys. They are drawing attention away from Will's car and over to the red light." I listened closer to the yelling and I recognized it. "That man is Logan. Of course, he would go over there and put himself in danger," I whined.

I looked back toward Will's car to see if it worked. At first glance, one wouldn't think that it was working. There were still so many surrounding the car. I noticed a few of the stragglers—the ones that were several rows back from the car—had turned in the direction of the red light. A few were moving, but not nearly enough to get everyone out of the car safely. Logan's screaming stopped. He was no longer holding the flare. It was on top of a car. It was light enough outside that I could now see Logan running around hundreds of feet away.

"What's he doing?" Elana asked. Logan had gone over to another car. I scanned the highway and the other guys were still not in sight. I looked back and Logan and the flare were gone. It must have died out. I felt useless watching as everyone else risked their lives. I desperately wanted to break my promise to Logan and get out of the stupid SUV to help.

"I can't do this anymore. I can't sit around and watch, it's not right," I said.

"I feel the same way. Let's go." Elana sat up, preparing to head out into the chaos. I went for my door handle when an explosion went off. The car that Logan had been messing with exploded. I glanced at Will's car. I hoped the explosion distracted the undead, and it did. The majority of the undead simultaneously moved toward the flames. They wanted the noise, the fire. A few stragglers had stayed at the car, determined to get inside. There were five undead surrounding the car banging on the glass and two undead were almost in the car from the back broken window. Will held a sheet up for protection.

Quinn, Evan, Doug, and Carter had weapons in their hands, prepared to approach the chaotic scene.

Logan tapped on the window, making us both jump in surprise. I opened the door to hear what he had to say. "I'm going to hot wire a new car if I can. The others are getting them out of the car and Carter is doing a quick check over to make sure none of them are bit or scratched. Stay here, don't move!"

Elana and I watched as the guys took care of the undead that surrounded the car. Evan and Doug pulled the two undead out from the back of the car while Carter and Quinn punctured the brains of the others. Once the undead were disposed of, the men began pulling Will, June, and the kids out of the car, checking for scratches and applying pressure to the cuts from the broken glass.

"We should help, we have some medical supplies in the back," I said looking over at Elana.

"Logan told us not to move, let's try and wave them over." Elana wanted to help as well. We both got out of the car and began waving our arms to gain their attention, not wanting to scream and alert the distracted mob of undead. Carter noticed us and began ushering everyone in our direction. Elana and I got out the medical supplies and began to help tend to the wounds.

Aside from a few minor cuts, everyone appeared to be okay, but shaken up. The baby was fine. She was small enough that they were able to put her on the floor to keep her safe. Will had some minor scrapes on his arms from leaning them against the glass while holding up the sheet. June had a gash across her face that bled a lot.

"Does this hurt, June? Are you feeling dizzy or anything?" Carter asked her while assessing her injury.

"No, it's fine really. My eyes are burning a bit from the blood getting into them. Other than that, it's okay. It's worse than it looks," June answered. Blake was hugging her leg, still crying almost uncontrollably. His mouth was pressed against her leg, so his cries were muffled. "Shh baby, it's okay, we're okay, we'll be out of here and safe in no time. You just have to be quiet, so the monsters don't come back, okay?" June tried to console her son. I nervously glanced over to where the undead were—they were still distracted.

"But Mommy, it hurts. It hurts so bad. Oh please, mommy help," Blake sobbed into his mother's leg. Carter knelt to his level to talk to Blake. Blake had a nasty cut on the inside of his right arm.

"Did the glass cut you buddy?" Carter asked Blake.

"Yeahhhhh," Blake whined. Carter took a bandage and pressed it against the oozing cut and wrapped it up tight.

"This should help for now. Once we're settled somewhere, I will take a better look at it." Carter turned back to June. "Be sure to keep pressure on it. Who was sitting in the back seat, you and Blake?" June nodded her head.

I looked back over to where the car had exploded. It was steadily burning, but it wouldn't burn forever, and we needed to leave. When I finished that thought, Logan drove up.

"Let's go guys! Quinn, how about you ride with Will, June, and the kids. I don't think it's is a good idea for them to drive right now. They are a bit shaken up," He said as he got out of the car.

"Sure! Let's go, we need to get a move on," Quinn said to the others. Will, June, and the kids followed behind.

Will turned to Quinn and said: "It's really okay, I can drive. I don't mind at all."

"Nonsense. Hooper drives the car, chief, now get in!" Quinn hopped into the driver's seat and began nervously tapping on the steering wheel. He constantly looked at the burning car—which was flaming out. Will, June, and the kids piled in the car after him.

"Come on, get in, we've got to go, the flames are dying. The fire is losing their attention. They're starting to come back over here," Evan said. I snapped back to reality and rushed back to the SUV. We piled in and took off, with Quinn following directly behind us. Logan drove with Elana and I crammed into the passenger seat, with the three guys mushed into the backseat. As we pulled away, the undead had caught up to us and grabbed for the back of the SUV but were too slow. They fell, which earned a small laugh from everyone in the car. It was nice to have outsmarted them without losing anyone. It was just what our group needed to lift our spirits.

Our uplifted spirits quickly deflated. We were exhausted. We had a terrible night's sleep in uncomfortable cars, interrupted by a screaming baby and the undead. The silence hung thick. I knew Logan wanted to find Lilianna and so did I, but we needed a break. We were mentally and physically exhausted. We needed somewhere safe to relax for one day. We needed to continue tending to the others' wounds before their cuts became infected. Those few days had been nothing but dreadful, stressful, and life changing. No one said anything about stopping, no one wanted to be the one who pissed Logan off. I knew it had to be me. I had to speak up for the rest of the group.

"Logan, can we just find somewhere and rest for today? I can't be stuck in this car, crammed tight all day again. I'm tired—everyone is tired. I can tell everyone in this car is exhausted and I'm sure the other car is worse. The kids need stability. The kids need to rest, I need to rest. Everyone needs to just rest—including you."

"It's like you read my mind. I just didn't want to have to be the one who said something. But I am so freaking tired. I need to sit, have a smoke, and a beer." Logan diverted his attention from the road and winked at me.

"Amen to that!" cried the three boys in the back. At that point, everyone needed a drink, including me. I was looking forward to it, until I remembered I was pregnant and couldn't. I would settle for sleep and a nice warm fire. It was cold out. The closer we got to Indiana, the colder it was. Once the snow fell, traveling would become difficult. I could tell by the air that snow was coming soon.

"So, what should we do? Where should we find a house at? We don't know this area at all," I stated, looking at everyone for their opinion.

"Good thing we got all day to figure it out!" Said Evan with excitement. "I don't give a rat's ass where we go, just as long as there is beer. I will not. I repeat, will not, get out of this car unless there is beer, preferably enough for me to get wasted." His college boy demeanor shone through. I looked back at Carter to see his reaction and he chuckled and shook his head, he was enjoying himself.

"Alright, well then we will drive until we find some place. Far off the highway, with a full stock of alcohol. Any other requests?" Logan asked.

"A shower!" Elana squealed.

"OHHH Yeah!" Cried out everyone. We set off in search of a place to sleep that was far from the highway and had plenty of booze and a working shower. *What could be so hard about that?*

chapter fifteen

Who would have thought that it would be so difficult to find a place to stay? We drove by a couple of neighborhoods but didn't dare go into any of them. We could see some undead wandering around from the main road. There was no way we were going to chance that. We made random turns trying to find a backroad. Every road that we tried took us back into another town. Each town had more undead than the last. It was impossible to avoid them. We sped by the undead. By the time they noticed us, there was distance between us.

After another wrong turn into an undead infested neighborhood, I started to feel hopeless that we would ever find a safe place for the night. We sped down the street, avoiding the undead and rushing out of town.

"Wait! Did you see that back there? It was a beer distributor! We have to go back," Evan shouted.

"I saw it! Let's go back! We need to get beer!" Doug agreed.

"Beer is not worth risking our lives. This town is overrun. It's not safe to get out of the car here," Logan logically stated.

"I'm willing to risk my life. I need a freaking beer, man. You promised us we'd get a house with beer. This way we already have the beer. Come on, man. Just drop me off then come back and pick me up," Evan begged.

"I'll go with him. We're stronger in numbers. We'll be five minutes—tops," Doug said.

"This is the dumbest thing you guys have ever done," Carter said. "But if you're seriously willing to risk your lives over beer, then fine, just get me a case of Corona. We need to tell the other car what we're doing."

Logan peered around, making sure no undead were around, and there wasn't. He slowed the car to a stop and put his arm out the window, waving for Quinn to come up beside him.

"These two idiots want to make a beer run into that distributor over there. Why don't you guys hang back and stay quiet. I don't see any of the undead around right now, but you never know. There were a few stragglers a few minutes back. Stay alert!"

"Jesus H Christ, that sounds like the dumbest idea I ever heard. But while they're at it, might as well get me something good." Quinn winked at Logan. "Well, get to it then, daylight's a wastin'."

Quinn moved his car out of sight. Logan pulled up to the beer distributor. "Alright guys, be quick. If it's crawling with the undead, get the hell out of there. We'll be right here waiting. If too many of those things start coming, we'll honk, and you best get your asses out here."

"Got it, dude!" The twins jumped out of the car and ran into the beer distributor. About a minute passed by before they emerged, empty handed. They came running up to the car. Logan tensed, ready to speed off the second they jumped in. Instead they approached the passenger side window. I rolled my window down to see what they wanted.

"Dude, it's a gold mine in there. No undead, the place is completely untouched. The town must have gone to shit before anyone had a chance to scavenge the place. There are cases of water, soda, and cases of pretzel sticks! You got to back this bitch up so we can load it," Doug exclaimed.

Everyone was overjoyed about getting supplies—even if they weren't exactly nutritional. Logan threw the car into reverse and the rest of us got out to help. We made a procession line, passing the various items to each other then right into the car. Elana and I were the last to receive the items. We organized the items in the car to maximize the amount we could take. We also kept watch for the undead. Overwhelmed with paranoia, I kept looking over my shoulder. I expected to see a cluster of undead show up to end us over beer and pretzels—at least I could have the pretzels.

Stopping at the beer distributor was a success. Thankfully, we had no problems with any undead. We filled both vehicles up as much as possible with water, soda, beer, pretzels, and a few bags of chips.

"I can't believe how lucky we got," I said once everyone was back in the car. We each had a water bottle and a handful of pretzels. "This find couldn't have gone any better or come at a better time." We had just run out of food and water.

After spending half of the day stuck in the car, I was ready to stop and rest. "Okay guys, so now what? I'm tired of being in this car and I want to get somewhere and relax," I announced to the others.

"Already on it, Sis. Evan found a town map hanging up on a wall in there. Just got to be patient a little longer. We'll be out of this car within the hour, I promise." Logan and Carter peered at the map, trying to figure out the best route to take to get to safety. As they looked over the map, I had a gut feeling we weren't safe. I peered out the window in search of any undead. Off in the distance, an undead was sprinting toward the car.

"That's it!" Carter said, pointing to the map. "That's the road we need to take. It's pretty far from town. There are no businesses on that road—which is a good sign. It's our best bet. To get there, I think you need to go to that intersection and then head left." Carter pointed ahead.

"We need to move fast, the undead are back and running straight for us," I said, pointing in the direction of the undead man who was now much closer.

"Oh shit!" Logan put the car in drive, slammed his foot on the gas and drove toward the intersection, taking a left. I glanced back to make sure that Quinn was following. We traveled down the road a bit, hoping to lose the undead. My brother looked in the rearview, "Alright, I think we lost them for now. Carter where are we going?"

"I think you need to make a right a couple streets up," Carter instructed as he studied the map, turning it in different directions. Outrunning the undead turned us around a little bit, but Carter was good with the map. As he had instructed, three streets up, we made a right onto Spring View Lane. "Okay, pick out a house," Carter said. I looked out the window to view our choices. It looked like a quiet suburban street.

"I think we should pick one in the middle of the street and preferably one that sits a little off the road," Elana suggested. We inched down the street looking for a house far from the road. "That one! The yellowish one, that's our house." The house Elana chose had a long driveway that led up to a small ranch style house. The structure was yellow with blue shutters.

"Does anyone see any movement?" Carter asked. We looked out the windows and studied the house for any movement. From what we could see, it was completely still.

"Nope, nothing," Elana answered.

"Me neither, I don't see anyone or anything," I responded.

"Onward we go," Logan said, and started easing up the driveway.

Halfway up the driveway, I noticed a curtain move in the front room. "Wait, stop."

"What is it Mya?" Logan asked, slamming on the breaks.

"I saw the curtain move. Someone is in there," I explained. Everyone in the car began to look out the windows again. As I stared out the window, I saw a figure come out the front door and step on the porch. "Look!" I pointed to the man.

My brother put the SUV in park, opened his door and began to step out. "Logan what are you doing?!" Elana asked.

"I'm going to talk to him. He's clearly not undead. The undead don't open doors, they smash through them. Stay here." He closed the door. I rolled my window down to hear what was going on.

"Excuse me, sir," Logan cried out to the man. The man looked to be in his early 70s's and had a gray beard. He was dressed in flannel and looked like a hunter. He did not have kind eyes.

The man said nothing and continued to stare. The man then pulled a gun out from behind him and pointed it at Logan. Once Quinn noticed the gun, he backed out of the driveway and moved out of harm's way.

"Hey! Hey!" Logan immediately put his hands up. "There's no need for that, I'm alive, and I'm not one of those things. I'm unarmed. Please lower your gun sir. I just want to have a word with you." The man kept his gun pointed at him and the car.

"You's best get back in that car and get on out of here. You don't belong here," said the man, while he continued to point the gun at us.

"But sir, we're just looking for safety. We don't mean any harm. We don't have to stay here I just want to talk to you. Maybe you could point us in the direction of a better place to go." Logan tried to reason with the man.

Before anyone could stop him, Evan got out of the car to join Logan, in hopes of reasoning with the man. "Evan get back in here! Don't be stupid!" Carter cried out. Evan ignored him and stayed firm in his place.

"Please sir, we just need a little bit of help, we're good people, I swear it," Evan pleaded with the man.

"I said get back in your car and leave!" The man was getting angry and raised his voice.

Logan raised his hands in defeat. "Okay, man. We'll leave." The man must have not heard him, or maybe he just didn't care, or maybe the sight of Evan getting out of the car just really put him over the edge, because he fired his gun. He fired into the air and everyone shrieked and ducked down in the car. Logan lunged behind the car to take cover. Then he opened fire again and hit the side of the car. Evan fell to the ground trying to take cover. Doug opened the door and pulled his brother up into the car. Logan opened the driver's door and pulled himself up into the car. While we were still ducked down, Logan put the car into reverse.

Logan began to reverse, and the man fired another shot at us, missing. Logan was almost out of the driveway when the man fired again. This time he got a direct hit on the tire. We all felt the pressure and heard the POP as the tire blew out.

"Shit! He got the tire—we have a flat," Logan exclaimed.

"Oh my God, what are you going to do? We need to get out of here. We can't stop. This man is crazed, he might as well be undead. And now, his gun shots are going to attract the undead," Elana expressed. The entire car was in complete chaos.

"We're not stopping, we'll drive on a flat. It's our only choice. This guy won't stop until we're out of sight. Unfortunately, we won't be able to move fast or far. Carter, take the map out again and see if you can find another road like this close by," Logan instructed. I took the map out of the glove box and passed it to Carter in the backseat. Logan inched down the street. Quinn was already waiting up at the stop sign, unsure of what to do next.

"Okay, well you need to make a right at this stop sign, for sure. I just don't know where you should turn next. I'm still looking," Carter replied. Logan waved his arm out the window, signaling for Quinn to turn right. My brother continued to drive the SUV at a turtle's pace. The tire sounded worse the more we drove on it. I began to grow nervous that we were attracting the undead with the terrible screeching. It was only a matter of time before they found us.

"I think it's best to be at least a couple streets down from that guy in case he decides to take a drive and try to finish what he started. I would also like to keep some distance from him in case his gun shots did begin to draw the undead near," Carter suggested.

"Dude, I don't know if we can make it a couple more streets with this tire and all the weight that we have in here. We got six people and a trunk full of bottles, the car is heavy. Just find something quick." Logan was worried.

A minute went by and we were going at an impossibly slow rate. Quinn's car wasn't even moving anymore. He was up ahead of us and stopped just waiting. The road was slightly uphill, and the car was beginning to squeal louder. "Carter, let's go, tell me something. I can't keep driving along like this. We're going to attract unwanted attention," Logan demanded.

"Fine, turn down this next left. It's not very far away from that guy, but it'll have to do. Pick a house with a garage," Carter said, unhappy at the hasty decision. Not taking all the proper precautions meant that we had to be more alert at night, we couldn't fully relax.

Logan signaled out the window for Quinn to turn left. Quinn turned left and then pulled over, waiting for us to pass so we could pick out a place. As we made our turn, the tire screamed, and sparks shot out. We were riding on the rim; the tire was torn to shreds. We picked the third house down and pulled over in the road.

"I'm going to get out and scope the house out. I'm not putting any of us in danger like that again." Logan stepped out of the car and went behind the bushes, angling himself to walk up to the house unseen. The rest of us silently sat, waiting for Logan.

Evan made a sharp inhale, and Carter turned to look at him. "Dude, what's wrong?"

"It's my leg man. He got me back there!" Evan said in agony.

"What the hell, man, why didn't you say anything sooner, you dumb shit?" Carter tried to peer around to see.

"I didn't want to make a big fuss about it. I know I shouldn't have gotten out of the car. It's just a little bullet-hole. Nothing major was hit—I don't think," Evan said.

"Get out of the car, now," Carter ordered. He stepped out of the car, slammed his door, and walked around towards the other side. I knew Carter was pissed, but he shouldn't have been so loud and reckless. He could have attracted unwanted attention from the undead or that crazy guy.

I leaned out the window. "Can you keep it down please? You throwing a temper tantrum and being loud isn't doing anyone any good. I'd hate to have a repeat already. Jesus, don't you think? You're a doctor, you're supposed to be smart, use that brain of yours inside that thick skull." I didn't mean to sound so harsh—the hormones had taken over. It felt good to let that out, blow off some steam. I needed the release after that highly stressful situation.

Carter ignored me, only saying "whatever" under his breath. He tore Evan's pants apart on his left leg to examine the injury. He pressed down on the area. Evan tried to suppress a shriek of pain. "It doesn't seem that bad, just a superficial wound. No major arteries were hit, you're lucky. It went straight through your calf muscle, though, running is going to be pretty much impossible and walking will be extremely painful. Hopefully, this house will have pain medication. I can't really do anything for you right now, other than tie this around it to slow the bleeding. The most important thing right now is to make sure you don't bleed out. You're an idiot. You should have said something sooner. You could have bled out by now and you'd be dead. I'm a doctor, use me." Carter scolded his brother while he tied up his leg with the ripped part of his pants. Both men stood and Carter helped ease Evan into the car. Carter walked around the car, looking down the entire way. He avoided eye contact and climbed into his seat.

Not a minute later, Logan emerged from the bushes. "We're good to go". He backed up and turned into the driveway, the tire making its dreadful noise all the way up. Quinn pulled in after us. They parked the vehicles, and we clambered out, grateful to finally be able to stretch. Elana and I were happy to not be crammed any longer together in the front seat.

Doug and Carter helped Evan out of the car and placed him on the front porch.

"What the hell happened?" Logan exclaimed.

"Jesus H Christ, you were hit back there?" Quinn asked.

"Oh relax, it's just a little gunshot, I'm fine. The doc here already checked me out. I'm just a little pissed now because I'm pretty much useless." Evan said.

"We can all fuss over him later, let's get inside where it's safe. You all should go in. Logan and I will get the SUV into the garage and out of sight in case that maniac comes by," Carter instructed everyone.

"Quinn, did that guy see your car? Or do you think it's okay to leave it out here? It's a one car garage but I guess we could drive it around back if we have to," Logan asked Quinn.

"No, I don't think he got a good look at it. As soon as I saw him, I pulled away."

My brother nodded, satisfied with his answer and we all parted our appropriate ways.

"Logan, did you clear the house already?" Carter asked.

He shook his head, "No, just snooped around. I didn't see anything, but stay alert, you never know."

chapter sixteen

Carter and Logan successfully stashed the SUV away in the garage while the rest of us went into the house to check it out. We each had a weapon in our hands. I had Logan's baseball bat, Quinn had a hammer, Doug had a tire iron, and Will held a flare gun. Elana and June were handling Evan and the kids. We stepped into the foyer and examined the room. We were alert with wide eyes and open ears. Everyone stood quietly, listening for any noises.

Doug banged his tire iron against the front door.

"What the hell do you think you're doing?" Quinn questioned.

"Haven't you ever seen a zombie movie? Noise attracts them. I've seen people do this in a million movies, to try and draw them out before we go getting ourselves trapped," Doug explained.

"Hm, didn't think someone so stupid would have such an innovative idea," Quinn teased. We all listened to see if the noise provoked any movement. While we waited, Logan and Carter joined us in the foyer.

"Did you guys do any checks yet?" Logan asked.

"No, we were seeing if this genius's brilliant idea works," Quinn said pointing to Doug, "He's banging on the door trying to draw those things out."

"Not a bad idea, but we've been standing here for at least five minutes, so chances are, if there is anything that can walk out to us, it's not in here. Either this place is luckily empty or an undead is trapped in a room somewhere. How about Carter and I go and clear the upstairs, Quinn and Doug you guys clear this level and the basement and then we'll meet back up. Everyone else hang tight. We're not taking any more chances here," Logan instructed and everyone complied.

I felt a slight breeze and walked into the kitchen. I was taken aback at the scene in front of me. Fortunately, there were no undead, but evidence that there had been one. "Guys!" I yelled for everyone to come to the kitchen before they went off to check the house. Everyone came when I called and examined the floor, unsure of what to think. Logan went over to the back door, where the breeze was coming from, peeked his head outside, looked around, and then shut it.

On the floor of the kitchen was a huge dried up blood stain and, on the door, some streaks of blood. "What are you thinking, Logan?" I asked.

Carter answered instead. "Looks like someone was attacked here and then turned. By the looks of the door and the fact that it was open, they are hopefully long gone."

Logan shot Carter an annoyed look for answering for him. "Yeah, hopefully, or they're still in the house somewhere."

"We should go check the house. Everyone remember what they're doing? Girls, maybe you should clean this up," Carter said.

"I'm sure everyone remembers what to do, we just told them minutes ago—and girls you don't have to clean this up." With that, Logan walked away, and the other men followed. It was obvious there was some type of underlying battle for the leadership role there. *Men. Their testosterone levels always getting the best of them.* Elana and I looked at each other, rolled our eyes, and giggled.

As the men checked the house, Elana and I helped Evan onto the couch and made sure he was okay, propping his leg up to help cease the bleeding. He appeared to be in a significant amount of pain, and he was sweating profusely.

"How are you feeling, Evan?" Elana asked, while wiping the sweat from his forehead.

"Ah, you know, I've been better," He chuckled. "But seriously, I'm in some pain. Where the hell is that brilliant doctor brother of mine?"

"I'm right here, quit complaining," Carter said from over my shoulder. I glanced up at him. "Upstairs is clear. Now, let's take a look at this leg." Carter looked down at me. "Can you move? You're in my way." His look was hard and cold—he was still mad at me. I shuffled to my feet and backed out of the way. *He's acting worse than a child who got yelled at by his mother, he needs to get over it. His temper tantrum was too loud, it could have been detrimental. Men, sometimes they just don't think, they are too hot-headed and temperamental.*

Logan brought a case of water in from the garage and we sat in the foyer drinking our water while Carter examined Evan. We patiently waited to see what the results would be.

"It's a clean through and through. He'll be fine. It's going to be painful and there's a high risk of infection due to our situation, but he should be okay. I need to clean and dress the wound and we need to find something for the pain. Blake, can I look at your arm some more now?" Carter asked. Blake walked over to him and sat on the floor. Carter began to examine his arm and we waited again. "It's a nasty cut, already getting infected. But that's to be expected. He was cut with dirty glass and it hasn't been properly treated all day. He definitely needs an antibiotic and lots of water." Carter felt his forehead. "He feels a little warm. We need to keep an eye on it. He's a kid though, should bounce back easy. Search the house for anything we can use," Carter told all of us.

I got up off the floor and began to search the house. I went to the upstairs bathroom to check there, seemed like the most logical place. I opened the medicine cabinet and began to read the labels. I found some expired antibiotics and a bottle of Advil. I also found a box of Spiderman band-aids and a wrap that you would put on a sprained ankle. I grabbed them all and took them to the foyer where Carter was waiting.

"Here, this is what I was able to find upstairs. Did you guys have any luck down here?" I asked looking at Carter. He ignored me and someone else in the room answered instead.

"No, we weren't able to find anything other than some standard pain relief, like what you found," Elana responded.

"Carter, will these antibiotics work? It says they're expired," I asked Carter directly.

Without looking back at me he answered, "It's not ideal, but it's better than nothing. We'll give it a try, but no guarantee that the infection will stave off. Did anyone find anything that we can clean the wound with? Rubbing alcohol or anything like that?" Carter asked everyone.

"Oh, I forgot to look for that," I replied to Carter.

"You forgot to look? How could you forget to look for that? That's one of the most important things. Someone competent, go find me something to clean this wound!" Carter was definitely angry with me. I was not going to let him talk to me like that.

"Cut your shit out, Doctor Brooks. I know I yelled at you on the street out there, but this is enough! You were risking all our lives by throwing a temper tantrum like a child. I am not your servant, go get your god damn rubbing alcohol yourself," I screamed at him, probably louder than necessary. Carter looked at me, a bit stunned, and just nodded his head and returned his focus to Evan. I stood there glaring at the back of his head and realized how quiet the room was. I looked around at everyone as they stared at me like I was crazy. I pretended like I didn't notice and sat back down in the corner of the room, drinking my water. Elana got up to get the rubbing alcohol.

She returned not even a minute later and handed the bottle to Carter, who began to clean the gunshot wound and the cut on June's head and Blake's arm. While he fixed them up, we discussed what the next move should be.

"What do we do about the SUV? We're safe for now, but we can't stay here forever," Doug asked. "Is there a spare tire in there?" He looked at me while asking.

"No, unfortunately there isn't," I answered. "Was the owner's car in the garage?"

"No. Looks like we're going to have to hang tight here for a little. We spent a lot of time on the road today, so I imagine it'll be getting dark soon. I can go out in the morning and look for a tire somewhere. I'll take the other car out," Logan offered.

"I'll go with ya," Quinn offered.

"Sounds good, man. I'm going to take the first watch shift. Why don't you guys start showering and see if there is any food for dinner." With that, Logan turned and went toward the front porch to keep watch.

"June, why don't you and the kids and Will take your showers first? I know you guys have had a rough day," Elana offered up.

"Yeah, there are two bathrooms up there and three bedrooms." Carter added.

"Do you mind if we take the master bedroom with the bathroom in it, the four of us will share it?" Will asked.

"We don't need to ask their permission," June snapped, as she walked toward the steps with Blake in tow. Will looked stunned by her reaction. I, on the other hand, wasn't surprised at all, *typical June.* Will followed her, carrying baby Rose. As he walked by, he mouthed 'sorry'.

We waited for them to finish walking up the steps before we started our discussion again. "Well isn't she a peach?" Quinn joked, smiling. "That leaves two bedrooms and a bathroom available. Who wants what?"

"Do you mind if Mya, Logan, and I share a bedroom? I'll wait for now to shower and Logan is keeping watch, so someone else can shower," Elana offered.

"That sounds fair. That leaves us men one bedroom and a free shower," Doug responded. "As for me, I'll sleep down here on the other couch with Evan, I don't want to leave him."

"The other room has bunk beds. Quinn, why don't you and I share that room? And Quinn, you go shower first, you smell like rotten fish guts," Carter announced. I couldn't tell if he was joking or being serious.

"Ha, funny Doc. Maybe the little lady here wants to shower first?" Quinn offered to me.

"No that's okay. I have a kitchen floor to clean, remember? Plus, I'm going to try and cook up some dinner. You guys can all shower first, you all have a lot of blood on you," I said, wrinkling my nose at them. With that, everyone separated. Quinn went up to shower first, then Doug, Carter and then it would be my turn. Elana and I went to work in the kitchen. We scrubbed the blood off the floor as much as possible, making minimal progress. Instead, I moved the doormat over it and sprayed some air freshener—problem solved. As for dinner, there were plenty of canned vegetables and a box of rice. The house had a gas stove top so we could cook. We made a form of stir-fry, our first real meal in days.

The men had finished their showers and came down in time for dinner. Elana took her dinner to the porch to eat with Logan. I quickly ate my dinner, then headed upstairs for my turn to shower. Before I went to the bathroom, I knocked on the master bedroom door.

"Hey," I said as Will opened the door. "There is plenty of food downstairs, an actual meal." I smiled at him.

"Thanks. I'll head down and get some for us. Blake's feeling a little under the weather. Is there anything that might be good for him?" Will asked.

"Eating will be good for him. It's just rice and vegetables. We also have soda from the beer distributor that might help settle his stomach," I advised.

"Thanks Mya," Will said as he closed the door behind him and headed to the kitchen. I went down the hallway and into the bathroom. I turned the water on and waited for it to warm up. As I stood there waiting, I wondered why it wasn't getting any warmer. *Oh, that's right, no electricity, no hot water heater, so no hot water. Looks like it's going to be a quick cold shower.* I briskly showered and hopped out. I stood in front of the mirror, staring at my body. It was beginning to change. The features of pregnancy becoming evident. My breasts were becoming fuller and my abdomen was beginning to slightly expand. I tried to imagine what my baby would be like. *Will it be a boy or a girl? Will he or she look like me or Scott?* I daydreamed about my baby while I began to towel off.

I crossed the hallway in a towel and went into the bedroom in hopes of finding something to wear. Fortunately, the room's previous tenant appeared to be a young woman. I rummaged through her things until I found some appropriate, clean, and warm clothes to wear. Once I was satisfied, with my new attire I sat down on the bed to think for a moment. I wondered who once lived here, whose clothes I was wearing and what had happened to her. Was it her blood that I was just scrubbing off the floor? My thoughts were interrupted by laughter coming from downstairs—a sound I wasn't used to hearing. I made my way downstairs out of curiosity.

chapter seventeen

I walked down the steps and into the living room where the men were sitting around—and of course, drinking. There was a fire burning in the fireplace that warmed the entire downstairs. Evan was laid out on the couch with a bottle in his hand and the other men were sitting on the floor, leaning against the couch and the adjacent wall, all with a beer bottle in their hand. They each had a smile on their face, I had forgotten what one looked like. They laughed and joked with one another—even the uptight Doctor Carter.

"God! This sucks! Why did I have to go and get shot?" Evan exclaimed.

"Because you're a dumbass. You're lucky that you still have your leg," Carter replied.

"You want to drink you say?" Quinn asked Evan who eagerly nodded his head in agreement. "Well, we'll drink to your leg!"

"And I'll drink to your leg my friend!" Evan said, excitedly holding up his bottle, already intoxicated.

"How about we all drink to our legs then!" Quinn said, holding up his bottle as well. The others followed in suit. "To our legs!" they cheered. *Drunk idiots.* I was about to get by without being noticed when Carter spotted me.

"Hey there, now don't you look all nice and clean," Carter said to me. I smiled and walked toward the kitchen. "Did you hear me? I said you look nice," He said again, a little louder.

"Yeah, I heard you, I'm sure the whole house did. You're very loud. There are young kids upstairs trying to sleep and Blake isn't feeling well. Where's my brother and Elana?" I gave Carter the cold shoulder, punishment from when he was an ass earlier.

"They're still outside, keeping watch," Quinn responded. I left the drunken scene inside and joined my brother and Elana outside where it was peaceful.

"Hey, how's it going out here? You guys must be freezing." As I spoke, I could see my breath.

"Yeah it's a bit chilly out here. I'm getting kind of tired and so is Elana. Would you want to keep watch for a while?" Logan asked me.

"Yeah of course. I want to straighten up the kitchen first if that's okay. Also, do I have to stay out here? It's freezing. Can I watch from inside?" I asked my brother.

"That's fine, we're going to head up to bed anyways. It will be fine if no one is keeping watch for ten minutes; there has been no action since I came out here, not even a loner. There is a window seat in the front room, why don't you just sit there and look out the window?"

"Okay, sounds like a plan, brother." I gave him and Elana a goodnight hug and went back inside to straighten up the kitchen. The men (or should I say, boys) were sitting on the floor—they were obnoxious. Evan had too much to drink and was passed out on the couch with a bottle in his hand. "Why don't you guys go sit in the kitchen, you're being loud and now Evan is asleep. He really needs his rest." The men turned their heads and noticed for the first time that he had fallen asleep. They made their way to the kitchen. Once they left the room, I grabbed a throw blanket off the couch and covered Evan in it. I took the bottle from his hand and placed it on the floor.

When I entered the kitchen, Quinn and Doug seemed to have fresh, new bottles in their hands while they sat around the table. Carter was at the sink washing dishes. Instead of cleaning the kitchen, I decided to take a seat at the table with Quinn and Doug.

"Well there, little lady, why don't you have a drink in your hand?" Quinn asked me.

"Oh, I'm not much of a beer drinker." I lied, I loved beer. Especially the Corona that Carter had picked out for himself. Logan and Elana walked in.

"Don't be so modest, sis," my brother said to me, then turning to everyone else. "She could drink any one of you under the table, without a doubt. Carter, didn't you pick up Corona? That's her favorite. Goodnight, guys." I silently cursed at my brother for mentioning that.

"Why didn't you say so!" Doug jumped from his seat around the table and went to the garage. He came back in with a bottle of Corona. He handed it to me, and I hesitated to take it. "Well, go ahead, take it. Kick back and relax. Have a drink with us."

I smiled in return. "Thanks, but I'm really not in the drinking mood."

"There is no such thing as a drinking mood, every mood is a drinking mood." He twisted off the cap. "Here you go, drink."

I knew I wasn't about to get out of this one easily, so to please him, I took the tiniest of sips possible and looked at him. "Happy?"

"Thrilled," He responded with a huge smile. I turned in my chair and noticed Carter listening to the entire exchange. Shit, I hope I didn't just blow my cover. Desperate to change the topic, I looked at Quinn—he was an easy conversationalist.

Quinn was wearing a button-down shirt, but the entire top half was unbuttoned exposing his chest hair. "Quinn, how did you get that scar?"

"Oh, this thing here?" Quinn pointed to a scar on his chest. "Well, Marcy Eliza Michael, she gone went and broke my heart," Quinn said it real serious and broke out into an infectious laughter. When the good laugh was done and over, Doug and Quinn slugged down the rest of their bottles like it was a competition. It was obvious they were both intoxicated. Carter finished the dishes and took a seat at the table. As soon as he sat, I stood and finished up the little cleaning that needed to be done in the kitchen. I was looking for an excuse to not have to sit anywhere near Carter, I was still pissed at him.

Quinn slammed his fist down on the table, which startled me and caused me to jump quickly and turn around. He began tapping out a beat on the table and started to mumble a drinking song about being drunk and needing to go home. Carter and Doug joined in the singing and all three of them were carrying on, singing about how the drink went to their heads and they needed to go to bed. They weren't wrong.

"WILL YOU SHUT THE HELL UP?" June yelled down the steps. The guys instantly stopped singing. "There are children here that are trying to sleep! ASSHOLES!" We heard her stomp her feet and slam the bedroom door shut—which startled the baby into crying.

We all burst out laughing. I agreed that the singing was loud, but her reaction was priceless.

"You heard the Queen, keep it down. I'm going to go keep watch in the front room," I told the men. I left my full bottle in the kitchen, went to sit on the window seat and looked outside. It was dark and still. No peeps to be heard, not even the hoot of an owl. I could see no smoke from any nearby chimneys nor hear any growling from the undead. The longer I sat looking out the window, the quieter the house became. There was no noise coming from the upstairs and the men in the kitchen had lowered their volume to an almost whisper. I got up from the window seat to go and check on them to make sure everything was okay.

Quinn was passed out on the table and Doug was sitting at the table with his head in his hand, struggling to keep his eyes open. Carter sat there, silently playing with the label on his bottle, lost in thought.

I walked up to Doug and placed my hand on his shoulder. "Doug, why don't we go lay you down on the couch, you'll be more comfortable there?" His response was a bunch of mumbles. He stood, staggered a bit, and Carter jumped up to help. We walked him into the living room where Evan was sleeping and put Doug to sleep on the adjacent couch. He was instantly snoring. I grabbed a throw pillow from the couch and brought it back into the kitchen and placed it under Quinn's head.

The entire house was asleep except for Carter and me. Without making any eye contact with Carter, I went back to resume my place on the window seat to keep watch. I sat with my back against the wall, with my knees up in front of me. Carter, uninvited, came over and sat down opposite of me, mirroring my position so that our feet were almost touching. When I looked over at him, he had sad eyes.

"Can I help you?" I asked Carter, not letting my guard down.

"I'm sorry, okay? I shouldn't be such a dick all the time. I just sometimes can't help it. It's a self-entitlement thing, happens when you're an awesome doctor." He smiled at me, trying to joke and make nice.

I wasn't having it, "Not okay. I am a person, a person that you barely even know, at that. Watch the way you talk to people and order them around. If you want this living situation and travel arrangements to be pleasant, I suggest you take on a new approach of communicating with others."

"Fair enough," was all he responded. We sat there in silence for a while. Neither of us knew what to say next, now it was awkward. I was stone cold sober, and he had been drinking all night. I was surprised he was still awake.

I finally broke the silence, "You should check on Blake in the morning. Will said he wasn't feeling well."

"Yeah I will. His cut is becoming infected, which is making him feel sick. I think the same thing will happen to Evan. I'm going to try and tag along with Logan tomorrow when he goes out to find a tire and see if we can find a pharmacy or something with some real medication."

"That's an excellent idea. You should get some bandages, we're almost out and all they have here is Spiderman Band-Aids. While I'm up tonight, I'll try and think of anything else we might need." I glanced up at him and caught him staring at me.

"How are you doing Mya? Still dizzy and nauseous? Is there a reason that you didn't want to drink tonight? Are you feeling okay?" Of course, he was as observant as ever.

"Yeah, I'm good. Being out of that church and in a real house helps. It's amazing what a change of scenery will do for your health," I said to him trying to reassure him. I kept an even stare right into his eyes to try and make my lie seem true. "I'm good. Why don't you go and get some sleep? I'm going to take the night shift for watch. You'll need your energy for the trip with Logan tomorrow."

"Okay, fine, I will soon. But I am determined to get to know you better," Carter said, slightly slurring his speech.

"Okay, one question and then it's off to bed," I agreed. I would say anything to distract him from the truth.

"What did you envision for your future, you know, before any of this shit happened?" Carter asked me.

I sat there and thought about it. "A family," I said, pausing to imagine what it would have looked like. I felt a tinge of sadness that it would never happen the way I wanted. "A bunch of kids, happy healthy kids, as many as possible. It would have been chaotic, but it also would have been perfect." I looked down at my hands. "What about you Carter?" I looked up at him.

"I couldn't picture a future worth living for until now. Goodnight, Mya." And with that, he turned and headed upstairs, leaving me speechless. His response was blunt and straightforward—not what I was expecting.

I looked out the window into the dark night. I thought back to what he had said. What exactly had he meant? He was obviously drunk. I couldn't picture him as a family man. He was selfish and I was hung up on the idea of my old life with Scott. Carter wasn't all bad, he was brilliant and dedicated to taking care of people. His eyes were probably the most gorgeous things I have ever peered into.

I shook my head—I shouldn't be having these thoughts. My husband had died only weeks ago, but in zombie apocalypse time, it felt like years. So much had changed since the first day of the apocalypse. Our previous life was gone, and it wasn't coming back. I couldn't live in the past forever. I needed to think of my future and what would be best for my child.

Lost in thought, my eyes began to droop, I was getting tired. I adjusted my position, in hopes that moving would help to wake me up. Repositioning made me more comfortable and before I could stop it, I was fast asleep. I dreamt of a field of children who were playing and laughing.

chapter eighteen

I awoke with a jump. I opened one eye against the bright sky. Only, my eye didn't see the sun, it saw an ugly undead man. I quickly sat up. I had slept through the night. I didn't do my job. There was an undead standing outside the window desperate to get in. Logan was not going to be happy with me.

I quickly closed the blinds, hoping he would forget he saw me and move past the house. I then went to another window and peered outside to see if he was a loner or if there were others with him. I didn't see any other undead. We would need to do a full sweep of the perimeter. Historically, when there was one—more followed.

I went back over to the window seat and peaked through the blinds to see if the undead was still there. He was. I knew I needed to wake Logan up. I could have dealt with it myself but doing so could potentially put me in a dangerous situation. I needed to be smart and protect my baby.

I sprinted up the steps and knocked on my brother's door. He opened the door within seconds, fully dressed and ready for the day.

"Logan, there's an undead at the window. I'm sorry, I fell asleep—I didn't see him coming. I don't see any more—he might be a loner, but I can't be positive." I gave him the rundown.

"No problem. I was getting bored with resting anyway. Let the fun begin." Logan walked over to the window to get a better look of outside.

"What's wrong?" Elana asked from the bed as she sleepily rubbed her eyes.

"There's an undead at the front window" I explained. "Do you see anything Logan?"

"Not from here but a full sweep of the perimeter will need to be done. We're going to have to stay here at least another day considering I still need to go out and find a tire or another car." Logan went over to the bed, kissed Elana on the cheek, then moved toward the door.

"Is anyone else up?" Logan asked me as we made our way downstairs.

"No, and I don't think they'll be up for a while. They were all pretty drunk last night. Probably have a nasty hangover."

"Not an excuse. Everyone always needs to be on full alert. This is a different world now." Logan walked into the kitchen. I checked on the twins, who were lying on the couches. Doug was still fast asleep. Evan, on the other hand, was awake and moaning.

"Uhhh," Evan moaned.

"What's wrong? Do you need more pain meds?" I asked.

"Where's my brother? My leg is killing me and it's on fire." Evan clawed at his leg.

"He's sleeping. Let me get a look at it." I unwound his bandage to look over his wound. He was right it was hot and beginning to fester. It was infected. "You need antibiotics. I'm going to get you some pain meds and water and wake up Carter."

"Thanks," he replied plopping his head back down on the pillow. I walked to the kitchen to find Logan, when I rounded the corner, he wasn't there, only Quinn—who was unexpectedly awake.

"Have you seen Logan?" I asked Quinn.

"Yeah he came in here pissed off and woke me up. He's a real ray of sunshine in the morning. He went into the garage," Quinn replied.

I walked to the garage and found Logan lying on the floor. "What are you doing?"

"Trying to find the measurements for the tires on the SUV, so I know what to get. I'm hoping there's an automotive store in that town back there. If I know what to get, I can be quick, in and out and back, hopefully under two hours. Quinn moving his ass yet?"

"He's getting there. About you going into town… Carter needs to go with you."

"No, I work better alone. I don't need anyone else. I'll be fine." Logan was stubborn.

"He needs to get antibiotics. Evan's leg is definitely infected, and Will said something last night about Blake not feeling well and he has an infection as well. He's a doctor, he knows what to get."

"Fine, go get him. We need to check the perimeter before we leave. I need to make sure you will all be safe while we're gone," Logan ordered, clearly unhappy he couldn't go on the journey alone.

I grabbed four bottles of water and a bottle of pain medication from the SUV before heading back inside. I first stopped in the kitchen and handed Quinn a water bottle and two pain relievers for his hangover. I then went to the living room where the twins were and did the same for each of them and assured Evan that I was going to get Carter.

I made my way upstairs and knocked on the door to where Carter was sleeping. He didn't answer so I invited myself in. He was curled up in the bed still fast asleep. I threw up the blinds, "Good morning, time to get up." He jerked his head up from the pillow and looked at me.

"Hi," he sighed at me. He rubbed his eyes and sat up. He was topless. He tossed his arms up in a stretch. I turned away so he couldn't see me blush. I looked back at him and he had a smirk on his face. He was gorgeous and he knew it.

I tossed the bottled water at him and placed the pain relief on the night table. "For your hangover."

"You're a life saver."

"Actually, you are and that's why you need to get up. Logan wants to leave to go into town, he's getting impatient. I told him that you need to go too, for the antibiotics. Evan's leg is worse today, he definitely has an infection." I took a breath. "Also, there is an undead outside the window I was watching last night. He scared me this morning. Logan wants to take care of it and do a perimeter check before you guys leave, so he needs your help for that."

"Okay then, busy morning." He sighed again. "Should have known better than to drink that much last night." He looked at me and his eyes got wide. "Mya, I... uh... about last night..."

I cut him off before he had the chance to finish his sentence. "Don't worry about it. Listen, I'm going to go lie down. I'm exhausted. Be careful out there today." Before he had the chance to say anything else, I exited the room.

I decided to check on Blake before I headed into my room. I went to the master bedroom door, knocked lightly, and waited patiently. I could hear a baby crying and Will attempting to soothe her. June came to the door a few seconds later.

"What?" She questioned.

"I just thought I would check in. Is everything alright?"

"We're fine. Rose is just fussy this morning," June replied.

"And Blake, how is he feeling? Will mentioned last night that he wasn't feeling well." I was concerned.

"Well, seeing that you are not a nurse or a doctor or his family, I don't really see how that is your business," June snapped at me. She was clearly over trying to be friendly with me.

"She may not be, but I am. I would like to examine him," Carter stated from behind me.

"Of course, come in." June was immediately receptive to him. As soon as Carter was through the door, she shut the door in my face. I was confident that Carter had it handled so I turned to get some sleep.

Once inside the room I went to the window and peered outside. I saw the men outside walking around, securing the perimeter. I saw no undead from up here, which was such a relief. I knew that Carter and Logan would probably be heading off into town soon and I wanted to be awake by the time they got back. I pulled the blinds down, turned the covers down, and hopped into bed.

Lying in bed I rubbed my belly and hummed lullabies to my baby. I had yet to feel any movement, which made me nervous. I wasn't sure how far along in the pregnancy that you could feel the baby move.

I was still humming along when there was a knock on the door. I cleared my throat, slightly embarrassed. "Uh, come in?"

Carter opened the door and peaked his head inside. "Hey. Were you just singing?" he asked with a smile.

"Uh, yeah, you caught me," I admitted.

"What was it? It sounded familiar."

"Oh, nothing in particular. Did you need something?" I asked, changing the subject.

"I was just letting you know that I checked in on Blake, he's in pretty bad shape. His cut is severely infected, and he needs antibiotics. I'm going to grab Logan and tell him we need to go and get back as soon as possible. I just wanted to check in with you first to see if there was anything you needed or wanted."

"Trying to suck up for being an ass?" I teased. "I'm fine, I don't need anything. Be safe and watch Logan's back for me please. I'll see you when you get back."

"Okay," He mumbled, obviously embarrassed that I called him out. "Have a nice nap." Carter closed the door. I turned on my side and quickly drifted off into a peaceful sleep.

chapter nineteen

I woke to the sun, far to the west, blaring through the blinds. It was late afternoon. Carter and Logan should be back. I laid in bed and stretched out, feeling relaxed and rejuvenated. Once I had fully woken up, I got out of bed and began to make my way downstairs. As I walked down the steps, I could smell something delicious, I was starved. I hadn't eaten in hours. I walked into the kitchen and saw Elana standing over the stove with a spatula in her hand.

"Hey, what are you up to?" I asked.

"Getting ready to feed the wolves. How was your nap?" She responded.

"It was great, exactly what I needed. Are Logan and Carter back yet?" I asked.

She turned around and looked at me with a worried expression. "No. I'm beginning to get worried. They left hours ago. They should have been back by now."

"What should we do? Should we round up a search party? Where are the other guys at?" I asked as I looked around and noticed that we were the only ones in the kitchen.

"They are in the garage, drinking of course. Even Evan's dumbass is out there drinking instead of laying on the couch resting. June, Will, and the kids are still upstairs. I haven't seen them at all, except for this morning when Will came down to grab some water and food. I tried to check in on them a couple hours ago, but they didn't want anything to do with me." Elana shrugged it off.

"Weird, they did the same thing to me earlier. They did let Carter in though to look at Blake. He said that his cut is extremely infected, and he really needs the antibiotics. I wonder how Evan is doing. I'm surprised he's up. I would think that he and Blake would be feeling similar. I'm going to go check in with the guys in the garage and see what they think we should do about Carter and Logan." I left Elana in the kitchen to finish cooking dinner and made my way to the garage.

The guys were all just hanging out, standing around. Evan was sitting on a folding chair and they all had a drink in their hand. It was nice to see them just relaxing, and not drunk like last night.

"Hey Mya, what's up?" Quinn asked me.

"Just checking in with everyone. Have you been doing any perimeter checks?" I asked the group.

Doug answered, "Yep, did the last one about an hour ago. Haven't seen an undead except for the one this morning, seems like we picked out a good house."

"Great, that's good news. Evan how are you feeling?" I asked.

"I'm alright, the booze makes it a little better. My leg is killing me and is hot as hell, but it could be a lot worse. I heard that Blake is really suffering, so I can't really complain here. Looking forward to those antibiotics though, I'm also praying that he brings me back some crutches," Evan responded.

"I'm worried that they aren't back yet. I would have thought that they would have been back by now. What do you guys think we should do?" I asked.

"Logan was clear that we weren't to go after them if they didn't return," Quinn responded.

"I'm not surprised by that in the least, however, Evan and Blake really need those antibiotics, so we have to go. They won't survive without them. Sorry to be a downer, Evan."

"No, you're right it's the truth, I do need the meds," Evan responded and then turned to look at Doug.

Doug spoke up, "We already decided that if they didn't come back, I was going to go out and look for them. He's my brother. I can't just wonder about what happened to him for the rest of my life. Plus, Evan really does need antibiotics."

"You're not going alone. Logan is my brother so I'm coming with you."

"Mya, I don't know…" Doug began.

"Why? Because I'm a girl? I'm going. You can't go alone and I'm your best option. June and Will are totally out because of the kids. Evan obviously can't go. Quinn and Elana should stay to hold down the fort. We can't leave everyone here with no manpower to back up the house. There's no point in arguing, I'm going."

"Fine. When we find them, you make it clear that it was your idea to come because they will both have my ass for bringing you," Doug responded.

"Now that you figured that out, one more problem. There isn't another car, so how are you going to get there? Oh, and it's going to get dark soon," Quinn pointed out. I hadn't really thought of that.

"We can't wait until morning, we have to go tonight, no question about it. Blake can't wait another day and the longer we wait the less likely we are to find them," I stated.

"We can always walk. Again, if you're not up for it you don't have to come," Doug said.

I stood there quietly nodding. I began looking around the garage. Then I noticed two bikes mounted on the walls. "We're not walking, we're taking those." I pointed to the bikes.

"Brilliant," Doug responded smiling.

"Well, daylight's wasting. Get a move on." Quinn urged us to leave.

"Give me three minutes," I said and turned to run into the house. In the house, I grabbed my sneakers and my winter coat.

"Where are you going?" Elana asked me.

"To find them and get Blake the meds that he needs." Elana gave me a look. "Don't argue with me, I don't have time for it, I'm leaving now."

"Fine, but Logan is going to kill you. I'll wait up for you. Please don't be stupid." Elana pulled me into a hug. "I love you, be safe and come back soon."

I hugged her back, "I love you, too, and I will, I promise."

I returned to the garage, ready to leave. The bikes were off the walls and Doug was already sitting on his waiting.

"Ready?" he said to me. I nodded back and mounted my bike. I noticed there were water bottles already strapped onto the bikes. "Do you have a weapon?"

"In the backpack" He answered patting on his backpack as he put it on. "I've got knives, a lighter, the tire iron, a flashlight, and two granola bars in case we get stuck."

"Looks like you thought of it all, let's go," I responded.

Quinn opened the garage door and we rode out. We rode the bikes down to the end of the driveway and then to the end of the street. At the stop sign we paused. "Do you know which way town is?" Doug asked me.

"I think it's to the right," I answered and we rode down the street until we were on the outskirts of the town. I hoped that it was the right town we traveled through before. It was getting dark outside, and the area was confusing.

We again paused before going forward. "When we were at the beer store, I noticed a convenience store with a pharmacy sign," I told him. "That might be our best bet to find them," I heaved, pausing between words. I was terribly out of shape.

"We can ride by there. We're looking for the car they took. Make sure to pay special attention to the parking lots," Doug stated.

"Agreed. I need a drink of water and to stretch my legs before we move on," I told him.

"I have to piss, so we'll take five." We split up briefly. Before Doug walked away, he pulled two knives from the backpack. He handed one to me before I went to the right side of the road, where I also decided to do my business—in case I couldn't later—and he went to the left side of the road. While relieving myself, I made sure to look around and be aware of my surroundings. I didn't want an undead to get me while my pants were down. When I was finished, I went back to the middle of the road, stretched my legs, took a swig of water, and remounted the bike. Doug mirrored my actions.

He sighed, "Ready?"

"As I'll ever be." We took off toward town, heading into unknown and dangerous territory. We didn't know what kind of situation we were putting ourselves in. We didn't know who or what we might run into, but we were willing to risk it all to find our brothers.

chapter twenty

We silently rode through the town, careful to pedal lightly. While we maneuvered through the town, I pointed to each direction that we needed to go to get to the pharmacy. We were almost there. Ahead there was a cluster of undead blocking the street. It wasn't enough to be a problem, but it was too many that we couldn't get by undetected. We stopped the bikes and dismounted away from the cluster, careful not to get noticed.

"You go from the right and I'll attack from the left and we'll meet in the middle after." Doug created a plan of action, making hand gestures as he whispered. He pulled the tire iron out from the backpack and handed it to me. I doubled around so I could come at the undead from the right angle. I had two undead to take down before I met the middle. I hid behind a parked car and, just as an undead woman moved by, I jumped up and slammed the tire iron into the side of her head. She instantly went down with a thud. As soon as she fell, I backed up. I knew that I had caught all the undead's attention. The man that was directly next to the permanently dead undead woman was on the prowl for my flesh. He jumped at me and he was quick, quicker than I had anticipated. When he lunged at me, I pulled the tire iron out of her skull. The undead threw himself directly onto the tire iron severing his own brain. I let out a sigh of relief.

As fortunate as that was for me, my tire iron was stuck, impacted in his brain and it wouldn't come out. I didn't have time to finesse it out. I dropped the tire iron along with the undead man onto the ground and made a run for it. As I ran back toward the bikes, I shot a glance over at Doug, who had already taken down his two undead men. I stopped running and watched him finish the job. He made his way to an undead woman, who was in the middle of the cluster and the only undead remaining. He let her come at him and, as she made her lunge, he side-stepped and shoved his knife into her temple.

He looked up at me and then we both did a quick glance around to make sure that there were no more undead around us. When he was satisfied, he came back to where I was standing by the bikes.

"You okay?" he asked me.

"Yeah, I'm good, except I lost the tire iron. It's stuck in that guy's head," I said pointing to the undead man.

"No problem." Doug walked over to the man, put his shoe on his face and gave the tire iron a good yank. It made a suctioned sound and popped out of the skull, dripping with brain matter. "Here you go." He said with a cocky smile trying to hand the tire iron back to me.

"No thanks, I'll just take the knife back," I said, trying to suppress a gag. Thank God I didn't eat before we left. "If I'm right, the pharmacy is just ahead," I said as I mounted my bike.

We pedaled toward the pharmacy. I was hopeful that we would find our brothers. I could see the pharmacy; it was only a few yards in front of us. In the parking lot sat several cars. Hopefully, they were there. Prior to approaching the pharmacy, we pulled the bikes over to the bushes and crouched down.

"That's the car right there. They're in there," Doug said, excitedly.

"If their car is here and they are in there still, why? Something had to have gone wrong. Otherwise, they would have been home by now. They must be stuck—cornered or something."

"What should we do? If there are enough of the undead to corner them, then there are too many of them for us to take on," Doug pointed out.

"I say we spy on the place. Sneak around, peer through windows, and see what we are up against before we make any decisions. We'll start with the front door. If there is an overwhelming amount of the undead, then we back out and figure out a different plan," I proposed my idea to Doug.

"Let's do it," He responded. We hid the bikes in the bushes and made our way to the entrance. We both had a knife in each of our hands—armed and ready. We peered through the window on the front door. It was empty, no movement whatsoever. I looked over at Doug and shrugged, signaling for us to move forward.

Upon entering, the store was deserted. No one, dead or undead, in sight. The place was completely trashed and ransacked. Someone had been here searching for something. We checked down every aisle in the store and made our way toward the back of the store, where the manager's office and the pharmacy were located.

As we reached the back of the store it was obvious that there was nobody in there. Our brothers weren't there searching for things, they weren't trapped or fighting for their lives—they weren't there at all. Who knows if they had ever even been in there?

"Now what?" I asked.

"Well, we are here, we might as well grab whatever we can and throw it into the backpack before we continue on. What do we need?"

"I worked in a hospital. I'll look through these meds and you should go find some first aid supplies. But try and keep it quiet. I don't want to attract any unwanted attention. Who knows what happened to Logan and Carter? I have a feeling they're in trouble, but, where are they?" Doug nodded in response. I ransacked through the scarce stock of medication and grabbed what I thought could be helpful. When I was satisfied with what I took, I brought the meds to the front using a shopping basket.

As I approached the front of the store, I noticed Doug on the floor, sitting on his knees staring outside. He heard me approach, turned around, and put his finger to his mouth, signaling for me to remain silent. I slowly put the basket down and crawled on my hands and knees to where Doug was.

I glanced out the window and was, at first, confused by what I saw. I was expecting to see a cluster or mob of the undead walking by, but instead it was people, real alive people. Four men were pacing with torches in their hands and rifles slung over their shoulders.

The men were talking and loudly laughing. Loud enough to catch Doug's attention and, probably, the attention of any undead that was within the vicinity. They didn't seem concerned at all; they didn't have a care in the world.

I moved away from the window, sat with my back against the wall, and motioned for Doug to come join me. "What do we do?" I asked.

"Grab the shit from the basket, put it in the backpack and fast. I say we follow them. They are acting like they run the town, so maybe they do. They walk with authority and their loud laughter shows comfort and arrogance. I say that if they run this town then there is a good chance that they have seen Carter and Logan," Doug explained.

"Okay, so why don't we just ask them?" I was having a hard time following.

"Don't you remember that guy with the shotgun who shot Evan. Something ain't right here, that guy was afraid of something. We don't know who these people are. We need to follow them. It might be a dead end and a complete waste of our time. Or it might be the path to our brothers." Doug handed me the backpack which was already almost full.

I shoved the medications into the bag as fast as I could. "Let's go." We both kneeled up and peeked out the window for the men. They were not visible, but I could hear their laughter and see the faint glow of their torches down the street to the left. Once I spotted the glow of the light, I pointed it out to Doug and mouthed 'that way'.

He nodded and slowly opened the door and then we were off to stalk our prey and find our brothers.

chapter twenty-one

Following the men, we were careful to stay in the shadows and keep completely silent. We followed them for two blocks before they slowed their pace. It was easy to keep track of the men because of their torches, but it was difficult to see where they were going because of how dark the town was.

The tallest man of the group completely stopped in his tracks and turned. "Did you hear that?" He asked the others.

"No, what?" said the man in the red shirt.

"Don't know, just thought I heard something," the tall man replied.

"Want me to double back and take a look?" Asked the youngest looking man.

"Nah, we're almost there. If it's a biter, then we'll deal with it when it's ready to show its ugly face," the tall man replied, it was clear that he was the leader of their group. "Come on, keep moving, they'll be wondering where we're at." The men continued forward.

He used the word they, which meant there were more of them. Up ahead there was a soft glow. The men continued forward, and we decreased the gap that was separating us. Once at their gathering place, we hid in the tree line behind a parked car.

There were roughly ten people including the four men. Of the six other people three of them were men and three of them were women. They were in an intersection with torches tied to each surrounding stop sign. Surrounding the intersection were dozens of dead corpses. It appeared that they killed the undead and arranged them in a circle around the intersection. Then at each road leading up to the intersection there was someone keeping guard. This group was smart they had thought of everything.

In the center of the intersection were two people blindfolded, gagged, and hog-tied with a shotgun trained on them.

"What are the chances that those two people are Logan and Carter?" I whispered to Doug.

"I'd say pretty damn good. It's hard to tell from all the way back here, but who else would it be. It has to be them." Doug was certain. "What should we do? There are too many of them for us to take on alone."

"We'll have to take a page from Logan's book and create a diversion. A diversion will have to take most of them away from here and hopefully we can handle the remainder," I stated.

"What kind of diversion did you have in mind?" Doug asked. I sat there, pondering it for a moment as I studied the scene that was in front of us.

"We need a gun," I said.

"As awesome as that would be, that doesn't seem like a viable option," Doug stated the obvious.

"We need something that is going to drive their attention away. If they heard gun shots, they would be curious as to who is shooting and leave to check it out."

"Well what about an explosion?" Doug suggested. "I brought a lighter. We passed a gas station about a block back. I can't get more creative than that."

"That would work, back at home a gas station exploded, and it was huge. The only problem with that is that it's going to attract all the undead from the surrounding area," I pointed out,

"That's their problem, we'll be on our way back home by then. We blow it up, take the guards down, rescue our brothers and hit the road."

"How are we going to do the explosion? Can you run fast?" I asked.

"I was a track star in high school, don't worry about me I'll take care of that. I also went through a pyro phase as a teenager."

"Sounds like you've got it all worked out, then. Come back as soon as you can, make sure you stay in the shadows, so they don't see you. I'll start the take down of the guards if possible."

"Don't be stupid, Mya. You should wait for me to get back to start that. I don't need you getting hurt in the process. Plus, we need to define the taking down of the guards. We're not going to kill anyone here, right?"

"It'd be stupid to wait, that would be wasting precious time. We'll see how it goes. Of course, we're not going to kill them. We'll just knock them out. Leave me the tire iron and, when you come back, use either the flashlight or something you find along the way and knock them out with that." Before Doug could protest any further, I urged him to go. "Get going, as soon as you ignite it, start running. Be careful and be as fast as you can." I hugged him.

Sitting there waiting made me nervous and jittery. I didn't want to hurt anyone, especially people who were alive, but, obviously, these were not good people. Good people wouldn't kidnap innocent men. I needed to keep reminding myself of this. My heart was pounding with anticipation of what could potentially go wrong. *What if Carter or Logan got hurt in the process? What if they were already dead?* It was impossible to tell if they were alright from this far away. *Was that them—hog tied in the middle of the road?* There were too many unknowns. I reminded myself that I was pregnant and couldn't put myself into risky situations. That was a risky situation.

After a little while had passed, I began to worry. What the hell was taking him so long? The explosion should have happened by now. He took forever and I grew more nervous. I glanced up to look at the moon, which was bright against the black night. I closed my eyes and let out a sigh. *What was taking him so long?* Maybe the lighter was dead or maybe… BOOM. Sparks flew out into the black night sky, shooting embers out in all directions. The explosion was higher than the tree line. I was able to see the huge flames as they burst with anger.

I quickly stood and watched the group for their reaction. Their senses were immediately on alert and they instantly started scrambling around barking orders at each other.

"What the hell was that?" I heard one of them shout. I watched as they huddled, creating their own plan of action. They pointed fingers at different people giving each person a task to do.

My insides were bursting with excitement that our plan was working. Within minutes seven of their members had gone off to see what the disturbance was. That left three remaining members of their group on guard of their prisoners. One person had their gun trained on the prisoners. Another person began pacing around in circles checking the perimeter around the intersection. The third person was down the road in the direction the explosion had come from. He was standing there as if he was waiting for someone to jump out at him— armed and ready. I decided my best target was the person doing perimeter checks. I got down on the ground and began to crawl towards the intersection. I tried my best to remain quiet and move quickly.

Five feet from the intersection, there was a car that was tipped over on its side. I hid behind the car to wait for the perimeter checker to walk by. I crouched down, leaning against the car waiting. I could hear the crunching of his footsteps as he began to approach the area in which I was hiding. I heard him pass by and, as soon as he did, I sprang into action.

I snuck up behind him with the tire iron held above my head and wailed it down on the top of his back. He was instantly knocked out and slumped down. Before he dropped to the ground, I caught him to soften his fall so that I wouldn't be heard. I dragged his body behind the car and peered over the top of it to make sure no one noticed me. I looked back down at the man I just hit, feeling guilty. I knew it had to be done. I took his gun and looked back to where the other guards were.

I was too far away to see the guard who was facing the direction that the explosion had come from. However, I was awfully close to where the other guard was standing with the prisoners. Now that I was closer, the prisoners looked like Carter and Logan. The guard was a woman with long, black hair. She was frantically looking around, but her gun was still trained on the men. I was unsure if she saw me or not.

"Julian!!" She shouted. "Julian!!" she shouted again. That must have been the guy I knocked out. I looked down at him. I checked his pulse just to make sure I didn't kill him. I put my fingers to his throat and felt his blood flow. He was alive. I turned my attention back to the black-haired girl. She was distracted now, her gun no longer on the men. Instead, she was spinning in circles checking her surroundings.

"Brass!" She shouted. I assumed Brass was the other man on guard. "Brass, I can't see Julian! Something's wrong!" She was now staring in the direction in which the explosion came from, waiting for Brass to answer her. "Brass!" She was really panicking now.

"Good" I said to myself. Brass not answering was a good thing, which means that Doug came back and took care of him.

"Oh, screw this." The girl said and she started sprinting in the direction of the explosion. The second she made her move, I made mine.

I ran out from behind the car to the men. "Logan! Carter!" I dropped to my knees, set the gun down and ripped their blindfolds and gags off. "Oh my god are you guys okay?"

"Mya!" Logan was surprised to see me. "What the hell are you doing here? I told them that no one was to follow us."

"I'm saving your ass, that's what I'm doing here," I replied to him as I tried to free his arms and legs.

"You came here alone? In your condition? What the hell is the matter with you?" Carter scolded me. I was taken aback by what he said, 'my condition'. Did he know?

I brushed him off, "I'm not alone. Doug is with me. He's the one who created the explosion. I don't know where he is though."

"Right here!" Doug said as he approached us. He took out his knife and immediately went to work on the ties on their arms and legs. "We got to go, now. They're right behind me. They figured out quick that it was sabotaged. I also ran past a cluster of undead who are also right on my tail. I'm hoping that the two groups slow each other down." Doug quickly cut them out of their restraints, and we helped them to their feet. They briefly stretched out their limbs and then we heard people approaching.

"Quick, we got to go!" Doug said tugging on Carters sleeves. We began to head to the tree line.

"Wait, the medication! Did you get it? Did you raid the pharmacy?" I asked Carter frantically. "What about the tire?"

"Oh shit. The bag, where is it?" Carter asked Logan in a panic.

"They took it. I don't know where they put it. Quick, everyone look around, we don't have much time," Logan ordered. We all spread out frantically searching.

"Looking for this?" It was Julian, now conscious again holding a duffle bag.

"Give it here and you won't have to get hurt. Just leave it and walk the other way," Carter tried to reason with the man.

"I don't think so. This is ours now," Julian replied with a sinister smile. "And you are running out of options, my friends are almost back. Bitch, you did quite a number on me—you'll pay for that I promise you."

"You leave her out of this," Logan warned, taking a step towards Julian.

Julian pulled a pistol from his waistband, "Ah, ah, ah. I wouldn't take another step if I was you. No one is going anywhere, or I'll shoot her. I know how valuable a woman is nowadays. Wouldn't want to have to shoot such a pretty one, but I will." Logan back tracked to us and stood in front of me.

I tried to remember what I did with his shotgun that I pulled from him. I tossed a look over my shoulder and noticed that it lay on the ground only two feet from us.

"Jesus, what the hell is taking them so long?" Julian was now talking to himself.

"AHHHHH" we heard the cries of someone in their group.

"What, you got more people out there?" Julian asked us.

"No, it's the undead," Doug replied.

"The what? Oh, you mean the biters." Julian looked between us and the area that the screams were coming from. It was apparent that he was torn on what he should do. Should he keep us prisoner or should he go help his friends. While Julian was distracted struggling with this internal battle, Logan kicked his foot back and dragged the shotgun to his feet. He snapped down, retrieved it, and aimed at Julian.

"Give me the bag and I let you live," Logan demanded.

"I don't do well with threats," Julian warned and pointed the gun at Logan ready to fire. Before Julian had the chance to get off a shot, Logan fired, blowing his wrist clear off.

Julian dropped the duffle bag and his gun and fell to his knees. He clutched his wrist, writhing in agony. Logan ran over, retrieved the bag, punched Julian in the face, and said, "You're lucky I didn't kill ya." He turned towards us and started running, "Let's go, and get back to the car."

"Wait, Logan, what about the tire, we need that to leave this house to get to Lilianna!" I asked, worried that we would need to do this all over again.

"We got that first, it's already in the trunk of the car. Now come on, let's go!" Logan urged us on. We could hear screams closer than before. I started to see shadows, faint outlines— people or the undead, it was hard to tell. I didn't want to find out either.

We ran through the town using the tree line and broken-down cars as coverage, shielding us from the group of torturers and the cluster of undead. Getting back to the car was a breeze and we had no complications, surprisingly. Once at the car, we all jumped in. Logan started it up and took off for our temporary home.

The entire car was silent. Everyone was exhausted, struggling to catch their breath, and, I'm sure, a little shocked by what we all just went through. I knew I was. I couldn't believe that those people would kidnap Carter and Logan. I couldn't believe that I got violent with another human. I couldn't believe that Carter figured out my secret and almost spilled the beans in front of everyone. I couldn't believe how ruthless Logan was. He shot that guy's hand off and punched him in the face afterwards. Unbelievable things happened in the new world.

chapter twenty-two

We made it home without any issues. When we pulled up the driveway, Elana was pacing back and forth on the porch. "What do we tell them?" I asked.

"The truth," Logan stated. "They need to know—they need to be on alert in case those guys seek out revenge. Everyone needs to be prepared."

Logan turned the engine off, and we all got out of the car. Elana came running over to us and jumped in his arms, kissing his face all over. "I was so worried. What happened? You guys took forever, and then Mya and Doug left, and they were gone forever. We've been worried sick."

We filled her in on what had happened.

"We shouldn't stay here, it's not safe. Those guys are crazy," Doug replied.

"Evan and Blake aren't well enough to travel right now," Carter stated.

"I'm afraid it's only gotten worse since you left. Evan is okay, he is in some pain, but Blake. I don't know, I'm really worried about him. So is June, she's acting like a lunatic. She was freaking out about where you were and when you were coming back," Elana explained.

"I'll administer the medication right away. It should kick in fast and in a few days the infection should die down." Carter grabbed the bag of meds and went inside.

"I'm going to sit with Evan for a while." Doug walked into the house.

That left Logan, Elana, and I to chat. "I can't believe you came after us," he spat out at me. He was pissed. "And I can't believe that you let her!" He said to Elana.

"Oh, come on Logan, it's not her fault. We were all worried. Whether you came back or not, we were going to have to go out for the medications. Plus, you needed us. Without us you'd probably be dead right now. Get over yourself. This is a new world that we live in. At some point or another, every single one of our lives will be put into jeopardy—and more than once. You're just going to have to learn to live with it," I argued with him. "Now if you'll excuse me, I'm starved." And with that, I stomped inside and went to the kitchen. I rummaged through the cabinets looking for something to eat. The others must have finished the food from earlier. I settled on a pack of pretzels, it wasn't the healthiest option, but it was the fastest. I sat at the kitchen table and began to eat.

Logan and Elana passed by, "I moved the cars around, the car is now in the garage and the SUV is in the driveway, that way the guys won't know where we are. We're heading to bed. Do you mind keeping watch for a little?" Logan asked.

"Nope," I replied, still pissed at him. He nodded and continued towards the steps. Elana was about to say something, but before she could, he tugged on her arm forcing her to go with him. I was alone again in the kitchen—left with my thoughts. I finished my pack of pretzels and threw out the wrapper. I went into the garage to grab a bottled water and another pretzel pack, then headed for the window seat where I sat the night before.

I stared out the window as I ate my pretzels. I thought of how the population had adapted. No one was safe anymore. Between the guy with the shotgun and the group that kidnapped Carter and Logan—no one could be trusted. I was fortunate that I ended up with a great group of people early on.

I looked out the window at the trees. I missed the scarlet oak tree from the church. That tree felt comforting to me, almost like home.

"You know those really aren't the healthiest option for you. I'm sure that there is something more nutritional in the kitchen." Carter said as he approached me.

"I know, but I was starving. Couldn't help it." I said guiltily.

"Here, I got these for you." Carter handed me a bottle of pills. I took it from his hand and read the label. They were prenatal vitamins.

I looked up at him, "When did you figure it out?"

"I've suspected for a while. At first, I didn't want to make any assumptions, there were subtle signs. I highly suspected back at the church when your sense of smell was ridiculously good. Then, the other day when I heard you humming lullaby's, that pretty much confirmed it for me." Carter said, proud of himself for putting it together.

"I have no idea how far along I am. I had just found out the morning that all of this started. Talk about timing. Scott died before I had the chance to tell him. Logan doesn't know either." I said to Carter.

"Uhm, I think that I may have let that slip. I didn't know that he didn't know, and, well, when we were about to die, I may have said something about it." He looked at me, slightly ashamed.

"Well, that explains all the animosity toward me." I sighed, looked out the window, and scanned the lawn—no movement.

"I'm sorry. I'm sure he'll come around. I don't think he's mad about the baby. I think he's mad because you put yourself and your baby in danger." Carter explained.

"I know. I know how he is. He will come around. He'll probably apologize to me by the end of tomorrow." I said with certainty. "So, did you happen to do any rotations in the obstetrician or prenatal area? I'm kind of freaked out."

"Yes, briefly. I can't say that I am completely educated on it, but it's better than nothing. I knew to get those for you." He said, pointing down at the prenatal vitamins.

"What kind of doctor are you anyways? I don't think that I've ever asked," I asked.

"I'm just a general surgeon. I work with a little bit of everything," Carter said modestly.

"Oh, just a general surgeon. You say that like you're not proud of it." I looked at Carter, who just shrugged his shoulders. "That's something to be proud of, especially now. You have all this knowledge and special traits that none of us have, and you have the abilities to save lives."

"Yeah, I guess. Listen, I want you to keep me informed about your pregnancy. Anything that doesn't feel normal or even things that might feel normal. I'm not going to lie, it's going to be difficult without any medical technology, but people have been doing this for thousands of years. You're going to be okay. I'll help you get through this, and I know Logan and Elana will, too," He said, trying to boost my confidence.

"Thanks, Carter. This is my first time so I'm not exactly sure what is normal and what isn't, but if I had to guess, I would say, so far, normal." I looked out the window to scan the front lawn. Still nothing. We needed a quiet night. "How are Blake and Evan?"

"Evan is okay—in pain—but once he takes these meds and antibiotics, he'll be okay. We're going to have to make him some crutches or something so he can get around better. He probably won't be able to walk on it for at least a month," Carter explained.

"Wow, a month. He's going to be vulnerable in difficult situations. We'll have to keep him in the car with the kids. How's Blake?" I asked.

"He's not doing well, and I don't know why. He could have an infection from the cut, but it's worse than I would have thought. I started him on antibiotics, and I found an IV bag at the pharmacy, so he's on an IV drip to get some more fluids in him. I'm equally as

158

worried about June as I am him. She is beyond worried about him, and I can't blame her. But still, it isn't healthy. She is also not eating and won't leave his side. She needs to get out of that room for a little while, just to take a breather," Carter suggested.

"I'll talk to her tomorrow and I'll have Elana help, she's good at dealing with distraught people. Maybe she can take her out of the room for a little bit, maybe get her to take a walk for some fresh air, and I'll volunteer to sit in with Blake," I offered.

"That sounds like a good idea. The problem is getting June to go along with it," Carter stated. I scooted my body back against one of the windows and rested my head. I was angled in a way that I was comfortable and still able to keep an eye on the front lawn. Still nothing.

"You can head off to bed," I told Carter, "I volunteered to keep watch."

"You should really be getting some rest," Carter said.

"I know, and I will tomorrow."

"Fine, but I'm starving. I'm going to make something. I'll bring some for you too."

"Sounds good." I smiled at him as he walked away. I looked out the window again. It was peaceful outside; the area was completely still. My eyes were beginning to get heavy. I worried that I might fall asleep and then I remembered that Carter was making me food, so I needed to stay awake.

I scanned the front lawn again and my heart skipped a beat. The undead were everywhere. I tried to scream to get someone's attention, but I couldn't find my voice. They were bashing on the windows trying to get in. I scooted away from the windows to protect myself and scooted too far and fell from the window seat.

chapter twenty-three

I hit the ground with a thud and looked up. There was nothing there, no undead, no windows, no window seat. I had been lying on the loveseat sleeping. But how did I get there? I don't remember going to sleep. My stomach growled—I was still starving. I stood and looked out the window. It was sunrise. I slept through the whole night, again. I was not a good overnight watch guard. I would have to come clean to Logan.

Sitting at the window seat in my place was Elana.

"How did I get to the loveseat?" I asked her.

She shrugged her shoulders, "I don't know. My guess is Carter, he was keeping watch before I took over. He slept on the other couch for a while. I think he's upstairs now." She turned her attention back toward the front lawn. She was mad at me, I could tell. I made my way over to the window seat and sat beside her.

I put my head on her shoulder, "Don't be mad at me."

"Why didn't you tell me that you were pregnant?" She was blunt and went straight to the point, which I liked.

"I just didn't want to bother anyone else with it. It's hard in a normal life, it's even harder in this life," I explained.

"I get that, but you have us, you always will. We're family, we will take care of you and the baby together."

"I just didn't want to burden you guys with my mess. I was going to tell you guys eventually—I was just waiting until we were safe and settled."

"It's not a burden, it's a miracle," She said to me, looking me straight in the eye.

"Okay. You think Logan will ever forgive me?" I asked her.

"I already have," He said from behind me. He walked up and gave me a hug. "I'm sorry for the way I acted last night. I was just frustrated that you didn't tell me earlier so we could have taken better care of you. I was also pissed that you put yourself and my little niece or nephew in jeopardy."

"I understand. But you're going to need to understand that probably won't be the last time we are in danger before he or she is born—and even after he or she is born. The world that we live in now is dangerous. There is no way to change that, we just have to accept it and adapt," I explained.

"I know. We will worry about all that the next time it comes, but for right now, I am just thrilled that you both are okay." He gave me another tight squeeze, let me go, and was ready to get down to business. "So, the agenda for today, I'm going to fix the SUV and prepare it for us to leave. We've spent too much time here and I'm worried about those guys from last night. The longer we stay here, the more of a target we become."

"Okay, I agree but we need to wait for Evan and Blake to get stable. I need to be honest with you Logan, I'm not good at this overnight watch thing. I always fall asleep and that means I'm risking everyone's safety."

"Okay, not a problem. You are off night duty. We'll find a different shift for you to take," Logan said.

"What are we going to do about the flat tire?" I asked Logan.

"I'm going to change it today at some point. I want to do it sooner than later that way we can leave in a moment's notice," Logan responded. I nodded in agreement.

"Elana, I have a special task for you today. I was talking with Carter last night and Blake isn't doing well—and neither is June. We were hoping you could get her out of that room for a little while. Get her to take a break, maybe get her to eat something?" I explained.

"I can certainly try. I don't know how successful I'll be. She won't stay away from him for long," Elana replied.

"I know, but anything is better than nothing. I'll sit with Blake and make sure he's okay," I said. Will walked by carrying Rose as we were talking. "Good morning, Will. How are Blake and June doing?" I asked.

"It was a difficult night. I'm afraid that Blake isn't any better and June is just wrecked with worry. The room is even beginning to smell a little odd in there. I want to be there to support her, but it's not a good place for my little Rose to be—and she is my first priority. I think we are going to go sit on the back porch and enjoy some fresh air." Will walked to the kitchen. His comments made me nervous.

I looked at Elana, and I could tell by her expression that she was already thinking the same thing—something just wasn't right. "Elana, this is probably our best opportunity to get her out of there. Let's go try." Elana followed behind up to the bedroom where Blake and June had been living in.

Elana knocked on the door, while I stood off to the side. While we waited, we heard shuffling coming from the other side of the door and then June pulled the door open.

"Elana, what do you need?" June asked.

"Hi June, how are you holding up?" Elana asked in her sweet-but-professional voice.

"It's just so hard," June admitted, her voice filled with agony.

"I'm sure it is, I cannot even begin to imagine what you are going through. Have you been eating or sleeping?"

"No sleep, I watch him all the time. I don't know about food." June gave her a blank stare.

"How about you come downstairs with me and we get you some coffee and maybe a bite to eat and we can talk some more about what's going on?" Elana offered her, coddling her.

"But I can't just leave Blake like that," June responded, hesitantly looking back into the room.

"Mya has offered to watch over him so you can get some food. She worked in a hospital, and she's great with kids. He'll be well taken care of," Elana offered a solution and stood there for a minute while June pondered it. It was obvious that she was desperate for a break.

"Okay, he is still sleeping, so just for a few minutes, half hour tops. He's just too sick for me to be gone for that long." June had made a compromise.

"Half hour it is, not a minute more. Come, let's get you some coffee."

"You take good care of him, get me if anything happens, even if it's just his eyes opening," June demanded from me.

Elana and June went downstairs, and I went into the room. I entered the room quietly, hoping not to wake him. The room was in complete disarray. There were items and trash thrown all about, and the floor was barely recognizable. The odor of the room was as if something had rotted, maybe spoiled food or old trash. The aura of the room made my stomach do somersault after somersault. I walked over to the window and opened it for some fresh air. The air was brisk, but the stench needed to be released.

I went to the bed where Blake lay peacefully sleeping. I sat down on the chair that was next to the bed and just stared at him. He looked sick. His forehead was covered with sweat and there were red rims around his eyes. I peeled the blanket back and looked at his cuts, none of them appeared to be healing. The cut on the inside of his right arm hadn't healed either, in fact it was extremely infected. There was puss coming from it and an unsettling odor. It looked as if it hadn't been cleaned in days. The skin around the wound was a greyish color.

I put the covers back over Blake and watched as his chest rose and fell with each breath he took. Up and down, inhale and exhale, up and down, inhale and… Blake made a weird struggled noise and his chest hadn't fallen, he hadn't exhaled. "Blake!" I said and tried to shake his shoulder to wake him, but it was unsuccessful. I began to panic. I needed Carter.

I rushed out of the room and went to where I hoped Carter was sleeping and burst in the door. Carter shot up in bed.

"I need you, hurry up!" I was too panicked to explain.

"What's wrong? Is it the baby? What are your symptoms?" Carter shouted out at me while he followed me down the hallway.

"No, it's Blake. I don't think he's breathing." I was finally able to spit the words out. He quickly pushed past me and ran to Blake's side and placed a hand on his chest and his ear to his mouth to listen. He shook his head and began CPR.

I stood there anxiously watching Carter trying to save Blake. The longer the CPR went on the more anxious I became. Carter was compressing nonstop and Blake was still completely unresponsive. Carter began to slow his movements, slower and slower, until he was no longer compressing.

"What are you doing? Why are you stopping?" I asked.

"He's gone," Carter said as he hung his head in despair.

"How? I don't understand, he was just alive a minute ago. He took a deep breath and then it all just stopped. What happened to him?"

"The infection must have shut down his body. The antibiotics didn't work. He just didn't make it, he's gone." Carter became silent and pulled the sheet up over his face, kneeled on the floor next to the bed and rested his head in his hands. I stood there in shock. My feet were planted where I was standing but my body felt as if it were floating. So many thoughts ran through my mind, there were too many to articulate.

"June…" I finally formulated a thought, an important one. "I promised June I would take care of him, and now…" I struggled to say the words, "Now, he's gone, and I broke my promise. Poor June, she is going to be devastated. What do we do?" I began to cry a little. "Why did this happen, Carter?" I was upset. I had watched a little boy die for no reason.

My emotions consumed me, and I was inconsolable. Carter rose from where he was kneeling, walked over to me, put his hands on my shoulders and looked me straight in the eye.

"I know you are upset, but you need to calm down. I need to think," He said. I looked past his stare, over his shoulder to where Blake's body was lying. In death, he did not look peaceful—he looked worn and disturbed.

I focused my attention back on Carter's face. "What do we do?" I asked him again in a calmer tone. He took his hands off my shoulders, put them on his knees, and bent over in thought.

I looked from Carter to Blake's body again. I tried to imagine what I would tell June. While I gazed over his body, I thought I saw something…but *it wasn't possible*. His hand had jerked. He's dead. Dead people don't do that… but the undead do.

Before my mind could fully comprehend what was about to happen, Blake was out of his bed. Blake was undead and, on his feet, and heading straight for Carter.

"Carter!! Watch out!" I exclaimed. The words came out of my mouth too late. Carter looked at me confused, then looked back towards the bed where Blake's body had been lying only moments ago. Before he was able to process what was happening, Blake tackled him to the floor.

Carter held Blake away from his body with his right arm and scrambled to search the floor for a weapon with his left. "Mya!" He yelled at me, snapping me out of a trance and into action. I ran about the room, frantically searching for something. I did not want to kill Blake, just knock him off Carter so we could get the hell out. I searched the tops of the dressers and left them empty-handed.

"Mya! Under. Bed," Carter growled at me. Now, he had both of his hands at Blake's throat, defending himself from his hungry opponent. Blake was strong and eager to get his first taste of blood.

I kneeled beside the bed and saw what Carter was trying to grab, a metal baseball bat. I stood behind Blake, then swung so that the impact hit his stomach and sent him flying across the bedroom. The doctor instantly leapt to his feet, grabbed my arm, and headed for the door. Blake was quick to recover from the blow and was up and coming for us. We just squeezed through the door with no time to spare. As we closed the door, Blake flung his body against it. Carter grabbed the doorknob and held tight, so Blake remained locked in the room. We stood there trying to recover from the intense situation we just survived. "How?" was the only word I was able to formulate and spit towards Carter.

"I don't know," Carter said, his mouth hung open, completely dumbfounded, staring at the door in disbelief.

"What happened? What did you do?" June shouted as she ran up the steps. At the door, she collided against Carter, who was still holding the doorknob. She was trying to force her way into the room. "Where's my baby?" She screamed frantically.

"June, I am so sorry…" Carter began. But it was useless; she hit him hard, trying to get through. Her outburst attracted the attention of the entire house and everyone made their way upstairs. She continued to fight her way through him until Doug grabbed hold of her.

"June, I'm sorry. I'm sorry this happened but you don't want to go in there," I said looking her straight in the eyes. "Do you hear that? Listen, that is not your Blake anymore. Your Blake wouldn't make those sounds." The entire hallway was silent as we all listened to the growls and shrieks that came from the other side of the door.

"I. don't. care," June sobbed. She melted into the floor in a wave of grief, sobbing into her knees. Elana sat on the floor next to her, comforting her. While June was slightly distracted, the guys began to whisper back and forth on what to do.

"How do we take care of this?" Doug whispered to Carter.

"We surely can't leave him like that, that ain't right," Quinn whispered back.

"He's just a boy, we can't sever the brain of a child," Will announced.

"There is no other option," Logan stated. "I'll take care of it. I'll just need some help to work up the courage."

"You can't hurt my baby. Leave my baby alone. He's a good boy, please," June begged, not really knowing what she was begging for. I gave Elana a look that told her she needed to take June away.

"June, they aren't going to hurt him, okay. Let's just go get some tea. That will help calm you down and we can come up with a solution," Elana consoled her.

"I'll come too, come on, honey," Will said. June sniffled and nodded. She leaned against the door and kissed it. "Mommy will be right back baby," She said to the undead boy. "We'll figure out how to save you."

chapter twenty four

"Jesus H. Christ. What a crooked-ass situation," Quinn said once June was out of earshot.

"What the hell are we going to do?" I asked the others.

"We're going to take care of it," Logan responded.

"How can you just say that? How can you act like it's no big deal? I know you have seen and done unspeakable things in your life, but this?" I spat at him, crossing my arms.

"This is what we have to do to survive. We can't stay here—he will kill us all," Logan stated.

"Can't we just keep him in this room?" Quinn asked.

"No, look at Carter's hands. They are practically purple from gripping the handle so hard. The undead are smart, they can get in and out of doors. It doesn't lock from the outside and, in time, I bet that his need for food would overpower his little body enough that he would find a way out. The only way we don't take care of this is if we leave right now. But the day is halfway over, so that is not an ideal option." Logan sighed, looked down at the floor, and then back at all of us. "If that was your kid, would you want him to live like that? He isn't a person anymore, he's undead."

I refused to accept this fate for that sweet little boy. Then I looked up at the door and how tightly Carter was gripping the handle and how much the door was rattling. Blake wasn't a sweet little boy anymore. He was gone and this new thing had taken over his body.

As if reading my mind, Carter spoke up, "He's right, Mya. It needs to happen. It's the only way."

"I know." We all took a moment of silence to gather our thoughts.

"This is insane. When they turn, it's like the person isn't even there anymore," Quinn stated. He seemed to be in a bit of shock at the situation. "The thing that freaks me out is their eyes. They have lifeless eyes—black eyes, just like a doll. It's like they aren't real, except when they want to tear your flesh off with their teeth." Everyone stood silent, reflecting on what Quinn had just said—he wasn't wrong.

"What is the plan then?" Doug was the first to finally speak up.

"I'm going to need a sofa cushion, a pillow, and a long, strong object—like a fire poker," Logan stated. Doug, Quinn, and I went off to gather the things Logan requested.

A few minutes later we met back at the doorway to the master bedroom, where Carter was still gripping the handle and Blake was still banging against the door. I brought the pillow, Doug had grabbed the sofa cushion, and Quinn had found a fire poker.

"Now what?" Quinn asked.

"I'm going to need Carter to throw open the door and immediately step back. Then I am going to need two of you there in his place with the sofa cushion to push him back and hopefully knock him off his feet. I'll slip my arm in the pillow and use that to defend myself and then swing around with the fire poker," Logan stated and we all nodded, agreeing with the plan.

"Be confident and swift in your movements, otherwise, this could go downhill fast. In fact, we should have a backup plan." Logan pulled the gun from his waist band and handed it to me. "If for whatever reason, he gets past all of us, you shoot him. In the head, remember."

"Uh-okay," I said nervously, not wanting the responsibility of holding the gun.

Carter held the doorknob still, but stood off to the right, as far from the door as he could. Quinn and Doug held the sofa cushion up in front of them in the doorway. Logan slipped his arm into the pillow, and stood behind them, armed and ready. I stood in the back, aiming the loaded gun, and praying that I did not have to use it.

"Ready?" Logan asked.

"Yes," we said, together.

"Carter, now!" Logan shouted.

Carter flung the door open and fell to the side. Blake flung against the wall with the door and was immediately at his feet again. Quinn and Doug held up the sofa cushion and pushed onward, knocking the boy down. He got right back up again. Quinn and Doug were confused and couldn't decide what to do.

"Again!" Logan shouted over the loud growling that was coming from Blake. Quinn and Doug knocked into Blake again and sent him flying to the other side of the room, giving Logan enough time to step in. The pair quickly crawled out of the room. Logan leapt in the room and immediately started swinging for Blake. Blake was on his feet again and heading straight for Logan. In defense, Logan lifted the pillow just in time. The boy collided with the pillow and sank his teeth into the cotton. With him temporarily distracted, Logan swung the fire poker over his head, and directly into his skull.

Blake's body immediately went limp and blood burst from the wound, spraying the pillow. Logan dropped the pillow and fire poker, which sent Blake's body tumbling to the floor. My brother walked past us, ignoring everyone, and went straight for the bathroom. We heard him turn on the water and slide the shower curtain as he entered the shower. He was shutting us out and shutting himself away. He needed to grieve.

The three of them looked at me questioning what was happening. "He just needs a minute. He's emotional and has been through a lot. His way of dealing with things is to shut them out," I awkwardly stated. "Let's clean this up. June can't see this." I approached the room and looked over the gruesome scene not sure where to start.

Carter came up next to me and put his hand on my shoulder, "We should wrap his body. There is no way to hide that we just shoved a fire poker through her kid's brain," he said to me. His vulgar words made my stomach flip and I gagged loudly.

"Are you okay? You shouldn't do this; it's going to make you sick."

"Who wouldn't feel sick over something like this?" I spat at him.

"Whatever you want to do," Carter said to me and knelt next to Blake's lifeless body. He tried to remove the fire poker from Blake's skull, but it was stuck. "I can't get it out," Carter said looking up at Quinn and Doug for help.

"Here let me try," Doug said. He went up to Blake, put his foot on his head, grabbing hold of the fire poker, and yanked it. The fire poker removed a chunk of skull and a matted thick piece of hair. The removal of the fire poker made me lose it. I rushed over to the bedside trashcan and vomited all the pretzels I had eaten the night before.

"Told ya..." Carter started to say.

"Shut it," I replied right back at him. I looked down at the bedsheet and had an idea. "Let's wrap him up in this. That way, June can see his body and know that he is there, but she won't have to look at it. She really does not need to see this." The men agreed and I removed the sheet. We wrapped his small body up in the sheet and wrapped a pillowcase around his head to stop the bleeding. I studied his tiny mummified body as tears strolled down my cheeks. By the time we were done, Logan returned from the bathroom. He brought with him a cleaning product and a towel. Without saying a word to anyone, he came into the bedroom and began cleaning the blood from the floor. Thankfully, it was mostly hardwood with a small carpeted area, which most of the blood had missed.

Just as we finished up cleaning, June began her ascent up the stairs. "How's my baby?" she asked with tears in her eyes.

I walked up to her, with tears streaming down my face, "I'm so sorry, June." With those words, she pushed past and went to the bed where her child was put to rest.

"NOOOO!" She sobbed repeatedly. Each sob tore away at my heart.

"Come on, guys," Carter said to the group of us. "We should give June some privacy to grieve." In agreement, we all turned toward the door.

"I'll keep an eye on her in case she needs anything," Will said, as we passed by him on our way out.

"Okay buddy. Let me know if you guys need anything at all," Carter said, patting Will on the back as he passed him.

We all migrated downstairs and took a seat in the living room. We filled Evan and Elana in on what had happened with Blake.

"God, that's awful," Elana said. "I knew what you guys were going to have to do, but just hearing that it actually happened, it's—I don't know, not real," Elana said, at a loss for words.

"What's our next move?" Carter asked Logan.

"We need to leave here. We shouldn't be here anymore," Logan stated.

"We need to bury Blake before we do anything. I agree that we need to leave, it's not healthy for June to be staying in that room anymore," I added.

"The sun is still high in the sky, so I say we dig the hole now," Quinn replied.

"We bury Blake tonight and we leave here first thing tomorrow. Girls, why don't you pack up the cars? Get whatever you can and shove it in there. We'll dig the hole. Carter, can you tell Will what our plan is so he can explain it to June?" Logan gave each of us a job to do.

The men went into the garage, grabbed shovels, and went to work. Elana and I sat on the couch, frozen with sadness.

"I can't believe that happened. Blake was such a sweet boy," Elana said.

"How did this happen? Was he bit and we just didn't know it? Or is it just anyone who dies turns undead?" I asked Elana. I thought back to each person that I knew who turned undead and each one was definitely bit or scratched.

"If he was bit, June didn't say anything about it," Elana rationalized.

"What if she did know about it though and kept it a secret?" I suggested. "She had to have known that he would eventually turn, so why didn't she say anything?"

"Fear," Elana simply said. I nodded back in response.

"Come on, let's get packing." I stood from the couch and headed into the kitchen.

chapter twenty-five

Over the next few hours, as the sun slowly began its descent, we were busy at work. By sunset, the cars were almost completely packed, the burial plot was dug, and dinner had been made.

"The hole is ready. We should bury him tonight," Logan said, walking in from the garage covered in dirt.

"Okay, we kind of made a big dinner—like a reception. I figured we could have his funeral and then all eat dinner together in remembrance of him. Plus, we really should eat well tonight. We don't know when we'll get a house like this again," I replied.

"I'll go tell June that we're going to hold a little ceremony for Blake tonight and hope that she agrees," Elana said, standing up from the kitchen table. She strode over to the steps and made her way to June.

Logan and I waited in silence for Elana to return with June. Elana was back downstairs in less than three minutes, alone.

"Is she not going to come?" I asked her.

"She's coming. Will is going to walk her down. The boys should bring his body," Elana said, turning toward the garage where the boys were hanging out. I grabbed my coat and followed her outside to wait by the burial plot. A few minutes went by before June, hardly capable of standing on her own, was escorted outside and into the chair that had been put out for her. There were tears streaming down her face as she sat in silence. Immediately following June were the men holding Blake's lifeless body. They gently placed him into the burial plot. No one had the courage to properly speak up, like how a traditional funeral would go. Everyone stood around, staring at his little body in the hole, in complete disbelief. No one foresaw that was how things were going to turn out.

"May he rest in peace," Quinn said, finally breaking the silence. June stood, bent down, and placed a toy car into the burial plot on top of his body.

"I love you, sweet boy," She said as she placed the toy. She fell back on the ground, defeated with grief. Will was by her side in an instant. "I'd like to go to my room," June mumbled.

"Okay. Come on, honey, I'll take you there." Will escorted June back inside. The brief ceremony was now over, and the sun had almost completely set.

"Come on guys, we need to fill this before it's pitch-black out," Logan said, retrieving a shovel.

"I'm going to go make sure the food is ready. Elana, want to help?" I asked. Elana nodded and followed me into the house. While the guys finished burying Blake's corpse, Elana and I put the finishing touches on dinner. I made up a separate plate for Will and June and asked Elana to deliver it to them. When she came back, we sat down to eat and decided to not wait for the guys. It felt good to eat a real meal—even if it was random foods thrown together. I had a feeling it would be our last real meal for a while.

The boys were done filling the grave quicker than expected and were able to get a hot meal. Everyone ate in silence, no one in the mood for a lively discussion. Once dinner was concluded, we said goodnight to one another. Everyone went their separate ways to get some much-needed rest before we set out on the road again.

"Make sure everything is packed and ready for tomorrow morning. I'll send a wakeup call for everyone at the crack of dawn," Logan warned. Everyone dispersed to their sleeping quarters. Carter insisted that I stay in the room he stayed in and he would sleep in the living room with his brothers.

As I made my way up the stairs, I passed the master bedroom where Blake died, and June grieved. I gently tapped on the door. Will emerged. "Yeah?" he asked me.

"I just wanted to check in and see how she's doing."

"She's devastated of course. Her crying is disrupting Rose from getting any sleep. I'll probably take Rose downstairs. Can you just keep an ear out for June in case she needs anything?" Will explained.

"Yeah, no problem. Go spend time with your daughter. I'll check in on her in a bit," I replied.

"Thanks, Mya." Will closed the door to tuck June in. I went down the hall to the spare room and lied down in bed. I picked up the watch on the side table—it read 9:20. I decided to get up at 3 am to check on her. I couldn't imagine the pain she was going through. I hadn't even held my baby yet and I couldn't imagine going through that. I placed my hand on my little belly and rubbed it, thinking of the little one inside—and of Scott. *It feels like forever since I last saw him.* I closed my eyes, hoping to dream of him and our baby, and live in pure bliss for a few hours...

Several hours later, I exited a beautiful dream filled with a little girl with curls and bubbles—I so hoped that was my future. I turned over in bed and grabbed the watch off the side table. It read 4:40 am. I needed to get up and check in on June. I crept down the hallway, careful to be quiet so I wouldn't wake anyone. I gently tapped on the door. Not hearing a response, I slowly opened the door and peeked my head inside. The bedside lantern was giving off a soft glow across the room.

What I opened the door to was completely and utterly unexpected.

In the middle of the room, dangling from the ceiling fan was June, with a bathrobe belt looped around her neck, and a chair tipped over at her feet. She had taken her life. I stood in the doorway in complete shock. How did she do this and why? Blake wouldn't have wanted this for her.

"Logan!!" I cried out. Logan and Elana both came running into June's room.

"Oh God!" She shrieked. "Logan, get her down!"

Logan rushed over to where June's body was limply hanging from the fan. He grabbed the chair, stood on it next to her body, and began to work her neck free from the homemade noose. Our commotion attracted more attention from the house and the others began to file into the room.

Carter was the first to make an appearance and immediately jumped to aid Logan in the removal of June's hanging body, "Oh My God! Is she breathing? Are there any signs of life? Quickly get her down so I can try to revive her." Carter was in doctor mode instantly.

Evan, Doug, and Quinn entered the room speechless, silenced by the shock of what she had done. It was obvious that she was upset about losing Blake, who wouldn't be? But for her to do this, why? Coming up behind the boys, was Will.

"What's the commotion guys, is June okay?" Will asked. The boys were on the defense and blocked Will's view of the unsettling scene.

"You shouldn't go in there," Doug warned Will.

"Why? Where is June?" Will demanded answers.

"I'm sorry man, the pain was just too much for her," Quinn replied. Will understood and the tears began to flow. He didn't flip out or melt into a puddle of tears, he just quietly grieved for the woman who had been his companion these last few weeks.

"I left Rose downstairs. I should go be with her." He turned and went to be with his daughter to grieve in peace.

Logan finally got the belt undone with Carter's help and slowly brought June down. They carried her over to the bed, where Carter instantly got to work on CPR. He worked to try and revive her. We anxiously stood around watching, hoping that she could be saved, but already knew she was gone. After several minutes of trying to revive her, the doctor sat back in defeat. Logan pulled a knife from the waist band of his jeans and was ready to take care of her when she turned.

"She wasn't bit," Doug said to Logan.

"I know that. But Blake turned, we don't know if he was bit or not," Logan responded.

"I think he was bit—or scratched. The cut that he had on the inside of his arm was so infected and very warm, it had to have been the cure of doom," I added in.

"If she doesn't turn, then we know that Blake was bit or scratched by an undead and that's why he died," Carter stated. We watched her corpse, waiting for it to jump up at us, but nothing happened. She laid there, unmoving, and definitely dead.

"Blake must have been bitten or scratched and we just missed it," Elana said solemnly.

"There was nothing we could have done anyway if we had known about the wound. He was going to die regardless—it's inevitable when they get you," Carter explained.

"Whether it's sinking their teeth into us or clawing at us, the second they touch you and break skin, you know your life is over and soon you'll be undead. It might take your life right then in that moment, or it'll wait until you think you might just live and then consume you," Quinn said.

chapter twenty six

It had been about an hour since I discovered June's body hanging from the ceiling. Logan, Carter, Doug, and Quinn had come back inside after digging up Blake's grave and burying June's body with his. Everyone sat around the kitchen table drinking coffee and relaxing before we left.

"Today is the day we cross the state border into Ohio!" Logan said cheerfully. He was pumped and ready to go. "Let's finish packing and hit the road." He left us and went into the garage to finish loading up the SUV. The rest of us gathered our belongings and packed them into their proper place.

"Who's riding where?" Evan asked.

"Logan, Elana and I will take my SUV. Evan, Carter, Doug, and Quinn, take the car. Will and Rose can come in the SUV with us. And that's everyone. Our group keeps getting smaller," I said.

Will spoke up. "It's about to get a little smaller. Listen guys, I'm sorry but I think that Rose and I are going to stay here. Her teething is bad and there's a lot of crying and I can't risk taking her out there. We're just going to stay here. There are plenty of supplies. I appreciate everything you guys have done for us. When you're done getting your sister, feel free to come back."

"Are you sure, Will?" Doug asked him.

"Yeah, it's the best decision for us right now," Will stated.

"Okay, I guess this is goodbye," Elana said to Will and hugged him. Everyone else said their goodbyes to Will and Rose.

Logan walked back in from the garage, "Everyone ready?" he was excited. "Hey, what's going on?"

"I have decided to stay here with Rose. It's for the best, but please come back and visit once you get your sister. This is goodbye, man, best of luck to you." Will extended out his hand to shake Logan's.

"Good luck to you too, buddy," Logan said, clasping his hand. "Okay, let's hit the road." We followed Logan out to the garage and piled into the two cars. Looking back at the house as we drove down the driveway, I saw Will standing on the porch, holding Rose, waving at us. I waved back and focused my attention on the new journey we were about to embark upon.

While we were packing up, I found maps of Pennsylvania and Ohio. I needed to find a map of Indiana. I opened the glove box and retrieved the Pennsylvania map and began to direct Logan on which way to go. "If you make a left and go straight for a few blocks and then make a right, it should dump you out onto the main street, which looks like it should take us to the highway. Reading maps was not my strong suit. "I miss the maps app on my cell," I told everyone. We had it easy before. I vowed I'd never complain about stupid things again when this was over—if this ever ended.

The new world was complex, every move you made mattered. Make the wrong move and it was the difference between life and death. Any simple mistake could kill you. It almost happened to me several times as well as most of our group. I witnessed a lot of death since the cure of doom began—I didn't see that changing. Whether I witnessed someone getting eaten by an undead or I had to kill an undead, death constantly surrounded us.

Logan followed the directions I gave him. We drove on Main Street searching for the highway. The town that we drove through seemed like a nice quaint area. It had a small-town feel with local businesses on every corner. House after house, row after row, they all looked similar with some type of flag flapping in the wind. Aside from the cute businesses and identical houses, the town was a wreck. There were collisions of cars in people's lawns, random blood splatter and pools of blood in the street and on the sidewalks. There were even random body parts spread about, mainly bones with the flesh mostly chewed off. The undead demolished the town.

"Are you guys keeping your eyes open for any movement? I don't want to come across those guys that took Carter and me," Logan said to us.

"I've been looking. I haven't seen anything. We aren't near the area where they held you hostage—this is new territory," I replied.

"I don't know what they look like. I saw an undead person crawling down an alley back there. Aside from that, I haven't seen anything," Elana added. I continued looking down alleyways and crossroads, making sure not to miss anything. As we approached another crossroad, Logan began to slow down. There was a flipped over truck in the middle of the intersection, there was no way around it. Logan put the SUV in park and got out to talk to Doug, who was driving the other car. Elana and I stayed in the car, patiently waiting for them to figure out what they want to do.

"Did you see that?" Elana asked me, her eyes scanning the area.

"See what?" I asked back.

"I don't know. It looked like a child peaked its head out from around the corner of that tall, tan building over there," Elana said pointing to the building. I turned my head in the direction she pointed and began scanning the area for any sign of movement.

I continued to stare in that direction, but nothing happened. Everything around us was still. I looked in the rearview mirror at Logan, who was still discussing with the guys in the other car. They were pointing in different directions, looking for a way around—out of harm's way. I focused my attention back ahead of us, to where Elana had pointed.

It happened in a quick second. Had I not been looking in that direction, I wouldn't have noticed it. I saw a small tip of a shoe pop out from where Elana had said she saw a child. It was out and back in, in a quick flash, but I saw it.

"Did you just see that?" I asked Elana this time.

"Yeah I did. We should tell the others," Elana suggested, exiting the car. We got out of the car and joined the men in their discussion.

Before we had fully reached them, Elana began to talk, "We saw something."

"What? What did you see?" Logan asked her.

"I'm not sure, I think it might have been a child," She replied.

"Where?" He asked. Elana pointed in the direction of where she saw the head and I saw the tip of a shoe. "Stay here." Logan crept away from us and went to where the child was seen. I anxiously watched him. He snuck up to the building and peeped his head around the corner. He looked back at us, giving us a hand signal, holding up one finger. Logan then walked out of sight.

"What's that supposed to mean? Does he mean wait one minute or there is only one person?" Quinn asked the rest of us.

"We're just going to have to wait and see," I replied. We continued to wait for Logan. I heard a rustling to my right and looked down the nearest alley. I was surprised to see him running up the alley. "Look guys," I said, turning their attention to where he was sprinting towards us.

"How did he get over there? Why is he running towards us?" Elana asked.

"Or what is he running away from?" Evan added.

Logan continued his sprint towards us and began to wave his arms. "Get in the car!" He shouted. That pretty much answered the question. He was running away from something, but is it dead or undead?

"Everyone back in their cars," Carter said, repeating Logan. "You should probably turn the cars around. We're not getting through this intersection with the accident." Everyone dispersed. Elana and I ran to the SUV. I hopped into the driver's seat, whipped the car around, and began heading in the opposite direction. I parked the car at the end of the alleyway where Logan was running and peered down. He was almost to us, but right at his feet were the undead, chasing after him. I looked in the rearview mirror, making sure that we weren't about to be surrounded. I expected to see the undead, instead I saw a child. Accompanying the child were several men—the same men who had abducted Carter and Logan. They were riding bikes and skateboards, coming toward us fast.

I beeped to alert the others, who were now in front of me. They needed to move first before I could go anywhere. I rolled down the window and began shouting out to them. "DRIVE! We are about to be surrounded. Just go, we will catch up!" Carter made a hand gesture of thumbs up and drove away.

I now directed my attention at Logan, "Come on, Logan! They are coming!" Logan was close now, just about 20 feet away. He was sprinting awkwardly, favoring one leg to the other.

"What's wrong with him?" I asked Elana.

"He must have hurt his leg. Oh god. I hope he's not bit," Elana said, already worrying. There was nothing I could say to comfort her because I felt and thought the same thing.

The undead were basically at his heels, an undead man was just centimeters away from grabbing him. That man was incredibly fast, he outran the others by several feet. He was as fast as my brother and was closing in on him. Logan approached the car and reached for the door. The undead man grabbed hold of the hood of his sweatshirt and yanked him back.

"Nooooo!" Elana screamed. Logan popped right back up and began to search his waist band for a weapon.

Two shots rang out. The undead man's head exploded, and his body dropped. Logan, Elana, and I all were confused on where the gun shots had come from. We began to look around. My eyes immediately went to the rearview mirror, where I saw the group of men from earlier in the week. They were getting closer. They saved Logan. Maybe they were looking for a truce.

"It's the men from the other night," I shouted at him. "They must want a…" Before I could finish my sentence, another shot ran out. The bullet hit my brother in the left shoulder, and he dropped down.

"LOGAN!" Elana and I screamed together. I peeked my head out the window and noticed him struggling to get to the SUV. The undead behind him were gaining more ground and the angry group of men were continuing to get closer.

Another shot rang out and the back window to the SUV exploded into tiny shards. "Keep your head down!" Logan yelled at us from the street—he was almost there. I reached for the back-door handle to open the door for him. I moved my head up slightly to look out the side mirror and made direct eye contact with the shooter. He smiled at me and then shot the mirror off the car. Logan flung himself up from the ground and into the SUV. Directly following him into the vehicle was an undead woman, thrashing her arms about. Still keeping down, I put my foot on the gas and took off. As I put my window up, an undead teenager smashed their face against it, leaving a deep, crimson blood smudge across the window. Thankfully, it didn't break the glass.

Logan, in the backseat, was kicking the undead woman with the heel of his boot directly in her face, attempting to kick her out of the car. As I picked up speed, the open door was swinging back and forth, crushing the undead woman with each hit.

Bullets rained down on us, impaling the SUV. I continued to drive, putting more distance between us with each passing second. I prayed they didn't shoot a tire—that would put an end to us. We would be as good as dead, whether it was from the undead or the group of men.

Now, with a decent amount of distance between us, Elana and I sat up in our seats. Logan was still battling the undead woman in the back seat. "Elana, help him!" I whined at her. "There is an umbrella under your seat, use that!" I told her.

She reached under the seat and pulled the umbrella out. She extended the handle but did not open it. With the extended handle, she turned in her seat and hauled the umbrella over her head and directly into the undead's head. The umbrella was not sharp enough to puncture skin. It just disoriented the undead, making it easier for my brother to kick her out. The two worked together—Elana with the umbrella and Logan with his boots. Together they evicted the undead from the car.

With the growls and screaming from the three of them now gone, I realized that I wasn't hearing any more gunshots. I looked in the rearview mirror and was pleased to see that no one was behind us. We were safe.

Elana crawled over the passenger seat and into the back with Logan. She reached over him, pulled the door closed, and immediately began to tend to her boyfriend. The left shoulder of his sweatshirt was soaked in blood and his jeans were torn in several places. Elana yanked a pillow from the trunk and began to apply pressure to the wound on the shoulder. "Are you bit or scratched" She began to ask him.

"I don't, I don't know…" Logan said, shutting his eyes.

"What did he say?" I asked her, tears streaming down my face.

"I don't know, he's not awake. Oh my God, is he dead?" She began to freak out.

"Feel his neck, he might have just passed out," I instructed her. I continued to watch her in the mirror, keeping one eye on the road and one eye on them.

"I think I feel something" She said with hope. "Where are the others? We need Carter."

"I told them to go on without us, I have no idea how far they went or what direction they went in." I put distance between us and the hell hole that we had left. I was frantically searching the side streets for any signs of the others.

"Up there!" Elana said, pointing a bloody hand out from the back seat in the direction of where the others were. I sped up to get to them faster. As soon as I had approached the others, I threw the car into park and hopped out.

"Carter!" I said, as I ran up to the car. "Carter, Logan needs you! He was shot!" I said to him frantically.

"Where?" Carter asked immediately responding.

"He's in the back seat. Elana has pressure on it. The bullet hit him in the shoulder," I explained. I directed my attention to everyone else, "We need to keep moving. There is a mob of the undead coming our way. Those crazy guys that shot Logan are following us too. We need to keep going. Carter you're going to have to work on him in the back seat of the SUV."

Carter made his way toward the SUV to help Logan. I turned my attention to the rest of the men. "We need to keep going, and we need to get to the highway. Suggestions?" I asked the others.

"Do we have a map? That would be a good start," Quinn asked.

"Oh yeah, I do!" I said to them.

"Good, I'm actually really good at reading maps, must be because I'm so much older than all of you," Quinn added.

"Fantastic! I'll be right back!" I ran to the SUV and pulled the maps out of the glove box. "We're leaving in a few seconds guys," I said to Logan, Carter, and Elana. I ran back to the others with the maps and thrust them at Quinn. "Here you go, read them as we drive and figure out the best way, we trust you!" I turned, ran back to my SUV, and climbed into the driver's seat. I put the car in drive and waited impatiently for the others to make their move. I glanced in the rearview mirror and began to see movement. It was too far away to tell if it was the undead or the alive and I didn't want to find out. I pressed the palm of my hand into the center of the steering wheel over and over until they finally moved. I thought I had made it clear that it was crucial we moved right away? *Men*—great—I was stuck following a whole car full of them.

chapter twenty-seven

I split my attention between the road and what was going on in the backseat. I glanced back and forth between the make-shift surgery room in my backseat and the car in front of me. "Carter, can I have an update?"

"The bullet missed all his major arteries and organs, which is good. However, the bullet didn't go through and through. It is lodged somewhere inside of him," Carter began to explain.

"Get it out!" I snapped at him.

"I can't do this here. I need to surgically open him up and explore what damage might have occurred and if the bullet is intact or if it fragmented. I need supplies, monitors, and an operating room. He's unconscious I need him alert. And we don't have any medical equipment to monitor him while he's out."

"What are you saying, Carter?" Elana asked while she continued to cry for Logan. She was brushing his hair back from his face. She cared so much for him.

"I'm saying that we need a hospital. I need supplies."

"You fixed Evan without a hospital!" I argued. "Why can't you just do the same for Logan? We can't stop, it's too dangerous. Hospitals aren't safe, they are ground zero. It's going to be crawling with the undead. You've told us this over and over."

"Evan was a different case; the bullet wasn't stuck in his leg. His wound was straight through and I knew nothing was hit. With Logan the bullet is stuck somewhere inside. I don't know if it's whole or in pieces. He needs surgery. If I don't get the bullet out, he could die," Carter said bluntly.

"I don't know where we are, I don't know where the closest hospital is. How long can surgery wait?" I asked.

"He needs surgery as soon as possible. I will try to slow the bleeding. If the bleeding doesn't subside, he could bleed out or lose his arm," Carter explained.

"Oh, hell no. He did not survive the war to lose his arm in this new crap world," I stated. I flashed my lights at the other car to get their attention.

Five minutes later, they finally realized, right before we were about to turn onto the highway. The guys slowed their car and I pulled up next to them and hopped out. I went around to the back of the SUV, pulled out bottled water and handed some to everyone. I also retrieved a clean towel for Carter to use to apply pressure.

"What's the update?" Quinn asked.

"Logan needs surgery, or he might not make it. We need to find a hospital," Carter explained.

"A hospital!?" Doug exclaimed. "That's a suicide mission. You know that dude. We can't go there, the undead overrun all the hospitals. Don't you remember how it was back at home?"

"It's the only option," I said, backing the doctor up. "You guys don't have to come if you don't want to risk your lives, I understand. This is what my brother needs and I'm going to make it happen as long as Carter is willing. It will be easier if you are with us. The more manpower, the better."

"Carter, are you really going to do this? You could die," Evan asked him.

"I'm a doctor. It's what I do, I save lives. They saved us. Now it's time to return the favor. If you don't want to come, then don't. Pick a place and we'll meet you there. This is what I was meant to do," Carter stated, taking my hand in his. That gesture made me feel supported by him.

Doug and Evan exchanged glances and nodded, using some secret, telepathic communication. "Let's kill some dead shit," Doug said with enthusiasm.

"You think we can find me a wheelchair there?" Evan asked with a smirk.

"Definitely," Elana stated.

"Quinn?" I asked him.

"Of course, I'm in. You'll never find your way there without me. What's the plan? What am I looking for?" Quinn asked.

"How far until Ohio?" Elana asked.

"Ohio?" I said to her.

"Yeah, Ohio. Logan said, 'today is the day we cross the border into Ohio'. He would be pissed if we didn't make it there because of him. It's what he would want," She stated.

I briefly thought of it and agreed, nodding.

"Ohio," Quinn said studying the maps. "It should take us a little over an hour, maybe less if we speed, maybe more, depending what is waiting for us on that highway. Then there is the concern of actually finding a hospital," Quinn said as he continued to study the map.

"The first hospital. I don't care how big or small. He doesn't have much time. I'm concerned that he's still not awake," Carter stated.

"Okay, give me a second to study the map here," Quinn said. While Quinn was mapping out our next move, I decided to dig out the pretzels from the trunk and pass them out to everyone. I sat on the bumper of the SUV, deep in thought, praying for Logan to pull through.

"He's going to be okay." I jumped, startled by the interruption. It was Carter, coming to console me.

"I know. I trust you." I sighed. "I'm just really scared. I need him, Elana needs him, my sister needs him and so does my baby. My baby doesn't have its father and now it might not have an uncle. No father figure," I said. I cried and patted my little belly.

"I'm here," Carter said awkwardly. "So are the other guys. We are all here." He took my hands in his. "We are all family now. There is no reason that, once this whole mess calms down, that we don't continue to stay family. I got your back and so does everyone else."

I was overwhelmed with emotion by his thoughtful and caring words that I couldn't suppress what I did next. I hastily put my arms around him and planted a big kiss on his cheek. Only it wasn't his cheek. Because he moved, not expecting my gesture, it turned into a full-blown kiss on the lips. I almost pulled away, but I couldn't. It felt too good. The kiss went on for a minute before I realized what I had done. *Was I ready for this? Should I be doing this?* I abruptly pulled away from our incredibly intimate moment. "I, uh..." I was speechless. I turned away, blushing.

"Guys, I think I found it," Quinn hollered over to us. I jumped up from the bumper, startled again and worried that they saw. I smacked my head on the raised back door of the SUV and collapsed. Of course, Carter was there to catch me before I hit the ground.

"Are you okay?" He asked as he put me back down and examined my head.

"Yeah, I think so," I responded, embarrassed beyond belief.

"You're bleeding," He said, concerned. "Are you dizzy at all?"

"I'm fine, let's go, Logan is more important."

"Dammit, Mya, you are important. Let me examine you," He said with a stern tone. I froze, sat back down, and let him examine me. I waved the others over to us, so we could multitask.

"What's the plan?" I asked.

"Oh my god, what happened?" Elana asked, instantly concerned when she realized that Carter was now treating my head wound.

"Nothing, I'm an idiot. What's the plan?" I asked Quinn again.

"There is a crisis center in Barnesville. I think there is a smaller hospital or urgent care that is closer to the border. The crisis center is right off 70, which is what we are about to get on. See here," He said, pointing to a spot on the map. "I think we are close to here, Taylorstown. Judging from the legend on the map, it should take

190

about an hour to the crisis center. Maybe a half hour to the other hospital," Quinn stated. "If you look further down the road, we can get back on route 70 and it will take us all the way to Indiana."

"There is no guarantee the other hospital will have what we need. The bigger hospital might have a generator, which will be beneficial," Carter stated.

"The crisis center will likely have more of the undead," I stated.

"They are both going to have a lot of the undead, I don't think we can avoid that," Quinn said.

"I vote the crisis center," Elana stated her opinion. "We know, for sure, that they should have what we need. What if someone already raided the hospital though?"

"Even if they raided the place, the things I need should still be there, like a heart monitor and a ventilator," Carter pointed out.

"I vote for the crisis center. It's in Ohio, which will make Logan happy. We're going to lose another day or two of travel because of this, so it's best to get as far as we can. Logan is going to hate himself and be pissed at us for fussing over him like this." I had to agree with Elana.

"Let's get a move on people! To the crisis center!" Quinn made a beeline for the car.

"I want to put a Band-Aid on this," Carter said to me.

"Is that really necessary?" I whined at him.

"Yes, quit complaining. I don't need to be distracted worrying about your head while I'm operating."

"Fine." I couldn't argue that. I reached into the medical bag and pulled out a band aide, handed it to Carter, which he so delicately put onto my wound. "Satisfied?"

"Yup." He stood up and offered a hand to help me up. He brushed the hair back from my face. Looking deep my eyes, he asked, "Dizzy?"

"Nope, I'm good," I replied.

"Good." He swiftly kissed my forehead and made his way to the backseat to monitor Logan again. He kissed me again and I let him.

What was I thinking? I got into the driver's seat and followed Quinn to the hospital, allowing my thoughts to drift off.

We pulled onto the highway and, to our luck, it was empty. Not a car in sight, no signs of the apocalypse that had damaged the rest of the world. The highway appeared to be untouched. I prayed to myself that for once, something would go right, and the rest of the ride would be smooth sailing.

chapter twenty-eight

God finally answered at least one of my prayers. We drove the entire length of the highway without any complications—a first for us. No cars blocked the road, no alive people shot at us, and no undead tried to break in and eat us. It had been smooth sailing as I hoped. About an hour had passed since we had been driving on the highway. The hospital had to be close. I was nervous, Logan couldn't wait any longer. I could see the anticipation, worry, and urgency in Carter's eyes every time I looked back at him. He was doing all he could for my brother, and I knew that, but there was only so much that he could do without the proper medical equipment.

Up ahead, Quinn had pulled the car over and was waiting for us to talk. I pulled up next to him and put the window down. "What's wrong?" I asked him.

"Nothing is wrong. We're almost there. We need to keep a look out for any signs pointing toward the hospital. We need to find a safe entrance. I don't want to put us right in the middle of an ambush," Quinn explained.

"How far up do you think it is?" I asked.

"Ten minutes," He answered.

"Dude," Evan said to him, nudging him, as if he were leaving something out.

"Quinn?" I questioned him.

"We do have one slight problem," Quinn started. "We are almost out of gas. We can barely make it there. If the place gets overrun, I don't think we're going to be able to take this car out."

"We will deal with that when the time comes. For now, let's focus on getting there and keeping Logan alive. Once that is done, we can figure out the car situation" Carter said, leaning over my seat. "It looks like we're going to need gas pretty soon too."

"Let's go. Flash your lights if you see it," Quinn said, putting his car back in drive. I put the SUV in drive and followed him down the last stretch of highway, until we were finally at the hospital. The closer we got, the more destruction we saw. The opposite side of the highway, going away from the hospital, was littered with cars, rotting bodies, and blood.

As we continued to drive in the direction of the hospital, signs began to appear, alerting us that we were close. Finally, we saw a huge sign that pointed toward the correct exit. I followed Quinn off the highway, scanning to see if there was any destruction or undead around. Surprisingly, there were no extreme signs of destruction, a few abandoned cars here and there and some expected blood spatter, but no dead bodies and no undead wandering around.

Quinn stopped at the end of the ramp and I pulled up next to him. In the distance, we could see the hospital, it was hard to miss. The building stood taller than anything else around.

"What do you think?" I asked Quinn.

"It's eerily quiet. I expected a lot of chaos, and this is almost nothing," Quinn replied.

"Maybe we just missed all of the chaos? Maybe it took the whole town weeks ago, and now there is nothing left so the undead moved on?" I suggested. My sense of time was gone, I had no idea what day of the month it was or how long ago the apocalypse began.

"We should proceed with caution. Stake it out and be on alert," Doug said.

"Of course, we're going to proceed with caution. We're not going to stake the place out. We are running out of time. Logan needs to be in there now," Elana exclaimed.

"We don't know what is in there! Do you want to risk all of our lives?" Quinn argued.

"Yes, I want to risk mine to save the man I love!" She said, with emotion.

"I agree to risk my life to save my brother's and you all should too. He risked his life several times to save all of you! Without him, you wouldn't have made it off the highway the first time—or the second time. Evan, without him, you wouldn't have gotten the antibiotics for your leg. He always puts himself at risk for everyone else. And he always takes care of difficult situations like with Blake." I made my argument for my brother's life.

"She's right, guys. If we don't make a decision and get him there soon, he isn't going to make it. His death will be on us, not this plague. It will be our fault for not doing something when we damn well could have." Carter backed me up.

"Oh please, you're just siding with her because you have the hots for her, dude," Evan argued against his brother.

"That was unnecessary. I'm siding with her because she's right. Without Logan, none of us would be here. Now, the four of us are going to keep moving forward and get into that hospital or die trying. If you want to be a bunch of pansies and hide out, then be my guest," Carter stated.

"Dude, I'm not a pansy. You're my bro, man, I'm going to have your back. This is just ass backwards and dumb. You really want to die man?" Doug asked.

"No, of course I don't want to die. I don't want anyone to die, including Logan, whose life is hanging on by a thread. We are stronger together." Carter stood his ground, knowing that he was persuading his brothers. They began to whisper back and forth to each other.

"I guess we're in, but what about Evan's bum leg?" Doug asked.

"We'll keep him safe and get him a wheelchair or some crutches or something," Carter answered.

"Quinn?" I asked.

"I'm done arguing with a bunch of people who are just lining up to be a hot lunch," Quinn boldly stated. "You're all stupid and I'll be laughing when you're getting eaten to death."

"Fine, Quinn, if you want to be that way, you can wait here—alone—and see what happens," Elana spat out.

"Alone? That's still suicide!" Quinn exclaimed crossing his arms with a stubborn look on his face. "Fine! If I have to go, I want a compromise."

"What do you want?" I asked.

"I want to take only one car. Yours. I'm not risking getting stuck behind," Quinn selfishly stated.

"Fine, get in," I said, not arguing about it anymore. We were wasting time—precious time that could be spent saving Logan's life. The three men got out of the car and hopped into ours. The twins sat in the passenger seat, smushed together and Quinn crammed into the back, in an incredibly awkward position. "Ready?"

"Just go," Quinn said angrily.

chapter twenty-nine

I drove at a slow pace off the ramp and through the small town, while Quinn directed me toward the hospital. The closer we got to the hospital the greater the destruction became. Buildings were burned down to the ground, dead body parts littered the streets, lawns, and sidewalks. The smell of death was overbearing.

"Oh God. What is that smell?" Elana asked everyone in the car.

"Death," I said plain and simple. I slowed the car. The road was blocked by several cars in a pile up accident. An ambulance was flipped over on its side with the back doors open and covered in blood. There was a small space between the flipped ambulance and the median, too small of a space.

"I'm going to squeeze through, it's too far to walk," I told the others. The twins in the seat next to me nodded nervously. I slowly began to ease my way past the ambulance, both sides of my SUV rubbed, creating a squealing sound, but we got through.

The entrance to the hospital was several yards ahead of us. There was no active movement, no active fires, or loud noises. Everything was still, frozen in a picture of mass destruction. Although all was quiet, the sight suggested that, at one point, it was a warzone. There were dead bodies, abandoned army tanks, blood splatter, and body parts. Not one inch of the pavement was visible. On the lawn of the hospital was a pile of wrapped up bodies—ones who must have died early on. As we pulled up to the emergency entrance, I studied the outside of the hospital searching for clues. Most of the windows to the hospital were shattered.

"Dude, look!" Doug pointed out of his window. We peered to see what he was pointing to. It was an undead man, hanging by his neck out of a window, kicking his feet and swaying his arms. He was still alive—well, undead alive. He must have been bitten and known he was going to change, so decided to end it.

"That is a horrendous sight. If possible, we should cut him down, that's no way for someone to remain for all of eternity," Elana suggested.

"He won't remain like that for all of eternity. His body will eventually rot off, detach from his head, and smack the pavement. The head might still be trying to chomp away though, who knows? These could be like super zombies that you see in movies," Quinn stated.

"There is something wrong with you, man." Evan laughed at him.

I parked the car in front of the emergency exit and examined the emergency room from the safety of my vehicle. There was no movement, just a lot of blood and to, my surprise, lights. Lights could also be a danger, drawing them in. "Carter, what is the game plan, here?" I asked.

"There are lights, that means there is a generator. We get in there and find the closest surgical room. There will probably be a map of the hospital on the wall. Most likely there's a surgery room on this floor, but by the looks of it, it's not going to be sanitary or loaded with equipment. It's better to go to a different unit, but it's also more dangerous. There are many corners and hidden places in a hospital. The undead could be anywhere," Carter informed us.

"What about Logan, who is passed out, and Evan, who can barely walk?" I asked.

"We need a stretcher for Logan and a wheelchair or crutches for Evan. He needs something; otherwise, that puts him in direct danger," Carter responded.

"Doug and Quinn, do you want to come in with me and help look for a stretcher, wheelchair, map, and elevator?" I asked.

"What do you mean?" Carter asked.

"It would be stupid for all of us to go into an ambush. We need to have a direct route cleared for you and to find the stuff before we get them out of the car. Elana, if we aren't back in 15 minutes, you need to leave," I instructed.

"You can't go, it's too dangerous in your state," Carter began to lecture.

"There is no time for this, I'm going and that's it. I'll be back soon." I hopped out of the car before he could say anything else. Doug and Quinn followed behind me. We grabbed the little weapons we had from the trunk and took off inside.

I walked through the emergency room doors and instantly began searching the walls for a map. Immediately on the wall to the right of the entryway, there was (what I assumed to be) the map. It was showcased in glass and, of course, completely covered in blood. I took the frame off the wall and threw it onto the floor— it shattered. The glass shattering on the floor echoed down the silent hallway.

"What the hell are you doing?" Quinn yelled at me in a whisper.

"The map was covered in blood and I needed it out of its frame," I explained.

"You're making unnecessary noise," He stated, clearly unamused.

"Better to know now if there is anyone in here, compared to when we're deep inside and stuck," I explained again. He nodded in response. "Wait here, I'm going to run this to Carter so he can study it before we go." I ran out to the car to hand the map to Carter. He was already getting out of the car to investigate the shattering glass.

"Oh God, I thought that something had happened to you already." He embraced me.

"Nope, I came to give you this. Study it, I'll be back." I awkwardly pulled away from his embrace and went back into the hospital before he could fuss anymore. Quinn and Doug were standing in the lobby waiting for me. About ten feet from where they stood were closed hospital doors that read medical personnel only. "We need to go through those doors" I said pointing to them.

"What's your plan?" Doug asked.

"You guys stand on each side of me and I'll kick the door open. Be prepared for anything that might be on the other side of the door. It sounds quiet, I don't think there's anything waiting for us, at least not down here. It looks like someone came through here at some point. Look at the bodies in the waiting area, they've all been shot," Quinn explained.

"They could have been killed when the army came through here when it all started. You saw the tanks outside, right? Don't let that kind of thinking cloud your judgement, otherwise, your ass might end up on the ground underneath a hungry undead," I warned. "Come on, this is taking too long. Let's do this."

We lined up as Quinn had suggested, Doug on the left, me on the right. "Ready?" Quinn asked and we nodded back. Quinn kicked open the door and we rushed it. Just as suspected, no undead were waiting for us. The hallway, of course, was a massacre: blood, guts, and bodies everywhere. The smell was godawful. At the end of the hallway was a stretcher flipped on its side.

"Look," I said, pointing to the stretcher, trying to breathe through my mouth and not my nose. The men nodded and we made a beeline for the stretcher. I carefully stepped over each undead, careful to not step on their bodies. When we reached the stretcher, we flipped it upright to discover that it was already occupied. There was a body of a woman strapped down to the stretcher, it was difficult to tell if she was ever an undead or not. Her insides were practically gone, basically just a hollow carcass. "Undo the straps," I told Quinn, I couldn't stomach to touch her. His hands fumbled over the buckle and he struggled to free it. His face was pouring sweat; he was nervous.

"Oh, for God's sake." He was taking too long. I ignored my urge to vomit and I took the knife out of my pocket and cut through the straps. I dumped the body off the stretcher and onto the floor. Her body landed with a thud.

"Brutal, dude," Doug stated.

"We're on a time crunch. Anyone see a wheelchair?" I asked.

"No, I looked in the rooms in this hallway, no wheelchair—just a lot of dead people," Quinn replied.

"Screw the wheelchair for now then. We'll have plenty of time to look for one upstairs. Either of you see a sign for an elevator anywhere?" I asked.

"Yeah, I saw a sign. It pointed down the hallway that was to the left when we came through the doors." Doug surprisingly was paying attention to his surroundings.

"Good job, let's go get them." We made our way past the hallway of bodies and through the waiting room back to the car. The environment outside was still quiet and calm. As we approached the car, Carter and Elana climbed out of the car ready to get moving.

"Wheelchair?" Carter asked.

"Couldn't find one, I figured we could look more upstairs. It's not pleasant in there, so prepare yourselves," I informed them. Doug helped Evan out of the car while the rest of us eased Logan out of the car and onto the stretcher. I grabbed a bungee cord from the trunk of my car to strap Logan down since I had cut the previous one. "We should just carry the stretcher, there is no point in trying to wheel it. There are too many bodies in the way," I stated.

"It's too heavy for you to be carrying," Carter snapped.

"With four of us, it'll be fine. Let's go, too much time has passed. Carter, did you figure out which floor we need to go to?" I asked.

"Fourth floor is best, but any floor would work. Elevator is through the doors to the left," Carter replied, his temper seething.

"Watch your backs while in there and try to breathe through your mouth," Quinn stated. With that, we began our mission to get Logan to the fourth floor.

chapter thirty

We quickly made our way to the elevator. I cautiously stepped over the dead bodies. Carter pressed the call button and we waited for the elevator to make its arrival, praying that it would be in operation.

"Are you sure this is a good idea? Taking an elevator in a hospital with power issues and the undead lurking—what if it's filled with the undead? What if something is blocking the way or the rope that holds the elevator is broken?" Evan questioned. Evan brought up some good points that I had not thought about. Did we really come all this way to save a life to all get stuck and die in an elevator?

"Evan has a point. The elevator is unpredictable. There are so many possible ways that could go wrong and then our lives are just done. We also don't know what's waiting for us on the stairs and carrying this stretcher up four flights of stairs seems impossible to me right now." I weighed our options.

"You're right. It is too heavy for you to carry. Especially up four flights of stairs," Carter said.

"What if Doug helps to carry him and I help Evan up the stairs?"

"Fine. The stairs it is. The elevator seems to not be coming, anyway. It must be stuck on another floor," Carter stated, heading for the stairwell.

"Hold on, let me scope it out really quick before we all pile in there," Doug said to the rest of us. Doug peered through the small rectangular window on the door to the stairwell. I had no idea how he could accurately see through it considering it was covered in splinters of cracked glass. Doug looked back at us and signaled for us to be quiet. He grabbed a metal pole that was randomly discarded on the floor. The pole was covered in blood, obviously having been used as a weapon before.

Doug placed his back against the door, and pushed it open, raising the pole in defense and started swinging. We anxiously stood waiting and listening. The only sound to be heard was the clink of metal hitting metal.

"Doug?" Carter called out, pointing to me to come hold the stretcher so he can further investigate. He eased the door open and found nothing. Doug was already up the steps investigating higher floors.

"HEADS UP!" Doug yelled down the stairwell. Down came an undead, flipping over the railing and landing with a thud at the bottom of the stairs, in front of us all. Carter had to jump out of the way before a dead, undead, man landed on him.

"Get your ass back down here!" Carter hollered up the stairwell. He returned to the hallway and resumed his position carrying the stretcher. "He's such a showoff, he'll get himself killed," Carter mumbled, mostly to himself.

Moments later, Doug reemerged. "The stairwell is all clear until at least the fourth floor. I couldn't really hear anything above me. It's kind of quiet up there. I tried to peek through the windows on each level, most of them are shattered. The third floor seems like a hot spot. I could hear growls through the door and the window was covered in blood, so we'll need to be quiet passing by there."

Carter replied only with a head nod.

"What, you're seriously pissed about that?" Doug exclaimed looking at the undead on the floor.

"You are careless. If anything would have grabbed you, you wouldn't have had any backup and you'd be an undead right now. You don't think, you just do, and that's dangerous," Carter replied, surprisingly calm.

"Noted," Doug said, with a nod, "Let's go."

Doug, Quinn, and Carter carried Logan on the stretcher up the stairs. Elana was responsible for helping at awkward corners and holding a backpack full of supplies. I helped Evan up the steps. He leaned on the railing and I supported him on the other side. It was slow moving, but it was getting the task accomplished. Shortly, we were approaching the third floor and, Doug was right, we could hear the growls through the door. They didn't sound close to the door.

Despite the chilly weather outside, we were covered in a sheen of sweat from the strenuous trip up the steps and lack of air flow in the tight stairwell. In addition to the sweat, I was also overcome with exhaustion from the lack of a good night's rest and food. The combination of the sweat and the exhaustion made the trek up the stairwell much more challenging.

"I need to put it down for a second, my hands are sweating," Quinn stated to the rest of us through winded wheezing.

"No, just wait one more floor," Carter whispered. "We can't stop right here, it's too dangerous."

"Fine, just a sec." Quinn leaned his side of the stretcher against the wall, holding it up with his knee as he wiped each hand, one at a time, on his pants. When he was finished, he nodded at Carter and resumed his position. They began to maneuver the stretcher around the corner of the third-floor platform. Just as the movement was almost complete, Quinn's hand slipped as he had predicted. The stretcher hit the railing, creating a loud clank between the metals.

We all gasped in surprise. Logan was fine on the stretcher, still knocked out. He was strapped onto the stretcher and the slip was caught by the handrail, which helped. For a moment, everyone was so concerned with the stretcher and Logan, that the threat behind the third-floor door was briefly forgotten. Everyone was fussing over the dropped stretcher and fretting without being conscious of how loud they were speaking. "SHHHH!" Evan shushed everyone. His notion instantly put everyone back on alert and everyone went silent. We looked at each other, hoping we went unheard. For a few seconds, it was quiet, we thought that we got away with it. After all, Doug was just in this stairwell minutes prior making noise and nothing happened.

THUD. The third-floor door shook violently as an undead slammed their body against it. The door continued to shake as one after the other undead slammed into the door, eager to get into the stairwell. There was no telling if the door would hold or not. It was still closed but had movement as each body attempted to plow their way through. Everyone started to panic, and we were not being mindful of our volume level. One by one, the undead flung their mangled bodies against the door.

"MOVE!" Carter shouted, and everyone began to run up the steps, there was no easing or taking care of Logan while we moved, no gentleness as the corners were taken. The stretcher was being moved and thrown in every which direction in hopes to get it up the steps as fast as possible. Evan and I rushed up the steps, awkwardly clambering and falling.

"Doug, what did you see on the fourth floor?" Carter asked.

"I couldn't see, the glass was splintered," Doug explained. Behind us the undead continued to heave themselves into the door, desperate for a meal. They were resilient. Within seconds, the door gave way. The door flung open, smashing into the wall, allowing the undead to trickle into the corridor, flooding the stairwell. The undead began their climb up the steps, chasing us—driven by their appetite. We had reached the platform for the fourth floor just in time.

"We're risking it. We'll be dead if we don't," Carter said to me as he nodded in the direction of the door. I positioned Logan's baseball bat into a batter's stance, took a deep brave breath and opened the door. The room was in complete havoc, just like the rest of the hospital. Not as much blood as the previous floors and no visible undead ready to eat us.

"Clear, hurry in!" I held the door open, helping Evan into the room. The growls from the undead echoed up the stairwell. They were getting closer. Next, Elana came through the doorway before attempting to get the stretcher through. Given that stairwells and narrow doorways aren't designed to accommodate stretchers, the guys were struggling. We were running out of time, the undead were approaching the platform.

"Flip it on its side and shove it through," Carter ordered. The others followed his instructions and effectively got the stretcher with Logan still on it through the doorway in seconds.

As the door was being pulled shut, an undead jumped at it, yanking it back into the stairwell. Doug, in a moment of surprise, fell onto the floor, letting the door go and giving possession of it over to the undead. The first undead made his way into the room. With Logan's baseball bat still in hand, I ran up, smacked him down and kicked him in the stomach back into the stairwell. I followed the undead man into the stairwell, standing in the door frame and gave another full swing, knocking the next eager body back. Doug quickly regained his composure and successfully closed the door, just before another attempted to make his way through.

"Do you think the door will hold?" I asked, breathing heavily. My arms and legs were Jell-O. My adrenaline was through the roof. For a brief second, I felt like Wonder Woman. I came back to reality and realized that one of those things could rip me to shreds in a minute, if given the chance.

"There's no way to tell. They are hitting it from the wrong direction, so that will help to prevent them from coming in. Are they smart enough to work doorknobs?" Quinn asked, half-joking and half-serious.

"This might slow them down." Elana grabbed an IV pole and stuck it through the door handle to help leverage the door closed.

"The floor is big enough that we can put some distance between us and them. Let's check the area for any undead and find an operating room. We need to get this bullet out now. It's been too long. We'll figure out what to do with the undead once we have taken care of Logan," Carter instructed.

"Which wing has an operating room?" Doug asked his brother.

"The map you gave me earlier didn't depict exactly where each room was in the building. I just predicted which floor would be best," Carter explained

I began looking around for any clues. "Here," I said to Carter passing him a map. There was a fire safety map on the wall which depicted 'you are here' and 'these are your nearest exits'. It also depicted where the operating rooms were.

"Perfect," Carter replied taking the map. He studied it for a moment turning it in several different directions to get a clear understanding of where we were. "It looks like it's a couple turns down that way." Carter pointed toward a hallway where the lights were hanging from the ceiling and flickering like they would do in a scary movie. The further down the hallway, the darker the area was.

"Everyone stick together and stay alert. The lights look dismantled down there, we could be going in blind. The good news is the operating room should be connected to a generator and the lights should be high enough that nothing could have broken them," Carter instructed us in a serious tone.

"Everyone got a weapon? Who is carrying Logan?" Evan asked.

We all situated ourselves and prepared to trek down the dark hallway and into the operating room to attempt to save Logan's life. The three men again carried Logan, Elana was again on the lookout, and I again helped Evan maneuver down the hallway.

chapter thirty-one

The width of the hallways was reduced by half due to flipped over gurneys, broken doors, abandoned medical carts, and, of course, dead bodies. We walked down the narrow pathway in a single file line. In the front was Doug, armed with the metal pole that he had discovered down on the first floor. Next in line was Carter, walking backwards, carrying the stretcher with Logan on it with the help of Quinn at the other end. Behind the two of them were Evan and me. I helped him shuffle along the hallway with one side of my body, while the other side sported the baseball bat, ready to take down anything that came my way. Pulling up the rear was Elana. She had a knife in her hand and the gun in her pocket as a last resort.

We crept down the dark hallway, careful to not alert the undead to our presence.

When we reached a dead end, we had a decision to make. To the left appeared to be brighter but there were questionable noises coming from that direction. To the right, it was pitch black with no working lights, but silent.

"I don't like either option, what does the map say is the fastest way to the operating room?" Quinn asked.

Carter signaled Quinn to place Logan down for a minute, took the map into the lighted area and began to study it again. After a few long seconds, Carter had a plan.

"It seems like both ways lead to an operating room. The dark way is risky, we are going in completely blind. The lighted area seems safer because we can see but there is something down there making the noise. I believe that the light wing is the better of the two and possibly the faster way to the operating room," Carter stated.

"Good enough," I stated, eager to get Logan into the operating room and back to normal.

The further down the lit hallway we traveled, the louder the noise was. The noise was confusing, it wasn't growls or scratching—it didn't sound like the undead. As we got closer, we located where the noise was coming from—a room on the left.

Doug pointed his weapon toward the door. The door was firmly shut with bloody fingerprints and claw marks all around it. Doug and Elana got on either side of the door, weapons up, ready to attack when it was opened. He looked over to her and signaled with his fingers, one, two, three!

He yanked the door open and started swinging his pole, hitting nothing but air. Once the door was open, there was a breeze and a noticeable change in the temperature. Elana peered through the doorway to investigate. The noise was still persistent and even louder than before.

"It's a phone, dangling from the cord." Elana laughed. "The window is smashed through and the wind is blowing the phone against the wall." We all sighed in relief. Elana hung the phone back up, and besides the whisper of a breeze, made the area silent again.

"Don't forget where we are. We are in a hospital, where a lot of dead and undead people have been at and still may be trapped. Be careful, watch each other's backs," I exclaimed to the group.

We made our way through the maze of hallways until we finally approached a door labeled 'OR'. Peering through the glass doors, the OR was filled with the undead wandering about, walking into each other, still completely oblivious that we were even there.

"What do we do? There are so many of them," Elana asked, frantically scanning the room.

"Is there no other way?" Quinn wondered out loud.

"This is the only option. We have to go through there to get to the operating table," Carter stated firmly, evaluating the scene in front of him. He was mentally calculating what he should do and how it should be done.

"We can let them out one at a time and then take care of each one separately," Evan suggested.

"Possible, but we run the risk of the undead overpowering the door and flooding right into us," I replied, playing devil's advocate.

"I agree with Mya, but there is no other option. I only see the door in front of us, the undead, and then the operating table. They are directly in the way of what we need and it's the fastest way to get them out of our way," Carter stated.

"What can we do to protect ourselves?" Elana asked.

"What if we use the privacy curtains in the rooms and throw them over the undead as they come out so they can't bite or scratch us? When their faces are covered, we shove the knife into their skull and then on to the next one," I proposed.

"I like the curtain idea," Quinn agreed.

"I think I counted about fifteen undead. Cover and stab seems to be the only option we have here. We'll have the girls throw the cover onto the undead, while the guys hold up the doors so they can't bust through." Carter gave us an outline of how things should go down.

"What about Logan and Evan?" I asked.

"We can store Logan in a room, and maybe Evan you want to sit with him and just keep an eye on things—make sure we aren't in for any surprises?" Carter asked his brother.

"Sounds good, man," Evan stated and began limping toward the closest open room.

"Grab as many of those curtains as you can. Quinn and I will place Logan in the room with Evan and try to start some IV fluids for him. Meet back here ASAP. We need to do this fast. Logan seriously cannot wait any longer," Carter instructed everyone.

Elana, Doug, and I began searching for as many curtains as we could, ripping them down off the metal poles they hung from. We were being loud and careless, but we knew that we needed to hurry. If we did it fast enough, then the amount of noise we were making would be irrelevant. Within minutes we returned with our hands full of curtains. Carter and Quinn arrived back at the same time.

"I was able to get some fluids going so he should be okay for a couple more minutes. Ready to do this?" Carter asked. We nodded in unison, ready to take on the undead. Doug, Carter, and Quinn leaned against the door, putting all their body weight against it. Carter held his hands on the handle ready to pull open the door. Elana and I stood at the door, waiting for it to open to throw the curtain over whichever undead came first. We both held a knife in our back pocket, an easy place to grab from when ready.

"Good?" Carter asked us. We positioned ourselves and nodded. Doug rapped on the glass, gaining the attention of the undead. The one closest to us turned automatically and began making his way toward us. The undead man slammed his body against the glass. He had a head start on his friend and approached us alone. Carter opened the door and the loner staggered out. They immediately shut the door, preventing anymore undead from escaping. The undead instantly charged at us, but before he could do anything, we threw the curtain over his head. Elana drew her knife and sunk it into his skull. His body went limp and fell to the floor. My adrenaline was pumping. Our plan had worked, and we were ready to take some more undead down.

The next several undead trickled toward the door. We took them out and put them down, one by one, with no problem. After we were about five undead in, the rest of the undead realized there was food for them to eat and they all came at once. There was no more slow progression, it was a full-on charge.

"Pick up the pace a little bit. We expected them to charge like this," Carter said as he slowly opened the door just enough for one undead to push his way out. I covered him in a curtain and took him down just like the few before him. I looked back to Carter, ready for the next one and realized that they were already beginning to struggle with holding the door.

I nodded to just let the next one out. Carter let the next one slip out but couldn't get the door shut immediately. Two ended up slipping out. Elana jumped back in surprise. Doug began to move away from the door to help us.

"No! Stay at the door. Keep it closed. Elana and I got this," I pleaded. We started backing away, knives up in a defensive position, ready to take them down. Using the knife without the curtains put us at risk. We continued to back up. My mind was running a mile a minute; I was beginning to panic inside. I backed as far up as possible until my back hit the wall. I reached my hand against the wall and felt a piece of wood. My heart swelled with hope and joy as I realized it was the baseball bat. In one swift movement, I picked up the bat and swung it at the undead woman who was closest to us, connecting with her skull on the first swing. The blow knocked her sideways, but not completely down. I took a step forward, reared back, and whirled the bat forwards again, this time putting her down.

As soon as she was down, I moved forward to the other undead woman who had pushed her way through. She was moving towards Elana quickly, she was desperate. Elana had her knife in her hands swinging it loosely in the air, hoping to make the connection. I used all my might and wheeled the bat, connecting with the base of the skull, ending the undead in her tracks.

"Nice. Great job girls. You good? We need to keep moving," Carter stated.

"Try to do one at a time. That was a little too close for comfort," I replied, sore from swinging the bat. Briefly, I was worried about the strain I was putting on my body and my baby. My attention was quickly pulled back to reality and the growls from the other side of the door that were deafening.

After that one little hiccup, we were able to successfully take them all down without any more incidences. At times, it was a struggle to keep the door closed, but the guys were able to do it as Elana and I stabbed each one. Once the last undead trickled out of the room, we got him down without any issues. We looked around at what we had accomplished. The room was filled with devastation. Even though the bodies were those of the undead, at one point, they were alive, ordinary people, and now, they were nothing but a pile of rotting corpses.

"Ready, Carter?" I was eager to get Logan on that operating table so he could heal and get back to normal.

"Let's go get him. Doug why don't you go ahead and sanitize the area. Elana, can you look for some surgical equipment—anything that you can find, and sanitize them as well?" Carter gave everyone some instructions, and everyone departed to prepare for the impending surgery. Everyone made quick work of their tasks and, within minutes, Logan was on the operating table, prepped and ready for the first incision.

"I'm going to need an assistant, sorry Mya and Elana, but it shouldn't be either of you. You both should go wait out in the hallway. This is something you don't want to see, and it's a lot of pressure on me for the two of you to be in here watching," Carter explained to us.

"I get it," I replied to Carter. I looked over to Elana, she was holding Logan's hand, sending up a quick prayer. She looked up to me fully understanding that we needed to leave. She bent down and kissed Logan's lips before she made her way back to the hallway of death. I stood frozen momentarily in place looking at Logan's still body. Carter approached me and ushered me out of the operating room. He took my hands in his and looked me in the eye, "I'll take diligent care of him." I nodded back in response. Still holding my hands, he led me out of the room. Once outside the door, he brushed my hair out of my face and kissed my forehead before turning to do his job—save my brother's life.

chapter thirty-two

As Carter went to work on repairing Logan, Elana and I remained in the hallway—the disgusting, filthy hallway full of dead bodies. The smell of rotting flesh was rank and made me nauseous. There was no place to sit that wasn't covered in blood or bodies.

"It's gross out here," I stated.

"Yeah, from us," Elana said, depression in her tone.

"I know you don't like taking them down, but there was no other option. It was for Logan and he would have been proud of the way we handled things," I replied.

"Yeah, I know, you're right. How long do you think this is going to take?"

"I don't know, but I can't stay in this room anymore. It's making me sick," I said as I overdramatically gagged.

"Let's get you and that little baby out of this hall. Why don't we find a vending machine? I know it's not the best food for a baby but it's better than absolutely nothing." Elana was eager to disperse her attention elsewhere.

"Sounds good." I grabbed the bat up off the floor and we made our way out of that slaughter room. We wandered through the halls in search of a vending machine. As soon as we exited the hall, I began to feel better. The nausea lessened and my stomach began to growl in hunger. I was starving and finally realized it—my baby needed food.

This world wasn't fair. I had not been able to enjoy the wonders and miracles of my pregnancy. Instead, it was one more thing I had to consider, which made it more of an inconvenience rather than a blessing. The only thing I did right, was take prenatal vitamins. I didn't have basic medical care. I hadn't had an ultrasound, so I didn't get to see my baby on the screen, and I had no idea if I was having a boy or a girl. I didn't even know how far along I was let alone decorate a nursery and think about names. All my attention centered on keeping myself alive—so this baby had a shot at being born.

Even with all the hard times, I wanted this baby so bad. It hurt my heart to know the baby will never know its daddy. But when I thought of the people I surrounded myself with during the apocalypse, I knew there were plenty of good candidates for father figures. This baby would be the future of the world—if humans could beat the undead.

"The baby kicking?" Elana asked me, pointing to my stomach. I hadn't even realized I was rubbing my belly.

"No. I'm just thinking about the baby, hoping that it's okay and developing normally. It's not fair that the baby will never meet Scott," I said to Elana with tears in my eyes.

"Oh, honey, I know. It's not fair right now, but that doesn't change that this is the way the world is now. We will always remember Scott, but you need to keep moving forward. It's not healthy for you or the baby for your body to be all stressed out about that—especially with everything else that is going on, like dead people constantly trying to eat us," Elana said as she hip-bumped me, trying to cheer me up.

"I'm glad that the baby will be surrounded by all these great people that we ended up with. Look! A vending machine!" I saw it as we rounded the corner into a staff lounge. We were fortunate we hadn't run into any undead for a while. I was thankful, I needed a break from all the death.

"There is no power to the machine," Elana said puzzled.

"Watch out. I hope this works." I stood back and readied to swing the bat at the machine.

"Wait! You shouldn't do that. You're worrying about the baby and now you want to exhaust yourself further when I'm right here. Give me that." Elana took the bat from my hands and picked up a random hospital gown then wrapped it around the bat. She positioned herself and lurched the baseball bat forward, shattering the glass. The vending machine was full, stocked to the max.

"I guess that no one ever wanted to risk coming all the way up here for some snacks, so now, they are all ours," I said greedily. I scanned the room searching for a trash can. I emptied the contents of the trash can onto the floor and began to fill it with the food from the vending machine to bring back to the others. Elana picked up a table and two chairs that were flipped on their sides and stood them upright so we could sit. I grabbed a bag of potato chips and took a seat at the table.

"Not to be nosey, but what is the deal with Carter? I saw the little kiss he gave you," Elana questioned.

"I don't know what the deal is yet. He's nice to me and he makes me happy," I replied.

"He makes you happy. That's all you have to say? Spill."

"What else should I say? We were just talking about my dead husband a few minutes ago."

"You know as good as I do that Scott would not want you to be alone forever and he certainly wouldn't want you to be raising that baby alone, either. I've heard those conversations. Scott was a good man. I'm not saying discredit him whatsoever. Carter is also a good man and he's here and alive. Take advantage of that. Life is too short—you don't know when that time could be up. He adores you. I see the way he looks at you. I see the way you look at him too. Stop being so tough on yourself, it's okay to be imperfect," Elana unloaded a world of advice on me.

"Thanks for the pep talk," I chuckled. "I'll do some serious soul-searching whenever we actually have time to stop and think without being eaten to death."

"Deal." Elana seemed satisfied for now. "Let's go see if they're done and want some food."

When we got back, the guys had moved the bodies to the side and were sitting in the middle of the floor waiting for us.

"How'd it go?" Elana asked eagerly.

"Great, as far as I can tell. He's still knocked out but he's stable. The bullet is out, and he's all sewn up. I think that we should move him into a more comfortable room, so he doesn't wake up on the operating table," Carter stated.

"Sounds like a wonderful idea. I'll go pick out a room." Elana skipped off, excited.

"Will one of you go with her please?" I asked Doug or Quinn. Doug leapt to his feet and followed Elana.

"Thank you for that. I appreciate it more than you know," I said to Carter. "I brought some snacks for everyone. I guess that we're going to stay overnight then?"

"That's probably for the best. I'm going to keep Logan hooked up to the IV and monitor him. I'm going to examine Evan's leg. And, I'm also hoping that I can find an ultrasound machine so we can look at that baby." Carter's eyes twinkled when he talked about the baby.

"We should pick out rooms to sleep in. Preferably far away from these bodies." I wrinkled my nose at the smell of them.

"Yes ma'am!" Carter was excited. Positive results from a surgery had him on a high. His excitement had me excited. Carter swept me up in a big embrace and I let him. It felt good to let someone hold me, even if it was only for a few awkward seconds in front of Evan and Quinn.

"I'm going to pick where I want to sleep," I said to Carter. I turned to leave, and he grabbed my wrist and whispered in my ear.

"Is it okay if I stay in your room? I don't want you to be alone in this place. No funny business, I promise."

"I guess that would be okay," I responded trying to suppress my smile. I left the room and began wandering the nearby hallways looking for a good clean room, preferably one that someone hadn't recently died in. I knew each room probably contained some sort of death—it was a hospital after all, but I preferred if there wasn't any current evidence of it. I also wanted a room where there were no broken windows letting in the frigid, winter air.

The first few rooms I looked in were either occupied by dead bodies or splattered in blood and random pieces of flesh. After several failed attempts, I discovered a room that seemed to be untouched. It was one hallway off the operating room and fully lit. We were close enough to the others that if something happened, we would hear it.

The room consisted of a medical bed, a TV in the corner, cabinets full of medical supplies, and a swivel doctor chair. There was a small closet filled with a few blankets and a pillow. I removed them from the closet and began to make the bed.

Once the bed was made, I decided to just take a break, lie down, and have some alone time to think some things through—mainly Carter. I needed to figure out how I really feel about him. I thought, if I can admit to myself how I feel, then how do I feel about those feelings? Elana had made some valid points. The world was ending, there was no denying that, and Scott wouldn't want me to be alone or raise the baby alone. He would want us to have a full life. I knew in my heart that I loved him so much, and even in death I still loved him. It wasn't healthy to dwell on that, especially while creating this little life inside of me.

I touched my stomach and thought of my little bean. I was excited at the possibility of seeing the baby today on the ultrasound. The fact that Carter was making that a priority showed how much he cares about me and the baby. Even though I didn't know Carter for very long, I knew he was a good person—he had integrity and compassion. I could imagine him as a good partner and father figure, if he even wanted the job.

After pondering my life choices, I was ready to let Carter in. Life was short—one of us could die at any time. If something happened to him, I would always wonder what it would have been like had we gotten together. I was ready to open my arms and heart to him and move on. It hadn't been long since I lost Scott, but that was okay. The rules in the new world versus the old world were different. They must be different otherwise the world really would just stop. Everyone in our group had lost someone they love since the beginning of the cure of doom. Everyone we knew was dead or fighting for their lives.

Lilianna... I suddenly thought. *I wonder how she is. I hope that she is okay. Is she fighting for her life? Is she already dead? Is this whole wild goose chase across the state for nothing?* I shook my head. I couldn't think like that. For my sanity and Logan's, I needed to be positive. *She's a strong young woman and she's a fighter. She has to be okay. I need her to be okay.*

I turned over onto my side, the bed was more comfortable than I thought it would be. I closed my eyes and tried to picture what Lilianna looked like. It had been a while since I last saw her—since she went back to school in August. She was supposed to come home for thanksgiving, obviously that wasn't going to happen. Thanksgiving might have already passed. I had no idea what month it was. The days were spent worrying about my life, the baby, and everyone else in our group. I constantly thought about how to keep everyone fed and alive. There was no space for worrying whether it was Monday or Wednesday or if it was November or December. One thing I did know—it was freezing cold outside; we were headed into the winter season.

Wow, December. Could Lilianna still be waiting for us if it was already December? She was a beautiful and smart young woman. God, I missed her. I wondered what she might be doing at that exact moment. My eyes closed and suddenly I could see her.

...Lilianna hovered in a corner, shaking from the freezing cold, and trembling with fear. Holding a knife out, all alone, defending her life. Covered in dirt, blood, and grime...

chapter thirty-three

"Mya." I slowly opened my eyes. Carter was leaning over me, brushing my hair out of my eyes, and gently caressing my cheek. I smiled up at him and closed my eyes again, not quite ready to open them. "I was worried about you. I couldn't find you. I was calling out your name."

"I'm sorry, I didn't mean to. I'm just so tired," I responded, still with my eyes closed.

"Don't worry about it, baby. I was just worried that's all. You sleep okay?"

He called me baby. That was weird, but in an enjoyable way. "I'm not sure. It felt good to sleep, but I had horrible dreams that I sincerely hope are not true," I said, with sorrow.

"What'd you dream about?" Carter asked, intrigued.

"Lilianna, my baby sister. I'm worried that we aren't going to get to her in time. It has been a while since everything went down, who knows how she's doing or if she is even still at school. How are we ever going to find her?" I started to cry; the tears streaked my cheeks. I turned my face toward the pillow to hide my sadness.

"Come here, sweetheart." Carter climbed into the bed and spooned me, holding me close as I wept about the possibility of losing Lilianna. I wasn't sure how I felt about the pet names he called me even though I appreciated his tender side and all the concern he had for me. I snuggled my backside into him and allowed myself to relax next to his body. His comforting arms eased my sadness and it felt so good to be held for the first time in months.

We lied there in silence for a while, him just comforting me and me just letting him. It was a nice new dynamic to our relationship. "You okay now?" He finally spoke, breaking the silence.

"I'm okay. Thank you and I'm sorry about all the emotion."

"That's what people do when they care about each other. I don't know if you've noticed, but I really do care about you. Your emotion is real, and I appreciate that. Without emotions, this world would be nothing but death," Carter opened up to me. "I'm fine with lying here all night with you, but I do need to go check back on Logan and I was able to find an ultrasound, if you're interested in seeing the baby?"

"Yes!!" I shot up with excitement. "Let's go, Logan first, baby second. Is he awake yet?"

"No, not since I last checked on him. His vitals are good and strong, but he needs to rest. I haven't known him from the beginning, but he strikes me as the type of guy who probably hasn't slept since it all began."

"Yeah, you're completely right. He's always concerned with other people and neglects his own needs. What about Evan?" I asked.

"I already examined him while you were sleeping, he's fine. I just gave him some more drugs, he's sleeping it off in some room," Carter explained. "Come on, let's go see Logan and that baby." His eyes twinkled as he spoke of the baby.

We made our way down the hallway toward Logan's room. Carter held my hand during our walk. When we arrived, he was still sleeping and Elana was asleep in a chair next to him, bent over his body holding his hand.

"Still asleep, just as I had suspected. I'm going to check his vitals and then we can look at the baby. It's best we just let them sleep, everyone is exhausted. Last time I checked in with the other three, they were getting ready to turn in for the night." He checked Logan's vitals and seemed satisfied. "Let's go down here, I set up the ultrasound already, expecting you to say yes." He took my hand again and led me down the hallway to where the technology had been set up for me.

"Lie down here and then I'm going put some gel on your belly. Then we should be able to see the baby. Before we start though, let me just ask a couple questions, okay?" Carter asked. I nodded in response. I felt nervous.

"You say you are not sure how far along you are?"

"No, it couldn't have been more than a month or two. I'm really not sure and I'm not sure how long it's been since we left home. My guess would be about four or five months, but honestly, I have no idea."

"Any medical illnesses that run in your family?"

"Not that I know of. My parents both died relatively young, too young for us to have had this type of discussion and, to be honest, Scott and I also never discussed illnesses on his side. I know his grandmother was sick but I'm not sure how," I explained, feeling stupid that I didn't have a better answer.

"Don't worry about it. Have you been feeling anything from the baby?"

"Every once in a while, I feel a flutter or a little tiny kick, or at least that's what I am assuming it is."

"Okay, let's take a look at this baby." He began to hook up the ultrasound and get all the wires going in the right places. "I'm going to put the gel onto your stomach now," He warned me.

I hesitated to pull up my shirt. I haven't shown anyone the bump yet and I was nervous to do so now, especially in front of Carter.

"It's okay, no judgment. I'm sure you look beautiful and if you want to see this baby, then I need to see that belly," Carter joked with me, putting me at ease. I lifted my shirt—exposing my stomach—and allowed him to squirt the gel all over and rub it in with the ultrasound wand. It took a moment to get the picture perfect and then, finally up on the screen was my baby.

"Things are looking good. This flashing spot is the heartbeat. There are the hands and feet, and the head over here." Carter began to point out various body parts to me on the screen.

"Oh my god, look at my baby," I said with tears in my eyes, so thankful that he or she was okay. "I thought you said you didn't work with pregnant women?"

"I didn't, but I am a doctor, Miss. I do know how to use an ultrasound and recognize what is what. I did go to med school for forever." He was a bit defensive, but there was a little sarcasm in his tone.

"Fair enough," I said, keeping my mouth shut. I didn't know what pushed his buttons or how far I could tease him. I didn't want to ruin, the most perfect moment that I have had since the cure of doom began.

"I'm thinking you are about five or six months. Like you pointed out, I did not work with pregnant women, so figuring out the stages by just a picture is a bit complicated. However, I do know how to tell the sex of the baby and I can tell, if you want to know," Carter explained.

"You really know that already?" I said, perking up.

"Yup! You want to know?"

I contemplated this for a moment. Did I want to know, or did I want to be surprised when the baby was born? There had already been too many surprises since all this began and I didn't know if I wanted anymore, even if it was a pleasant surprise. If I knew the sex of the baby, I would be able to prepare. I could also stop calling my baby an "it."

"I want to know," I said smiling at him.

Carter studied the screen, "It's a girl!" He was all smiles, beaming down at me.

"Really, a little girl?" I said, with tears in my eyes. I stared at my baby on the screen, full of pride. I could stop calling the baby an it. She was a girl! I could begin to picture what my future would look like if we survived the cure of doom. I leapt up and hugged Carter, overcome with excitement.

Carter was briefly surprised by my abrupt reaction. He recovered quickly and returned my embrace with twice the passion. "I'm so excited. She is going to be beautiful, just like her mother."

"You are really that excited?" I questioned him, testing him.

"Yeah, I am," He said flatly. "Why? You don't believe me?"

"I do, I'm just surprised. You're not the father and we haven't known each other very long." I pressed on. The conversation was awkward, but it needed to happen. I needed to know where he stood with me and my daughter. God, it felt weird to think that. *I have a daughter*, my heart swelled.

"I care about you. This little girl is a part of you—therefore I care about her. I obviously know that I'm not her father, but with respect, her father is not here." He paused before going on, finding his words. "I thought I made it obvious how I feel about you." He looked at me, took my face in his hands and gently kissed me. This was our first real kiss; it was sweet and tender. It was the type of kiss out of a movie and your feet want to do a happy dance after. I didn't want it to stop. He pulled away and looked me in the eyes, "I know we haven't known each other for forever, but I care deeply about you. I'm falling for you. You are beautiful, strong, and amazing. I want us to be a thing—to be together. I want to be a family."

I nodded at him, speechless by the amazing kiss and surprised by his confession. "I'm not sure what to say." I paused trying to get my thoughts straight. "I appreciate those kind words you said about me. I care about you, too, Carter." I kept it simple.

"But?" He said to me.

"But?" I repeated back.

"There sounds like there is a but there, like this isn't what you want."

"I'm sorry, I'm just taken by surprise. I'm not dumb, I knew that you were smitten with me, but loving me and wanting to be together, I'm a little surprised by that," I admitted.

"A good 'surprised'?"

"Yeah, I think so." I smiled slightly at him.

"If the world is ending, I want to end it with you by my side. With that baby, that precious little girl. I want to be there for her and to help raise her." He expressed his desires again with emotion written all over his face.

"I would like that," I stated.

"Really?" He said, his face lighting up with glee.

"Really. I have been thinking about this all day and I want this, too. This whole thing has shown us that life really is too short. I'm still not over what happened to Scott, but I know that I need to accept it and move on. He would want me to be happy, and he would want a family for our child. I, of course, wanted my baby to know her father, but that's not possible and she needs a father figure in her life." I paused briefly, nervous for what I was about to say next. "If you are up for the job, then I would love for that person to be you. You give me butterflies," I admitted to him.

"I could not be any happier to accept that job," Carter instantly responded. He embraced me and then gave me a tender kiss. He then turned the ultrasound machine off and climbed into the bed, spooning me "We're going to make this life work and it's going to be awesome."

chapter thirty-four

The next morning, I woke up in the small, uncomfortable hospital bed, with Carter's arms wrapped around me. At first, I was a bit confused on where I was and who was next to me. Then, I quickly came back to reality, grounded by the comfort of Carters body against mine. I shuffled in the tiny bed and looked over at Carter. He squinted and smiled.

"Good morning, gorgeous." He kissed my forehead. "I am so lucky to be able to wake up next to you every day from now till the end of time." He snuggled into my neck.

"Who knew that you were such a romantic," I teased him. "Do you know what we have to do today?"

"Get back on the road to get to your sister?" He guessed.

"Well, that would be nice. But we also need to tell Logan about us, and I'm not sure how he will take it. He is protective and he really hasn't allowed you to even be near me. It might come as a shock to him," I warned him.

"I know. I've talked to him," Carter stated.

"Really?"

"I've felt this way about you for a while. When Logan and I went into town for the meds, I told him how I felt about you when I thought we were going to die. He just doesn't know that my feelings are reciprocated."

"Wow, you are loose-lipped when you're on your death bed. Telling him about your feelings and the baby—you got balls, doctor," I joked with him.

"Yep." He grinned at me. "As much as I would love to lie here with you all day, we do need to get up and get going. Hopefully, Logan is awake and is stable enough to be moving. We can lay him down in the back of the SUV."

"What about the undead blocking the staircase?"

"We'll figure something out, we always do. Let's go talk with the others." Carter got out of the bed, I followed suit. We walked hand in hand to the room where Logan was recovering.

When we entered the room, Logan was awake. He and Elana were having a quiet conversation. I knocked on the door, gaining both of their attention. "Look who's awake," I said to Logan.

"Hey sis," He said with a smile, waving me into the room. I approached the bed, bent down, and kissed his forehead.

"How are you feeling?"

"I'm doing great. I don't really remember much of what happened. I know I was shot, that's about it. Wouldn't be the first time. Probably won't be the last." He joked in his macho way. "Starving though, I feel like I haven't eaten in days."

"It's because you probably haven't. I'll go get you some vending machine munchies," Elana stated before leaving the room, passing by Carter who still stood in the doorway.

"Come on in here, doc." He invited Carter into the room. "Thanks for saving my life man."

"It was my pleasure. I was happy to be doing some work from my past life, felt good. Now, let's not let that happen again though, okay?" I rolled my eyes at his lame doctor's joke.

"Of course man. Do you think I'm stable enough to get out of here today? We really need to get back on the road," Logan eagerly asked him.

"Let me do a quick examination." Carter approached the bed, lifted the sheet up and began to tear off the bandage, inspecting the wound.

"It's not infected, and the healing process has begun. In the real world, I would say absolutely no leaving. But in this world, it's your call. You are a liability though—you aren't going to be able to function as you normally would. You have to take it easy and be cautious, otherwise you're going to rip your stitches out and cause an infection," Carter warned.

"Understood," Logan replied.

"Do you understand?" I questioned him. "Because you are always putting yourself in danger and stepping up to be the leader— and you can't. You need to let us help you and let us do the heavy lifting and difficult things."

"How long do I need to be like this doc?" He ignored me.

"At least a couple days. I know it's unrealistic to tell you that you can't do anything, especially if its life or death. I'm going to take all the medical equipment that I can so I can re-stitch and give you antibiotics. I'll try to work around this, but there will always be the risk." Carter was trying to reason with him.

"Fine. I'll try, but there are no promises. Can we get going soon?" He asked. His stubbornness was pissing me off. As eager as I was to leave, I had to be realistic. I knew that Logan was alive and needed medical attention to survive. I didn't know if Lilianna was alive, as much as that hurt to admit.

"We need to find a way out," I stated, knowing there was no point in arguing with Logan.

"What do you mean?"

"We are on the fourth floor. We were chased up the stairwell by the undead and barricaded the door. Who knows if they're still there or not, but the third-floor door is open so I'm sure they are still hanging around in there. The other problem is that the elevator never came when we called it downstairs. We don't know if it's broken or if it's full of the undead. I'm sure there are other ways down, we just don't know where they are. The other half of this floor is in complete darkness, which we thought to be too dangerous to explore," I explained the scenario to him.

He was quiet, processing all the information in his mind, weighing our options, deciding what the best move was. "Clearly, the stairwell you already came up is out, as is the elevator. There is too much risk associated with the elevator. As for the dark area up here, I'm sure there are flashlights stored somewhere on this floor, in case of blackouts. Let's explore that area and look for a stairwell and hope it's clear." He had a plan all mapped out in thirty seconds.

"We have a standard map of the floor, so why don't I give that to you to look over to find where the stairs are before we go wandering around in the dark. While you're doing that, I'll pack up some medical supplies and have the other guys help me out. The girls can empty the vending machines and break rooms," Carter tweaked the plan and exited the room. I was happy they got along. This wasn't time for a "my balls are bigger than your balls" fight!

Elana entered the room with a bag of potato chips and a snickers bar. "Breakfast of champions," She joked, holding up the snacks.

"A Snickers!" Logan was genuinely excited about this. "Been forever since I had one of these."

"While you're both here, there are a few things that I wanted to tell you," I stated grabbing their attention.

"You guys finally together or what?" Logan laughed. It was weird to see him so calm and joking around.

I blushed, "Figured it out, huh?"

"That's what we were talking about before you guys walked in this morning. He asked where you were, and I said that you and Carter were in a room down the hall. Sorry I sold you out. He was worried. I had to let him know that you were in good hands. Then when you walked into the room holding hands, I mean that kind of confirmed our suspicions," Elana explained.

"Happy for you, sis," Logan shared.

"Thanks, I am relieved to have your approval," I said with sarcasm. "Anyway, the other big news I wanted to tell you both, is that we were able to do an ultrasound on the baby."

"And?" Logan tried to sit up straighter, wincing a bit. He was excited to hear about the baby.

"The baby is healthy as far as we can tell. We can officially stop calling the baby an 'it' and start calling it a 'her'. IT'S A GIRL!" I shouted with excitement. Elana jumped up with joy and Logan clapped his hands.

"Another girl in the family. That's fantastic, Mya. That little girl is now the future of this world. I can't wait to meet her. How long do you think?" Logan asked.

"I'm predicting that she is about five months along. I would say at least three more months to go." Carter reappeared in the doorway. "She's really beginning to pop. We need to get to your other sister soon and begin to look for a place to settle down, so she can nest and prepare for the baby."

"I couldn't agree more. I love you sis and I'm happy for you and I can't wait to meet her," Logan said to me, then turning to Carter, "Do you have the map? I'd say we should try to leave here within the hour." Logan was more eager as ever to leave now. Carter handed him the map—still in its frame.

Carter went back to the other guys to look for medical supplies. Elana and I tore apart the break room and emptied another vending machine. Logan studied the map searching for a new exit strategy.

chapter thirty-five

Everyone, including Logan with the map in hand, met up with the various supplies they were responsible for finding.

"It looks like this stairwell, here..." Logan said to us, pointing at the map. "...is the stairwell that you guys came up with the undead in it. This stairwell on the other side could be a potential option to get us out of here. The new stairwell is through the darker half of the floor. You guys haven't heard anything from over there?" Logan asked us.

"When we came up to this floor, there were a ton of undead in the operating room that we took over. We were pretty loud and no undead ever attempted to come over from that side and we never heard shrieking or growling." Carter filled Logan in on the little info that he did know.

"Hopefully, that's a good sign and you guys already took all the undead out. I say we head in that direction and see how it goes. Did anyone find any flashlights for us to use?" Logan made the final decision to move on.

"I was able to find three in a janitor closet," Doug spoke up, revealing the flashlights, handing one to Logan and one to Carter, keeping one for himself. "Also, I found Evan a quad cane that will hopefully help him get along better."

"Logan, I meant to give this to you. This will help with the healing and make you less tempted to use your arm." Carter handed him a sling to rest his arm in. Logan's arm resting in a sling was a hindrance to the rest of the group. He was one of our strongest members due to his time in the service.

The group gathered our belongings, each person taking something to carry. Everyone grabbed a weapon to arm themselves. Once everyone was situated, the boys turned their flashlights on, and we headed to the dark hallway. We treaded lightly, carefully stepping over any undead bodies or overturned equipment.

Further down the hallway, I noticed that while walking, our feet crunched with each step. I nudged Carter to shine the light on our feet so I could see what I was stepping on. The floor sparkled; we were stepping on shards of glass. He then turned the flashlight to shine above us and revealed that all the lights had been shattered. That explained why it was dark. *Why would someone want to break one of the only remaining sources of light left?* The generator won't last forever. Eventually the entire world will be dark. The thought chilled me.

Lost in thought, I was oblivious to the strange noise ahead of us. Logan on the other hand was, of course, always on high alert. He heard it and held up his hand signaling us to stop. We abruptly stopped in our tracks. I froze in fear of what was waiting for us in the dark. There were no windows nor were there any lights, just darkness and whatever was waiting for us in the dark.

"Psst, Logan?" I whispered, trying to be as quiet as possible, wondering what was ahead of us.

"I don't know, Mya," He whispered back, already knowing what my question was. We stood in silence, trying to figure out what was waiting for us— trying to prepare ourselves for what was to come. I took a deep breath, trying to calm myself down. My heart was about to beat out of my chest.

Logan, I think, felt the same way. Tired of waiting, he decided to make a move. He held his hand up and signaled us to start moving forward. He took the first steps and started to creep forward with his flashlight up, on high alert. Normally, he would be holding multiple weapons, but, due to his shoulder injury, he was unable to manage most of them. He did, of course, have his gun in the back of his waistband if need be.

As we inched further, Carter moved up next to him, with the baseball bat in hand, ready to pounce.

"I urge you to return from which you came." A loud and gruff voice came from the other end of the hallway. We all stopped. No one knew what to say or do. We stood silent.

"I said, return from which you came," The male voice said louder this time. My heart was hammering in my chest, we needed to turn around. It didn't sound like the voice was very far away either. Those of us with flashlights began to frantically shine them all over the place looking for the man. We still couldn't find him.

Logan cleared his throat, "We don't want any trouble. We can't go back that way. That stairwell is no good. There's supposed to be another one over here. We just want to get down so we can leave here. We don't want trouble; we're just looking for a way out."

"We can't help you with that, you need to turn around and leave," the voice said again.

"Come on Logan," Elana whispered, pulling at his sleeve. He stayed put.

"There is no other way, Elana, we're getting through," He whispered back. "Are you willing to negotiate?" He asked the man.

"You have nothing that we don't already have," the man flatly replied, unimpressed. I had an eerie feeling about this.

"I'm sure we can work something out," Logan again attempting to persuade this man. Logan still shining his light around, inching forward looking for the source of the voice.

"I doubt that," the man replied, then there were some muffled whispers being exchanged. He wasn't alone.

Then, out of nowhere, the man stepped into the light. He freaked us out, Logan jumped back and almost dropped the flashlight. The man appeared to be in his forties with large muscles and a lot of tattoos. He was dressed in green scrubs, as if he worked at the hospital at some point. No one followed him into the light. It was unclear how many of them there were. The man put a cheesy smile on his face, "Turns out I was wrong, you do have something that we want."

"Name it," Carter replied, eager to make this deal and be on our way.

"Rumor on the block is that you have a baby, my lady wants it," he stated. I gasped and now my heart was really going to explode.

"We don't have a baby," Logan responded.

"We did have a baby, but we don't anymore. The baby and the father stayed behind, miles and miles away, if that's what you're referring to," Carter spoke up.

"You don't have a baby, yet," the man chuckled, still smiling. I placed my hand over my stomach as if that was going to protect us. "You see, we've been up here. We have been watching you. You entered our home, that's the price you have to pay to leave. The unborn baby and the walking incubator stay." The smile was gone, replaced with a crazed stare that meant he was serious. I clutched Carters arm, terrified for my life.

"Not an option," Logan bluntly replied. He was done playing nice with this guy.

"Suit yourself." And with that the man stepped out of the spotlight and back into the dark. The guys started shining their flashlights all over in search of the man.

"I'm moving in," Logan stated. Carter followed behind, baseball bat raised and ready to swing. Logan made some hand gestures towards Doug, ordering him what to do. Doug replaced Logan's spot. Logan turned, slipping his arm out of the sling he went to search for his new target.

Carter, Doug, and Quinn continued to creep down the hall, ready to fight if needed. Elana, Evan, and I stayed behind, careful to stay out of the crossfire. Elana and I were holding hands, our hearts racing and our breathing labored. The guys took the flashlights when they went forward, leaving us in the dark with just a glimpse of light coming from the lit end of the hallway from which we had just come.

The hallway was quiet. The dead silence made me even more nervous and paranoid. I began to look around. I kept looking to Elana and Evan, trying to read their expressions. Evan looked at me with a strange puzzled expression. He seemed confused about what was happening. "Mya..."

Before either one of us could react, there were hands around me, covering my mouth to stifle a scream. I instantly started hitting and kicking, but he was powerful and fast. He dragged me down the hallway. By then, Elana and Evan were freaking out, yelling to get the attention of the others.

The strong man continued to drag me down a separate dark hallway that we didn't know was there. Once we reached our destination, the man opened an examine room door and threw me into the room, slamming the door shut.

I quickly scurried into the corner of the room with my back up against the wall. I was unsure of what was in the dark room with me. I blinked my eyes over and over again, hoping to force them to adjust, so I could see where I was. I had a strange feeling that I wasn't in the room alone.

chapter thirty-six

There was a sudden flicker of light—of fire. It was a lighter. Someone was in there with me.

"Please let me go," I pleaded with the hidden stranger.

"I can't do that sweetie. You have something that I need," A woman responded to me.

I started to cry. Getting out of this situation felt impossible. "Please just let me go."

"I'll let you go alright, straight up to the heavens once that sweet little baby is in my arms." She was just as twisted as the man. *Where are Logan and Carter?* I placed my head in my arms and cried. I prayed that we would survive. The creepy woman continued to flick her lighter on and off, freaking me out even more.

I finally heard voices on the other side of the door. Voices that I recognized. There were repeated loud bangs and the walls shuddered. The doors were being kicked in. They were looking for me. I sat up a little straighter—filled with hope. I was too close to the doorway. I needed to move to avoid being hit with the door.

I started to inch myself away from the door when the woman came up behind me and placed a knife to my throat. I immediately stilled and stopped breathing. Carter and Doug kicked the door in. I looked up at them, frightened for my life.

"Stop!" I yelled out to them. They shined the flashlight on my face and saw that a knife was pressed to my throat. Doug and Carter instinctively put their weapons on the floor and arms in the air, careful not to piss the lady off.

"Nobody takes one step toward us or she dies," the woman stated.

"You don't want to kill her. The baby won't live without her. You need her to stay alive longer for the baby. Like your husband said, she's an incubator," Carter tried to reason with the crazed woman.

"I know that. Now stop talking and back up. Where's my Jimmy?" *That must be her husband.* The duo shrugged their shoulders and stayed silent. "Move." The lady directed to me and forced me to my feet. "We're going to find Jimmy. You two in front of us so I can see what you're up to. Hands up in the air the whole time or I'll slit her throat."

We began our trek down the dark hallway. "Left down the next hallway" She directed. "Jimmy!" She started to call out. She was growing nervous.

At the end of the next hallway there were people standing and waiting. "Jimmy?" She questioned; hopeful it was him.

Approaching the scene, Jimmy was on his knees with his hands tied behind his back. Logan stood behind him with a gun to his head. There were two other men on the ground who appeared to be unconscious. My brother shifted his eye contact and looked at me. "Mya," he said. His eyes grew big as he noticed the knife to my throat.

"Let her go," He stated to the woman. How he was able to successfully pull that off with basically only one hand was a mystery to me.

"You let my Jimmy go!" she replied.

"Let her go now or I blow his head off," Logan stated again, removing the safety on the gun to show that he was serious.

"Linda," Jimmy stated, taking Logan's threat seriously and pleading with his wife. The woman continued to hold the knife to my throat, moving her head back and forth, weighing her options.

237

"Linda," He said again, a little more demanding this time. I could feel her grip loosen.

"Jim," she bluntly replied. "I want this baby."

"Not this baby, Linda. We will figure something else out." Jimmy was being reasonable, obviously scared for his life. He had already taken a small beating; his face was cut up, blood dripped from his eyebrow.

"Jimmy!" She yelped at him, not wanting to give in that easy. She tightened her grip, pressing the knife harder against my throat. I felt the blade slice open my skin, and warm blood began to surface. That excited the woman and she pressed harder.

Logan was ready to play the game. He moved around to the front of Jimmy, tilted his head back and placed the barrel of the gun in his mouth. "Is this really what you want Linda?" He asked.

I felt her breath quicken as she panicked. She pressed the knife harder; I felt the blood run down my neck. Suddenly, she let go and threw me to the floor. The second she dropped me, Doug was on top of her, knocking the knife out of her hand and Carter was on the floor next to me, applying pressure to my throat. The neck wound, mixed with the excitement and the blood loss, had me feeling a little woozy.

I laid on the floor and struggled not to pass out. Doug, Logan, and Quinn took care of the couple, ushering them away into another room. Elana rushed over to Carter and me—worry etched across her face.

"It's not as bad as it seems," Carter stated. "Neck wounds tend to bleed a lot. No arteries were punctured, she didn't cut deep. Elana, in the backpack that Evan has, there are gauze and alcohol wipes. Can you get them?" She took off to meet him, who was already hobbling over toward us. I laid there, lost in shock at the events that had unfolded. I felt like I was in a nightmare, except it was real life. Tears continued to stream down my face. I didn't even know I was crying. "Shhh, you're okay," Elana whispered to me, brushing the tears off my cheeks. Carter wiped the cut clean, which burned like hell, and applied a gauze.

"That's the best I can do for now, we need to move." Carter looked up and saw Logan making his way back.

He rushed over and got to his knees, taking my hand in his. "Mya. How bad is it?"

"Not as bad as it looks, I can tend to it properly later. She's stable for now. Logan, put the sling back on," Carter barked at him. He sighed and complied, returning his arm to the sling.

"We need to leave. I locked them in a room on the other side, it's only going to hold for so long," Logan stated. He helped me to my feet and hugged me. I lazily hugged back, still in shock. "This way." He began to usher the group in the direction of the other stairwell. Carter came up to me and helped me get to the stairwell. I didn't trust myself to walk alone, I felt delirious.

After several turns, we arrived at the infamous stairwell we had been looking for. "Here it is. Stay here, let me check it out really quick," Logan announced and went through the door. He was back within 15 seconds. "I don't see any undead and I don't hear any undead. Let's move."

We filed into the stairwell and began to make our descent down to the main lobby. Hopefully, the SUV was still there. Everyone was quiet as we went down, not wanting to attract attention from the undead or the crazed alive. Approaching the lobby level, I felt as if I could catch my breath, almost to freedom. We scurried through the lobby, made our way through the hallways and back to the ER entrance. We exited out the doors we entered through and landed directly into the harsh sunlight. Our eyes had trouble adjusting to the natural light after being stuck in the dark for so long.

Just as we hoped, the SUV was still sitting there untouched. Another answered prayer.

"I am so glad we survived that!" Doug happily stated, twirling in place with his arms outstretched.

"Now, only one more problem," Quinn stated.

"Yeah, what's that man?" Logan said slinging his good arm around Elana, pulling her in for a victory kiss.

"We still have to find us a new car."

"Piece of cake," Logan replied with a smile.

chapter thirty-seven

Logan, with his injured arm, was able to hotwire a car and scrounge up gasoline for the SUV that was starting to run low. It wasn't enough gasoline to fill it, but better than nothing. The new medical supplies gathered from the hospital were packed into the vehicles. Quinn and Logan studied the map, looking for the best route to continue our drive to Indiana. Doug retrieved what supplies were left in the other car.

Carter fussed over me, tending to my wound. "How is your throat doing? Are you in any pain?"

"I'm okay. Just a little shook up. I'm more worried about the stress that I'm putting on the baby," I responded.

"I'm worried about you right now. Let me look at your throat again, I want to thoroughly clean and redress it." He turned to the trunk of the SUV and dug out some of the new medical supplies we just collected.

"I'm going to apply these. They are like little tiny stitches but less invasive." He showed me the bandages. He cleansed the wound and re-applied the proper bandages. "It's bleeding less. Next time we stop, I'll redress it, so it doesn't get infected." He pulled me into an embrace and hugged me. I felt the tension loosen. Being in his arms I let the worry slip away and I was able to relax. Carter rubbed my back and kissed me on the forehead. "I'm so glad that you're okay. I was so worried."

"Ready, lovebirds?" Quinn inquired. "We're going to try to get back to route 70 and, hopefully, have a straight shot to Indiana." We broke our embrace and prepared to depart from the hospital with the crazy, alive people. I wasn't sure which was worse, the undead or people like that.

We separated into the vehicles; Quinn, Evan, and Doug in the car, and Logan, Elana, Carter, and myself in my SUV. Quinn was better with the map reading, so he led. We followed behind, with Carter behind the wheel. Logan's ego was too big to just allow him to drive. There was a small argument and we out-voted Logan, three to one. Carter drove and we allowed Logan to take shotgun.

Several turns later, we pulled back on the ramp, attempting to get onto the highway. The way from which we came was now blocked by an overturned semi-truck. The regular on-ramp was filled with cars littering the street. It was impossible to pass through and it was dangerous. There were undead trapped in cars, under cars, and, frankly, all over the place. There was blood spatter and dead bodies scattered around. Undead were strapped into their seat belts still banging on their windows to be let free to hunt. Pending we could get the cars through; this was absolutely not a safe travel area.

"Logan, this isn't a good idea," I stated. "There are undead trapped all over the place. If we start trying to push our way through, we could loosen them up or we could get stuck in the middle of all that, and I don't know if we'd make it out."

"I know. I'm thinking," he said, repeatedly scanning the area for any potential threat. Finally, he decided, "Back the SUV up," He stated. Once the SUV was back a decent amount of room, Carter flashed his lights at Quinn's car. Slowly, Quinn began to back up and eventually pulled up next to us to figure out our next move.

"I know you didn't want to do this, but it looks like we're going to have to take the long way around this mess," Quinn hollered over to our car.

"Looks that way. It's not even possible to try to get these cars through. Do you already know where you are going?" Logan inquired.

"Yep, just follow us. I'm going to try the backroads that run parallel to route 70, so we can eventually get back on," Quinn replied and took off in a different direction. Carter followed behind him, turn after turn. Multiple times we had to stop due to the roads being blocked by over-turned cars or clusters of the undead. It was best to keep turning around and avoiding them.

I was getting nervous; we hadn't made any progress. I felt like we were wasting gas and daylight. I kept glancing over Carter's shoulder at the gas gauge. Half tank.

"I feel like we are going in circles," Elana spoke up.

"It seems that way, doesn't it?" I responded. "I wonder what they are thinking in the other car."

Quinn pulled his car over and we pulled up next to him. He was studying the map and crossing off roads that we already tried and failed on.

"We're running out of options, here. We tried most of the routes out that I can see. The apocalypse must have hit this town hard," Quinn concluded.

"What other options do we have?" Logan inquired.

"I have three roads that we can try, otherwise we're probably going to have to go back and fight some undead so we can pass." Quinn circled the remaining three options and passed the map over to Logan for him to examine. He briefly studied the map and then came to a conclusion.

"I say we go for the middle route. Just a feeling I have," Logan replied, eager to be on our way. The longer we were stagnant, the higher the risk of more undead. He kept checking his side mirror. I turned around in my seat to see what he was looking at. The undead had heard us and caught up with us.

"Time to go," I announced to both cars. Quinn and Carter nodded at each other and both cars sped off in hopes of losing the undead. Unfortunately, it wasn't that easy to lose them. The undead had begun to evolve. Their food sources were becoming limited, they were desperate for a meal. They would chase cars for miles before something else finally caught their attention.

I caught myself staring out the back of the car, watching the undead chase after us. My body was tense, stricken with fear that the undead would catch us and overtake the car. Carter glanced at me in the mirror and noticed how tense I was. "Take deep breaths. It'll all be okay." He attempted to soothe me. I obliged and took a deep breath. I turned my attention and looked out the window at what we were passing. The scenery wasn't any better, mainly filled with destruction. The world had no vibrancy left, it was rubble—dark and dreary. The grass looked frosted like it gently snowed that morning. It was cold out. I looked up at the sky, it was dull—a dull winter sky, ready to release snowflakes any time. I was lost in thoughts of winter wonderland. Once I snapped back to reality, I looked behind us and, thankfully, we had lost the undead—at least for the moment.

"Did it work, Logan?" I asked.

"So far so good, sis. The destruction is less the further we go. We are moving further away from the city and into what appears to be a rural area. This means less people and hopefully less undead," He replied.

"Sounds like wishful thinking. How long do you think it will take to get through Ohio?" I hoped we would get to Indiana that day.

"Normally, not very long, about five hours." He sighed, "Now, after all of this, and given how long it took us to just get to Ohio, I'm going to say days, at least. It's winter and the sun is going to keep setting earlier. It's not safe to travel at night. It took us forever just to leave the city. I think that we're in for a long journey." He leaned over Carter and checked the fuel meter. "Gas is going to become an issue soon."

"What's our next move?" Elana questioned.

"Keep driving for as long as we can. I can already tell by the way the sky looks, that the sun is going to set within the next few hours.

244

Staying the night on any road is not a good idea. It didn't end so well the last time we did that. We lost Blake and June, and Will ended up leaving our group." He made valid points. Based on where the sun was in the sky, we had at least an hour of travel time before we needed to find a place to stay the night,

chapter thirty-eight

About an hour had gone by. The sun was beginning to lower allowing the moon to take its place above us, thus bringing on the darkness and the night creatures—giving the undead the upper hand.

"We should look for a place to stay the night," Logan said. Carter agreed and began flashing his lights at the other car. A couple minutes later, Quinn noticed the flashing lights and pulled over. Carter pulled up next to the car and everyone got out to form a plan.

"What's going on?" Quinn asked, stepping out of his car.

"The sun is starting to go down—we should pick a place to stay for the night. We also need gasoline," Logan responded.

"How low are you?"

"Under a quarter tank. We won't make it far tomorrow."

"Our situation looks similar—little more than a quarter tank."

I looked around at our surroundings. It felt like we were in the middle of nowhere. The trees were lined up and down the road and piles of leaves were strewn about. The fall foliage was taking over and there were no people left alive to maintain it.

"We are in the middle of nowhere, can't we just pick a house nearby. I haven't seen one in a while, but that doesn't mean we won't find one soon. People live out here in the sticks," Evan stated. "That handy map say anything about houses or gas stations?" He asked Quinn.

"Yeah right, dude, it's not a GPS system, it's a piece of paper," Doug mocked him.

"Doug's right, it just has the roads. No landmarks like houses or gas stations. I haven't seen an undead in a while. We can try to stay at a nearby house and get right back on the road tomorrow," Quinn replied.

"If we leave early enough, we might even make it to Indiana. Long shot but it could happen." Elana was trying to be hopeful.

"We have a solid plan. Next house, I'll pull in. Let's go, daylight's a wastin'," Quinn uttered his favorite slogan.

Everyone piled into their vehicles and we proceeded down the road hopeful to find a house. We traveled a few more miles before Quinn put his turn signal on, signaling he was turning into a driveway on the left. The house was set off the road; we couldn't tell if it was occupied or not. Both cars crept down the driveway at a painfully slow speed, extra cautious. Once we reached the house, I was happy to find that there were no cars in the driveway and the garage door was open and empty. That was a good sign that there were no living people waiting to shoot us.

"So far, so good," I announced to the car.

"We're not in the clear yet," Logan replied. Carter parked next to the other car and got out. Elana, Logan, and I followed suit. Logan pulled the gun from his waistband, prepared for whomever we might find. The rest of us grabbed our weapons and began to walk toward the house. We needed to get another gun—I hoped the house had one.

"Girls, stay here with Evan. Doug and Quinn, you two take the front door. Carter and I will take the garage. Open the door and bang on it and wait to see what happens, try to draw them out." Logan gave out his orders and everyone went their ways, except those of us that were forced to watch due to overbearing brothers. I had to admit I was a smidge perplexed that he always tried to leave me out of those situations, even more so now that he knew about the baby. I folded my arms over my chest and tapped my foot.

Elana caught onto my irritation, "He only treats us like this because he wants us to be safe. Don't be so offended." I said nothing in response, just glared at her. *She always takes his side.* I blamed the hormones. I took a deep breath and refocused on what was happening.

Each pair was at their assigned doors. The doors were open, and the guys were banging on the frame, using sound as bait. They waited a few minutes, and nothing showed up. Carter and Logan emerged from the garage.

"Nothing, it's time to go in," Logan stated. "Everyone clear a room and see what goods you can find while you're at it." He turned to the three of us, "Why don't you unload some stuff from the car—water and snacks."

"Sure boss," I responded sarcastically. I could not contain my attitude.

Everyone went their separate ways and Elana, Evan, and I began to unload water from the car. I walked into the house through the front door. It opened to a nice-sized living room with an open floor plan, which was nice; less places to hide. The house was not big, and the guys finished clearing the house fast. "Empty," Carter informed us.

"Anyone find anything useful?" Logan asked. Everyone shook their heads.

"Let me check out the kitchen." I made my way toward the kitchen and began opening cupboards. The cupboards were bare—completely empty. I checked the rest of the cabinets. Each cabinet only held dishes, no food.

"Also empty," I replied to the group.

"The owners must have taken everything and left when things went south around here. Explains why the garage was left open. Good thing we still have snacks and water." Logan was trying to look on the bright side.

"And beer!" Doug smiled, thrilled about the beer, per usual.

"I'm going to check the garage for gasoline." Logan went back to the garage.

"I'm going to check the upstairs for any leftover medical supplies." Carter made his way upstairs.

I sat on the dusty white couch decorated with pink roses. I looked around the room: older taste and lots of family photos of children. I assumed that an older couple once lived there. I wonder if they ever made it to safety. Given the pictures, they were probably trying to get to their children and grandchildren.

Within minutes, Carter and Logan were both back in the living room.

"Nothing." Logan was clearly disappointed.

"Nothing," Carter stated.

"Man, these people did clean house," Doug stated, opening a beer, taking a swig.

"Quinn, how much ground did we cover today. How far into Ohio are we?" I was curious to see what our progress was. He came over to me with the map so we could both examine it.

"Over here is where the hospital was in Barnesville." He pointed, "After all the turning around and different turns we had to make off track, staying as close to route 70 as possible, I think that we are right around Zanesville. Which looks like we are about a third of the way into the state."

"Only a third of the way?" I questioned. We were in the car all day and we barely made progress toward Indiana. Hell, we should have been there already.

"Like I said, with all the turning around and changing directions, not to mention pulling over to talk. The daylight fades fast in the winter, that's what I mean when I say daylight's a wasting. Hopefully, we'll make more progress in tomorrow's daylight." Quinn folded up his map and retreated to where he was previously sitting.

"The gas situation is going to be a problem" Logan announced.

"Babe, lets worry about that in the morning. There is nothing that anyone can do about that right now from where we are. Look outside, there is nothing around and we are two seconds from dark," Elana pointed out. I didn't even notice how fast the sun had finished setting. Darkness had taken over the sky.

"I refuse to do nothing." He was clearly frustrated and made his way upstairs in search of an answer.

"Let's figure out dinner," I said to Elana grabbing her hand and leading her outside. We dug through the random food in the trunk of the SUV—very slim pickings. Our stash had dwindled down to a few cans of veggies, some expired pasta boxes, pretzels, and vending machine snacks.

"This is barely a meal," Elana stated.

"I know, but it's the best we've got for now." I grabbed some pasta and canned veggies. That would have to do. Hopefully, we had a way to cook the food. We wandered into the kitchen, passing the guys who were sitting around and drinking—except for Logan. Once in the kitchen, I was disappointed to find an electric stove.

"What about a grill?" Elana opened the back door, which led to a small patio with a grill.

The back porch gave me the creeps. It was surrounded by woods. I felt like the undead could come out of the woods and eat me at any time. Elana must have caught my vibes.

"Let's have the guys help with this one," Elana responded, heading inside. The guys agreed and came out to start the propane grill.

"Lucky for us, this thing is running low, but still has enough propane left," Quinn informed us.

I started to shiver, the temperature outside was frigid. "Go ahead inside and prepare everything. We will get the grill going, bring it all out once you're ready," Carter said to me, rubbing my back to ease my shivers. The rest of the evening flowed smoothly. I put the pasta in a pot to boil on the grill and handed off the cooking to Carter.

Everyone ate as Logan filled us in on his new idea. "Backpacks." He presented to us.

"What about them?" Quinn asked.

"We need to load the backpacks up as much as we can, ditch the cardboard boxes—and probably the suitcases." No one responded, clearly confused by what he was saying. "Realistically, we are only going to get so far tomorrow. Given the path that we've been taking, there are not many places for gas and there are not many random cars lying around. We'll run out of gas tomorrow and we need to be prepared to finish this journey on foot."

"On foot!? That's so far!" I protested. "What about Evan? He's using a cane."

"I'd rather us be prepared for that than not. We'll drive until there are no other options and we break down, but I'm assuming that is what will happen. After dinner we will evenly divide the food and medical supplies into the backpacks. Everyone should find some warm clothes. It's going to be a cold walk for us. I'm sorry, Evan this is going to be difficult for you." No one responded, but we all understood. Our journey was about to get a lot more challenging.

After we finished dinner, we looked for backpacks. Afterward, we worked as a group, dividing up our goods into the packs. I was sad that I was going to lose my clothes and belongings that I had since the start of the journey. I made sure to transfer the few pictures I had from my suitcase to my backpack. Everyone finished packing their backpacks and retreated to bed for the night.

Logan and Elana took a room. Carter and I took another. The rest of the guys slept in the living room with each taking turn keeping watch. I was eager to get to bed early. I wanted to get an early start the next day. I wanted to see Lilianna. I kissed Carter goodnight and drifted off into the winter wonderland that was dancing around my head earlier.

chapter thirty-nine

The next morning my eyes fluttered open as the bright sun shone in through the window. It felt like it was early in the morning. Our internal clocks were off. We went to bed entirely too early and then we woke too early. I stretched in bed, preparing for the day. I was positive that Logan was already up and waiting to get on the road.

I turned over in bed, surprised to see that Carter was already awake.

"Good morning," I said with a smile.

"You are beautiful in the morning," He responded, pulling me into an embrace. I rested there for a second before making my move to begin the day. I wasn't ready to take our relationship any further. I was antsy to get on track and see Lilianna.

"Come on, get up. We got places to be!" I hopped out of bed, changed into some different clothes, aware that I would be leaving behind a lot of my personal belongings. Once we were ready, we headed downstairs to start the day.

In the living room, the guys were already awake, eating vending machine snacks.

"I'm surprised to see you all up already," Carter greeted the guys.

"Logan didn't give us much of a choice," Doug replied, obviously grumpy and probably hungover.

"Of course, he's up already. Where is he?" I asked.

"Outside, preparing the cars," Quinn responded. I wandered outside to find my brother and Elana packing whatever they could fit into the backpacks and the trunk of the cars.

"Ready to go?" I asked.

"Of course, been waiting on you. It's too hopeful to think that today is the day, but you never know. Today might really be the day that we finally get to see Lilianna again." He was unable to contain his excitement at the thought of seeing our sister.

"Part of me thinks you're too hopeful, but I feel the same way. I'll go tell those bums to get a move on and get in the car. How many hours do you think we have left in gas?" I asked, scared to find out that answer.

"Maybe three hours, tops. Who knows how long we could run until they just shut off. Hopefully, there's a gas station somewhere and that won't be a problem. No need to worry yet." Logan tried to play it cool. He shut the trunk of the SUV, signaling that he was ready to leave.

"I'll go get them." I went back inside and announced to the guys it was time to leave. The guys grumbled and got up, making their way outside. They might as well have been the undead with the demeanor they had.

Everyone piled into their respective vehicles. "Now Quinn, don't forget to stop for gas if you happen to see anything ahead of us, it's crucial," Logan informed him.

Just like that, we were back in the car and on the road again. The driving situation remained the same— Quinn drove the other car and Carter drove ours. We were still in need of a gas station. Deep down in my stomach, I knew it wouldn't be as simple as that for us, it never was.

They pulled out of the driveway, making a left back onto the same road we were driving on the night before. Still tired, I put my head against the window and gazed at the world.

Almost all the leaves were off the trees and there was evidence of early morning frost on the grass. The sky was a dull grey-blue color, like the color of a winter sky. *Maybe it will snow?* Back at the house I had to down-size my personal items, but I was smart enough to keep all my warmer clothes and my coat. It wasn't a parka, but it was better than freezing to death.

It had been an hour before we had encountered any undead. There was an old car accident that kept the undead trapped inside. They looked like they had been there for a while—the car was starting to rust over and the undead's skin was rotting away. They seemed to be able to live forever without food.

Quinn stopped his car in the intersection, as the accident was blocking the road. There were trees surrounding the area on both sides, there was no way around.

"Looks like we're going to have to come up with a new route. Let's see what Quinn wants to do." Logan hopped out of the car and went over to the driver's side window to chat with him. The rest of us stayed put, I didn't have the energy to get out of the car. While my pregnancy had been smooth sailing, I did have difficult days. My body felt drained, I didn't want to move at all. I wanted to play hooky on the whole situation and curl back up in the nice warm bed. Sadly, that wasn't my life anymore. I sighed. I knew I was being a little over the top.

"You okay back there?" Carter questioned, looking at me through the rear-view mirror.

"I'm good. Just having a mental fight with myself," I replied, simply. He gave me a puzzled look, like he didn't understand. Before he could question it again, I stated, "Pregnancy problems." That seemed to suffice, and he dropped it.

Logan finally came back to the car with the new plan in place. "We can't go straight, but from the map, that's probably the best way to go. I think we're going to go left at this intersection and hope to loop our way back around to this road." He peered over Carter's shoulder to check out the fuel status. From his facial expression, I could tell the situation wasn't good.

UNDER THE SCARLET TREE

Carter backed the SUV up, allowing room for Quinn to turn and make the left. We traveled down the new road. I was hopeful that we would continue to avoid the undead. I was eager to reach Lilianna. I was worried that we wouldn't be able to find fuel.

chapter forty

We made several turns, hopeful to find our way back so we could continue running parallel with route 70. We constantly ran into barriers which caused us to take more detours. We tried to avoid the undead at all costs. When there was one undead, then there were more nearby. Before you knew it, you were surrounded by a mob.

"Does he even know where he's going anymore?" Carter questioned Quinn's navigational skills. His tone of voice revealed his irritation.

"Who knows, but we are effectively wasting all our gas." Logan was equally as irritated.

"I can't believe we haven't passed a gas station yet. Or at least a car we can siphon off some gas," Elana added.

"We're in the middle of nowhere," I stated the obvious. We hadn't passed any landmarks. No stores, no restaurants, and hardly any houses. "If we stayed on the first road, we would have eventually come across something."

Carter flashed his lights at the other car, "We need to figure this out."

Quinn noticed the lights and pulled over. Carter pulled up next to him and rolled down the passenger window.

"What's the problem? We're going in circles. We're almost out of gas," Carter questioned.

"Trying to navigate the map and drive at the same time is hard enough. It's impossible to predict what these roads are going to be like and whether they are accessible or not. Don't give me shit. You have a try at it, then." Quinn was clearly frustrated and defensively threw the map into our car. He folded his arms and laid back in his seat.

Logan and Carter unfolded the map and began to examine it. Each of them taking turns pointing out various routes. More than once I heard them say "not that one, it dead ends way over here." That must have been Quinn's issue. Every road he picked resulted in a dead end or was forced to be a dead end due to the conditions of the world. The undead had been scarce that day. We had seen a few stragglers that we were able to outrun with the vehicles. No clusters or mobs, thank God. We had been successful at avoiding them and getting away from them unharmed.

"Why don't we just stay on this road for now and see how far we get. It looks like, eventually, we can cross over into Indiana. I don't know if that's exactly where we want to be," Carter proposed to Logan.

"Let's just get there. One more state border then we are that much closer to her. We can figure it out once we get there. If we ever find a gas station, we can look for a different map." They made a decision, finally.

"Follow me. We need gas, flash your lights if you see one," Carter updated the others. The tension in the car was high—everyone stressed that we were going to run out of gas.

I spent my time daydreaming while looking out the window. What would our new life be like? I couldn't wait to hold my daughter for the first time. I couldn't wait to see what she looks like. Would she look more like me or Scott? I had no idea how much time had gone by—I was consumed by my thoughts. *Ding.*

I snapped back to reality, "What was that?" Elana asked.

"The gas light came on." Logan's voice was filled with worry.

As if the world had perfectly aligned, I came back from the daydream and blinked. Had I just seen what I thought I saw? Or was I daydreaming? At the same time the gas light came on, I processed what I had seen—a gas station.

"Wait!" I yelled, a little too excited. I panicked Carter and he slammed on the brakes, causing Quinn to slam on his brakes and almost hit us.

"What's wrong?" Carter was worried.

"Sorry, I didn't mean to freak you out, but I think I saw a gas station back there," I stated.

"Where?!" Logan also got excited. Finally, our day was turning around.

"Not far, maybe that last side road. I swear I saw, like, a shell symbol. I think that's a gas station, right?" Now I was beginning to doubt myself.

"It's worth a look," Carter said, turning the SUV around.

Logan rolled down his window and yelled to Quinn "Gas station!"

I pointed Carter in the direction toward the shell symbol. Carter turned down the road. "I see it too." The car erupted with joy.

We pulled up to the deserted gas station, no undead in sight. There was leftover evidence that, at one point, the undead had come through here, but not for quite some time. Carter and Quinn pulled up to the pumps. Everyone got out of their cars, happy to be out of one stressful situation.

"I'm going to check out the inside," I announced

"I'm coming with you." Logan pulled the gun from his waistband. Inside, the place had already been raided, random leftovers littered the floor. Anything worth taking was already gone. I went behind the counter in search of a map, Logan followed.

Logan was pleased to discover a few boxes of cigarettes left and snagged them. I rifled through the pile of maps, looking for one of Indiana. I was able to find a map and, even better, in the corner of the place was a brochure stand. I studied it and uncovered a brochure for Indiana State University. On the back was a simple map outlining the best ways to get to the campus from different directions. I located the store address, which revealed the town we were in. We hit the jackpot at that gas station. We were set for the rest of our trip.

"It is possible that we might see her today," I said to Logan, my voice filled with hope.

"If not today, then tomorrow." He was also very hopeful that this journey was coming to an end and soon we would get to be with our sister again.

Then, my emotions took over and I began to tear up. "I'm sorry, I'm so goddamn emotional these days," I said, trying to toughen up for my brother and wipe away my tears. Damn hormones.

He rubbed my back, soothing me. "It's okay, and it's almost over. Once we get to her, then we can settle down somewhere and wait for my niece to make her arrival." I took a deep breath and wiped away my tears. I needed to get it together and get my head back in the game.

"We should go. I'm sure they're done pumping the gas." My brother took one final sweep of the place, confirming that there indeed was no food or drinks to be found. We then joined the others, who were finishing fueling the vehicles.

"Find anything?" Carter asked us.

"No food or water, but we did find a map and a brochure for the college," I replied.

"I guess that's better than nothing," Carter said, capping the gas cap.

"I figured out which town we are in." I unfolded the map on the hood of the car and began to search for the town. "We are here, in Westerville, which is on the outskirts of Columbus. That means that we're about halfway through Ohio. Now that we have gas, we might actually get to Indiana sooner than I expected!" I was super excited.

"Let's go, I'll continue to look at the map while Carter drives," Logan stated. Everyone got back into the cars. We were finally on the right path and things were starting to look up for us. Although the sky and weather did look a bit concerning, I was trying not to worry about it until it became an issue. I prayed that never happened.

chapter forty-one

We found our way back to route 70, however, we decided to stay on the side roads instead of taking the highway. It wasn't worth the risk. The highway had abandoned cars and the undead. The side streets would be safer and hopefully less congested.

We stopped for a bathroom break. Logan gave the map back to Quinn to examine. I hoped we would cross the border into Indiana before nightfall. "Looks like we are here, around Dayton. If we continue on this road, then we can cross the border into Indiana—around the Richmond area," Quinn pointed out.

We got back into the vehicles and drove the straight shot for Richmond, Indiana.

The car erupted with joy as we drove by the "Welcome to Indiana" border sign. As excited as I was to finally make it to Indiana, I knew we wouldn't get to Lilianna that day. It was getting late and the sun was about to set. Our entire day was spent driving and making random turns, hopeful we would end up in the right place. Thankfully, we had made it to Indiana.

"I am so happy that we finally made it here," I announced to the car.

"We aren't there yet—we still have a ways to go. We should find somewhere to stay the night," Logan stated and Carter flashed his lights. Quinn pulled over and my brother put down his window. "Let's find a place to stay tonight."

"Roger that." Quinn glanced at the map. "There's a side road up ahead that should put us in a good position for tomorrow." Logan nodded in response. Quinn began in that direction and we followed.

A few minutes had passed, Elana pointed out movement up ahead. Carter slowed down. "You guys see that up there?" She pointed ahead, nervously shaking her finger.

"Undead?" Logan asked squinting to see what it is.

"I can't tell." Carter creeped the SUV closer to the movement, trying to figure out what it was. Quinn had pulled over already.

"It looks like they are carrying weapons. They must be alive then, right?" Logan stated, pulling his gun out in a defensive manner. "Move closer, let's see who these guys are."

Carter inched the SUV closer to the figures. As we got closer, the figures became more distinguished. As suspected, they appeared to be two men carrying weapons. They were dressed in military uniform.

"They are military," Logan stated, lowering his gun. "Drive up next to them slowly. We don't want to spook them." He rolled down his windows and moved his arm outside of the car in an attempt to signal to them.

Once next to the men, "Soldiers." He saluted to them. "Corporal Logan Whitten, U.S. Marine Corps."

They both saluted back, "Private Bass, Sir." "Private Moyer, Sir" They said in unison.

"Where are you soldiers heading?" Carter asked. He made a move to get out of the car and the rest of us followed suit.

"Honestly, I don't know anymore. Every time we think we know where to go, once we finally get there, it's overrun," replied Bass, hanging his head in defeat.

"We've been going city to city, state to state, stopping at the military bases in search of something. Each time we come up empty handed," Moyer added.

"It's just been the two of you?" Logan inquired.

"There were more of us in the beginning. Now it's just the two of us," Bass answered. Again, his voice filled with defeat.

"If you don't find anything at these bases, what does that mean for humanity? When was the last time you spoke with anyone else?" Elana questioned them. Everyone was very eager for any news of anything happening in the world. All we had experienced was death and despair.

"As far as I'm concerned, civilization is gone. We haven't had contact with anyone else in months. We walked from place to place, each time losing more men." Moyer attempted to answer the questions.

"The world is essentially over? There are no safe havens anywhere? What about the places mentioned on the news when it all first went down? What happened to those places?" I joined in the questioning. I knew things were bad out there, but I didn't think they were that bad. I figured there was still somewhere safe to go. We had been so focused on getting to Lilianna, that I hadn't been thinking about what we would do afterward.

"To our knowledge and what we have experienced, the safe havens were overrun long ago, when the world first went to shit. I don't think those places stood a chance from the beginning. There were too many of those things—the people were massacred," Moyer explained, using air quotations when he said the words 'safe haven'. "Every time we try to go to another safe haven or base, we lose more men. The locations are overrun, and we walk right into an ambush when we get there. When there are too many of the undead, they easily overpower you and then it's too late."

"Man, sounds like you guys have been through a lot. I'm sorry dude," Doug sincerely stated. That news brought the group to silence, killing everyone's hopes of any type of normal life after this. No one ever mentioned it, but deep down we all hoped that life was moving on somewhere out there, we just needed to find it. There was nothing left. Just other random people, wandering about the world with no real purpose other than to stay alive.

"I'm Elana, by the way. It was rude of us to jump on you with questions and not introduce ourselves." In unison, we followed suit behind Elana, regained our manners and introduced ourselves to the soldiers.

"You are more than welcome to join our clan here. We are on a mission to get to my sister at Indiana State. After that, we really haven't figured that part out yet," Logan extended the offer to the men. The two men looked at each other and shrugged.

"Thank you, sir," Bass answered.

"We're in the process of getting off the road for tonight. We don't travel at night, it's too risky. Like yourselves, we have also lost many friends and we aren't willing to take any chances," Logan explained.

"We're on board with whatever you guys want to do. We're just thankful for the opportunity to join your group. It gives us purpose again." Moyer thanked him.

"Let's move, it's going to be dark soon and we need a place to stay tonight. There'll be plenty of time for talking later." Logan was all business again.

"We can find a house somewhere off of this road." Carter was trying to stay positive.

"They seem few and far between," Quinn responded looking around. I couldn't disagree with him.

"The next long driveway with a secluded house, we pick that one. Something that can't be seen from the road is our best bet," Logan concluded.

"Evan why don't you ride with us so the soldiers can stay together and ride with Quinn and Doug," Carter suggested. "Everyone okay with that?" Everyone nodded and went to their respected vehicles.

Not long into the drive, we came across a mailbox with a long driveway. As the sun was getting ready to set, we ventured down the driveway to discover a cute cottage. It wasn't big, but it would suffice for the night. The size of it also made it easier to confirm there were no undead inside.

We pulled up to the house and everyone got out of their vehicles. We immediately armed ourselves to face the undead. Our automatic responses showed we had adapted to the new world.

No one needed to say what the plan was, we already knew it. The guys would go inside and check the perimeter while Elana and I stayed with the car. They now had extra help with the addition of the soldiers. Given the size of the house, they were back fairly quickly.

"All clear," Logan stated. Elana and I began loading our arms with the essentials for the night, leaving most of our supplies in the car. We wouldn't be there long. Carter made sure to lock the car. Logan took two of the backpacks out of the car and brought them into the house.

Inside, we organized the essentials and scavenged the house in search of anything that would be useful. The supplies that we had wouldn't last forever. The size of the house didn't leave many places to look for items. The kitchen was practically bare to begin with, hardly any furniture or decorations; the cupboards matched. A few moldy pieces of food were found, but nothing salvageable.

Elana returned to the kitchen with a few items in hand, mostly first-aid related. "Any food?" She asked.

"Nothing edible," I grimly replied as I opened a can of beans. Meals were becoming slim. The two of us tended to the boring, typical apocalypse meal. The guys started to settle in, in the front room. Logan had positioned himself near a window and repeatedly checked—making sure we weren't followed. To the onlooker, the house was nothing special. We doubted anyone would turn up scavenging for food or supplies. There just didn't seem to be that many people around. Our noise could attract the undead, but they had been scarce lately. Maybe they started to die off?

"Have you guys seen a lot of the undead lately? I don't recall seeing them as much as normal," I asked the soldiers.

"A lot? I don't know if I would say a lot. We've seen a decent amount, though," Bass answered.

"Oh, I was hoping that maybe they started to die off from starvation." I was hopeful.

"I don't think that'll be the case for a while. There are a lot of them out there. They just hunt in large groups now. They don't linger. They're on the move in search of what they need," Moyer interjected. "Personally, I think they're going to adapt. In fact, I think they've already started to. I noticed that their hunting skills have improved since the start of this. They are more successful at finding what they want."

"Is that what the military is saying?" Elana asked.

"No idea, like we said before, communication has been down for a few weeks—months now, at this point. I don't even know if there is anyone else left out there to communicate with," Bass informed us—his tone grim.

The world as we knew it was gone and it would never be the same—not in my lifetime. To hear that news was devastating. Before hearing that we were filled with hope that we would find refuge and rebuild our lives. I wanted to be able to have a normal life.

After hearing this upsetting news from the soldiers, then processing it, everyone's reaction seemed similar to my own. I had lost hope. What were we going to do once we finally got Lilianna? Then what? What was our purpose?

chapter forty-two

After chit-chatting for a while and getting to know one another, everyone turned in for the night. We had crossed the border into Indiana and gained two new members of our group—it had been a successful day.

I felt safer at night next to Carter, knowing he was there to protect me. Lying in his arms at night kept me warm. His soul comforted mine.

That night was cold— the chill raw against my skin. It was going to snow any day. I was hopeful that the snow would hold off until we were able to reach Lilianna.

I lied in bed, next to my furnace of a boyfriend, trying to filter through my dreams in search of a happy one, away from all the despair. I dreamed of sunflower fields and the sun warming my skin. Suddenly, something in my dream made repeated loud bangs.

The final bang jolted Carter and I awake. Those bangs weren't in my dream, it was real life. I was dreaming longer than I had thought. When I glanced out the window, there was evidence that it was the early hours of the morning. The sun was getting ready to rise.

"What the hell is that?" I asked Carter, foggy from sleep.

"It didn't sound good." He hopped out of bed, briskly pulling his shoes and coat on. He was nervous.

Another shot rang off. This time Carter had more clarity. "Those are gun shots. The undead must be outside." I was putting my shoes and coat on, prepared to fight off the undead. We quickly left the room. Upon entering the hallway, we realized that Logan and Elana had already gone downstairs and I began to panic.

We cautiously made our way downstairs, but there were no signs of the undead around. Elana ran into the room from outside, shouting for Carter. She was covered in blood. Her face was pale, and she stumbled over her words. "Carter...Carter... We need...Now!" He ran outside.

My insides were turning upside down and my brain was speeding a million miles a minute, "Logan?"

"Not him." Was all that she was able to speak. I was silently and selfishly relieved. I sprinted after Carter, filled with worry at who was injured. I needed to see for myself that Logan was okay.

Upon entering the scene outside, everyone was out there with despair written across their faces. On the ground was Logan leaning over a lifeless body, blocking the face so I couldn't tell who it was. Next to him, was Carter attempting to stop the blood that was pouring out of the body's chest, he was panicking. Normally, he was calm and collected in those situations but not then. I looked around at everyone, trying to figure out who was on the ground. Then it hit me—it was Doug.

"Oh my God. What happened?" I asked anyone who would give me an answer.

"Those piece-of-shit traitor soldiers did this," Quinn boldly responded.

"What? That doesn't make any sense. Why would they do that?" I questioned. I could not wrap my brain around it.

"They got up extra early this morning and were trying to take the SUV. Doug noticed, stood up to them and then they opened fire. They took off with the SUV and all of our supplies," Quinn quickly filled me in. I looked around and noticed that they indeed did steal it and most of our stuff. Even worse, they hurt someone in our group. They broke our trust that good people still existed in the world. Soldiers did this—men that we were supposed to trust with our lives.

Evan was kneeling on the ground next to Carter, covered in blood, tears streaming down his face. "Evan saw the whole thing happen but wasn't able to get out here fast enough because of his leg," Quinn added.

"That's probably a good thing. Otherwise, they could both be in this position," I responded before approaching the scene.

"What can I do or get you?" I asked Carter.

"Towels, sheets, something, anything to stop the bleeding," He responded and I turned to find them. Elana was already running out of the house with a pile of towels. She rushed up to us and handed them to him. He applied them to Doug's bleeding body. The towels instantly became saturated with blood.

"He's bleeding too much," Logan stated. Doug was not awake. His eyes were closed, and his mouth was open.

"He's been shot in more than one place." Carter was searching for exit wounds. He lay Doug's body back down and checked his pulse again. "I can't feel a pulse!" He immediately went into CPR mode and was vigorously trying to save his brother.

Carter performed CPR for a while. Several minutes had gone by. We watched the horrific scene unfold before our eyes, too stunned to say or do anything. He pounded away on his chest, desperate to save his brother. Finally, after too much time had gone by, Logan gently touched his hands while he continued CPR.

"Carter," he said in a gentle tone. Carter paused at his touch, staring down at his brother's lifeless body in disbelief. He put his fingers to his neck to check for a pulse one last time. He held his fingers there for a few seconds and then shook his head in anguish. Doug was gone.

"No!" Evan yelled, preparing to fling his body onto his twin. Carter caught him just in time before he landed on him.

The two men embraced each other, "He's gone," was all that Carter was able to choke out to him. The group fell quiet, the moment filled with grief.

I didn't know what to say or do in that moment. I felt awkward. We had been in that situation many times and it never got any easier. There was no logic behind his death, especially since he wasn't killed by the undead. He was killed by an alive person—a soldier.

Elana, on key as always: "Carter, Evan, I am so sorry for your loss. What can we do for you right now?" She was gentle, but direct. "Maybe we can clean him up a little and cover him up."

Carter managed to nod his head. He was staring down at his hands, which were covered in his brother's blood. His eyes looked distant, as if his mind had vacated his body. He seemed to be in shock.

I approached him gently, putting my arms around him. "Come on, let's get you cleaned up." He said nothing but mirrored my body language and stood. "Quinn, maybe you can help Evan out. Do you know where his quad cane is?"

"I will find it." He was off in seconds, in pursuit of the cane. Elana and Logan covered Doug's body with a sheet.

"You don't think that he'll come back...?" Evan began to question, his eyes filled with terror.

"I don't think so. He wasn't bit, he was shot," Logan explained. Evan nodded and looked back down. I ushered Carter inside and upstairs to the shower. We passed Quinn heading outside, cane in hand.

In the bathroom, of course, there was no hot water. The shower was not as soothing as one would have liked it to be. Instead, I sponge bathed him as he sat lost in thought, still in shock. I tried to be gentle and not alarming with the freezing cold water. Even in shock, his body still flinched every time the cold rag touched his skin. He managed to get blood everywhere. His clothes were saturated with blood. I would find him new ones.

I wrapped him in a towel and led him into the room we had slept in. I sat him on the bed and ravaged the closet for men's clothing. I was able to acquire a long-sleeved shirt and pair of sweatpants. I presented him with the clothes and he finally began to cry. Tears were rolling down his face, his expression still flat, but the tears were there. I wiped his tears away and enfolded him into my arms. I softly rocked him side to side as he wept on my shoulder.

When the tears dissolved, I tucked Carter back into bed even though the sun was on the rise. "Why don't you just rest for a little bit? I'm going to go check on things and make sure it's all okay. I'll be back soon." Carter nodded and rolled over. He takes such good care of me. It was my turn to take care of him.

chapter forty-three

With Carter tucked in, I went back downstairs to see what else needed to be done. Out front, Logan and Elana were sitting on the porch step, huddled together, and whispering. They turned at the sound of the door opening and quickly separated. They looked extremely suspicious.

"It's just Mya," Elana stated.

"What's the secret?" I asked on edge.

"There is no secret. These are just sensitive times and we don't want to make any one worry. We're just trying to figure out what to do next. We're not in the best situation at the moment," Elana explained. I nodded in agreement and glanced around at my surroundings for some type of answer.

The sun had begun to rise and was high enough in the sky I could see my surroundings. As my eyes grazed the scene, they landed on the corpse wrapped in a bed sheet. The white sheet was soaked through with blood, despite their best efforts. It was nicely wrapped and lay waiting for the next step.

"What do we even do with his body?" I asked, looking around. The temperature was bitter, my nose was freezing. "You won't be able to dig a hole, the ground is completely frozen over."

"That's the least of our problems right now," Logan responded in a low tone, careful to not be heard. "We are stranded here. They stole the SUV and they slashed the tires on the car." Logan had an edge in his tone. I knew it was better to let him work it out in his head, so I only nodded in response and kept quiet.

I continued scanning the scene, looking for signs of destruction. My eyes finally realized that, yes, the tires on the car were definitely slashed. What terrible people—soldiers or not. I wouldn't be surprised if they were posing as soldiers.

"Hey, I just had a thought," I announced, "What if they were posing as soldiers and they really have no idea what the world is like. Maybe there are still some safe zones out there." I knew I was being optimistic.

"They seemed like soldiers to me, their mannerisms were on point. If they were acting, then they certainly deserved an Emmy or whatever. They definitely had me fooled." Logan sighed and looked down at his feet. He trusted those men and Doug ended up dead. I could tell that weighed on his mind.

"It's always a possibility they were wrong about the safe zone. Once we get to Lilianna we can regroup and see what everyone wants to do next," said Elana, also being optimistic. We both knew deep down that there were likely no safe zones. The world was not a safe place.

We sat quietly for a minute, each of us lost in our own hopeless thoughts. None of us knew where to go. I just knew that we weren't giving up—we were so close to Lilianna.

"Logan, what's the plan?" I finally asked, hoping he had thought about it long enough.

"Seems to me like our only option at this point is to walk. We have no car and I don't see any around here. I don't remember passing many abandoned cars on the road. Walking is the only option. Luckily, I did take two of the backpacks out of the SUV last night, so we at least still have some supplies."

I nodded in response. I was not happy. I was pregnant and exhausted. Add a million miles of walking and forget it. Not to mention the fact it was freezing outside.

"When do you think we should leave? I don't want to rush them out of here, their brother was just murdered. I think they need time," I proposed.

"We don't need time, we're fine. We need to get back on the road," Carter appeared from behind us and interrupted our conversation.

"And what about Evan?" I questioned.

"I know my brother. He'll be fine to go today." He looked down before speaking again. "We need to do something with his body, though, I can't leave him on the lawn like that. I know it's too cold to bury him."

"Why don't you discuss this with Evan. Let us know how you want to take care of Doug's body and whether you want to leave or stay another day. You guys let us know what you want to do. We'll leave the ball in your court," Logan offered. He didn't respond verbally, just nodded and turned to find Evan.

The three of us remained on the porch. I looked over at Logan and was surprised that he had the sling on. He had been compliant for the most part, as much as he could be.

"How's your shoulder?" I asked.

"It's healing. I keep messing it up every time we have some type of issue which seems like all the time. I'm trying to wear this stupid thing more. It'd help if people stopped trying to kill us," He responded, half- joking, half-serious.

I was tired of sitting outside in the freezing cold for basically no reason. "I'm going back in. It sucks out here." I was not happy about having to walk.

Quinn was sitting alone in the living room. "Where are they?" I asked in a whisper. He pointed toward upstairs. I was glad that they were up there—just the two of them. They needed to have a difficult conversation and decide what to do. Their brother had just been murdered and we were already talking about leaving. There was no time for them to grieve. In the new world, grief was expedited, and you needed to move on to survive.

Quinn and I sat in silence. I stared out the window, watching the sun as it finished its climb and parked itself high in the sky. The sun allowed the dew to evaporate off the frosted grass blades. Once the sun had finished rising, Elana and Logan made their way inside to see if any decisions had been made. They joined us on the couch, and we waited.

Carter and Evan finally emerged shortly after Logan and Elana came inside. As they walked into the room their faces were filled with sorrow.

"We recognize that it's not fair to ask the rest of you to stay here another day when we had a clear plan in place," Carter started. "In normal circumstances we would stay behind and properly bury our brother. In these circumstances, we know that is not realistic. We are okay to leave here today with you as long as you are willing to give us some time with his body and allow us to find our own way to put him to peace," Carter proposed a compromise.

"No problem, man whatever you guys need to do. You have done so much for us already and have saved my life. You are our family now too. Anything that you need at all just let us know," Logan replied, he was turning soft.

Evan was grief-stricken and wasn't talking. The room became eerily quiet—none of us knew what to say. We felt the loss, it devastated our group.

Quinn, who didn't do well in awkward situations, decided to get up and move around. He wandered casually towards the window and peered out it by habit.

"Hey guys, I don't think we have a few hours. We should go now." Quinn's voice panicked and he slowly backed away from the window.

chapter forty-four

We collectively rushed to the window to see exactly what Quinn was talking about. Once again, my eyes saw something that I could never un-see. The undead, a mob of them, were coming down the driveway. They must have heard the gunshots. It took them a decent amount of time to find us—they must have come from a distance. That proved that they were indeed evolving.

In addition to the mob that was making its way toward the house, there were some that already made their way and found exactly what they were looking for—a snack. Doug's lifeless body lay there, being consumed by the undead. I watched in horror as the undead fought over his intestines and picked him to the bones.

Everyone stood there, stunned by what they were witnessing. Logan, as usual, quickly snapped out of it and jumped into survival mode. "Quick, we need to go, and we need to be quiet. They are distracted right now, and we need to take advantage of that. Quietly grab your belongings and meet at the back door." Logan went to grab the two backpacks that he luckily removed from the now stolen SUV. Everyone dispersed quickly but quietly, even Carter kicked it into gear now. We were in immense danger. Evan, frozen, stared out the window as his brother turned into zombie food. I gently touched his shoulder to usher him along and he complied.

As we were instructed, we quickly grabbed our belongings and were all waiting at the back door less than a minute later.

"Run straight back into these woods and put some distance between us and them. Once we get far enough, turn left and continue to follow the same road we were driving on." Logan then addressed Evan. "Where is your cane? You're going to need that. It's going to be a tough trip for you man."

He finally said something, "I'll be fine. I'm good without the cane." He didn't seem to be in the mood to deal with anything—he was trying to just suck it up and move on. I knew how he felt. I didn't want to be out wandering around in the cold woods, either. I had bundled myself up as much as I possibly could. I raided the closet, stealing scarfs and hats. I was even lucky enough to find a pair of gloves.

Logan put his hand on the doorknob and signaled for everyone to be quiet, "One, two, three," he mouthed. On three, the door opened, and we all sprinted as fast as we could straight back into the woods. It wasn't as cold as it was earlier when I first joined Logan and Elana on the porch. The booming sunshine helped to warm the temperature above freezing.

We sprinted straight back into the woods and then curved to the left. Evan and I, of course, were the slowest—him with his bum leg and me with my pregnancy. Carter hung out in the back with us, being protective. He was on edge—on the highest alert—constantly turning his head looking all over the place obsessively for any signs of the undead heading our way.

His paranoia rubbed off on me and I found myself frequently glancing over my shoulder. Every time I did look over my shoulder, it was all clear. The undead must have been distracted enough to not hear us run out the back door. That didn't mean that they wouldn't be close behind—they were evolving more and more each day.

We continued our run for what felt like forever. In reality, it was probably only ten minutes. We were trying to put as much distance between us and the mob of undead as possible. While everyone else continued to run, Evan and I began walking. Running wasn't for us, given our current medical conditions. It was going to be a long trip to Indiana State.

There was a great distance between us and the rest of the group, with Carter hanging out in the middle of the two. Up ahead it looked like the group had stopped allowing for us to catch up. I again looked over my shoulder and was relieved that there were no undead trailing behind me.

As we caught up with the rest of the group, the others were already sitting around on fallen trees taking sips of water. Finally, able to take a break, I parked myself on a fallen tree next to Elana who offered me some water. We had hardly started our journey on foot, and I was already exhausted. As we sat catching our breath, Logan became increasing more impatient and began pacing.

"The point of this rest stop is for everyone to rest and catch their breath, stop pacing around," I tried to reason with him.

"We shouldn't be resting—we need to keep moving. The undead won't be far behind us and this is wasting time." He was unsympathetic.

"That's easy for you to say, you're not pregnant running through the woods trying not to trip. And poor Evan is still having issues with his leg. He did get shot in it, remember?" I argued with him.

Everyone else remained quiet, letting us siblings hash it out real quick. Carter began to pace and craned his neck around searching for the undead.

"This fighting isn't helping anything either. Come on, we need to keep moving even if we are only walking," Carter sided with Logan. I sighed at the situation. I felt irritated. I never wanted to walk in the first place. I was getting colder the longer we were outside. The sun was out, but it didn't warm the temperature much since it was the dead of winter.

I motioned that I was about to stand up and everyone else instantly followed. Logan, Elana, and Quinn started slowly jogging. I refused to run at any speed. I would be walking the rest of the trip. I had decided that's what was the safest for my baby. I didn't want to exert myself.

We continued through the woods, trekking over fallen trees and boulders for what felt like an hour. We were free from the undead. If they were following us, they were a decent distance behind us. Hopefully, they were caught up back at that house. With that thought I was reminded about what happened to Doug all over again. I had blocked that out, hoping to never think of that terrible moment again. It was heartbreaking what happened to him, but thank god for that distraction, otherwise we would all probably be dead.

Up ahead, the rest of the group was again waiting on Evan and me to catch up. Once we caught up, I was happy to break for a minute to rest my feet. They were getting sore from the walking. My sense of time was off, and I had no idea how long we had been walking for or where the hell we were.

"So, does anyone know where we are now?" I asked. "Do we still have a map or something?"

"I honestly hadn't thought about the map, I was just wandering around," Logan stated sarcastically. He cleared his throat and became more serious. "My top priority was getting us to safety and keeping us safe, not the route. We need to find a road before we can even determine where we are," He stated the obvious.

"Don't you think that maybe we should have looked at this a while ago instead of just wandering around in the woods?" I was not happy.

"Maybe if you could keep up, then you would have heard all of us discussing this during the walk. Quinn has the map and we already knew that we needed a road to figure out where we are," He rebutted.

"This is not going anywhere, and it is, again, not helping." Elana had heard enough and was going to put an end to it. Logan always listened to her. "Mya and Evan are doing their best to keep up. Logan you can't act like this because of that. Now Quinn, get the map out and let's see if you can at least predict where we are compared to where we started and how long we walked." She was taking control of the situation. Everyone stopped their nonsense. He dug out the map and began to study it.

While he studied the map, I took the opportunity to separate myself so I could think in peace. I knew that I was being hormonal. It was a high stress situation physically and I was freezing my ass off. My brother's sour attitude always pushed my buttons. I took a few deep breaths and, for the sanity of the rest of our group, I decided to drop the attitude with Logan.

I wandered back to the group and heard Quinn explaining the map, "I think that we were somewhere around here, back at that house. If we left through the back of the property into wooded area, then I am assuming that we came through this way and are probably somewhere in here." He pointed to various spots on the map, estimating where we were located.

"If your calculations are right and we are here, then where do we need to go and what are we looking for?" Evan asked.

"If I'm right, given that we have been walking for what feels like hours, we must be somewhere around Centerville," Quinn pointed showing us.

"That's hardly any progress." Logan's irritation continued.

Quinn ignored him and continued, "We need to continue down this way and find a road so we can verify that's where we are. If we are where I think, then we are still on track and heading in the right direction to the school."

"Glad that's figured out, let's move." Logan picked up the backpack and started in the direction of the school. As we picked up our pace, I wondered how much daylight we had left. The sun was high in the sky—it was past noon. I predicted we had a few hours left of daylight. Better make those hours count.

chapter forty-five

We had been walking for what felt like an eternity. We barely had any breaks, just a few minutes at a time. Most of the breaks consisted of the rest of the group waiting on Evan and me, so the two of us ended up not getting much of a break. We had been walking long enough the sun was setting and nightfall would soon take over. During our walk we found a road and verified that Quinn's predictions were correct. We were in the Centerville area. That had been hours before. I didn't know where we were anymore.

"How long have we been walking?" I asked Carter, who kept pace next to me.

"I don't know, maybe around three or four hours. We'll find a place to sleep for the night soon, the sun is going to set shortly," Carter responded. *Three or four hours.* I hoped we had covered a decent amount of ground.

Up ahead the others were waiting on us. Hopefully, they wanted to turn in for the night too. I could not wait to get off my sore feet. They throbbed with each step.

"We should find a good resting point," Logan stated as we caught up to the others.

"Has anyone seen anything? I haven't seen a building since we left," I announced.

"There have been some—they are few and far between," Elana mentioned.

"Maybe we should walk more in this direction and try to stay a little closer to the actual road and hope we come across something." Quinn pointed to the left.

"Why don't we look at the map again?" Evan suggested.

"The map doesn't show where houses are," Quinn paused, gathering his thoughts. "Without a landmark I'm not even sure where we are right now. Trying to find a road again would help, then I'll have some idea of where we are. We've just been wandering from wooded area to wooded area hoping we're on the right path," Quinn admitted.

No one was shocked at his admission. I didn't think any of us had any idea of where we were. We were in Indiana, that much I knew.

"We really don't have much of a choice but to keep walking until we find some type of shelter for the night. The sun will set in a little bit and then the temperature is going to drop even more." Logan pointed forward. "I say we continue on in the right direction, or so I hope, and I'm sure we'll find a place."

Without further discussion, Logan took off. Everyone was too exhausted to even want to discuss it further and followed suit.

We walked again for what felt like forever before Evan pointed something out. "Hey look, over there!" He shouted and pointed towards our left. The sun was definitely going down, dusk was taking over. Soon it would be dark, and we were still outside.

Logan rushed next to Evan to see what he was looking at. "Where? I don't see anything."

"Right there, that headstone," Evan said and again pointed.

"Uhm?" Logan was confused by how that was helpful.

"A headstone, it might be a cemetery. Cemeteries have mausoleums that you can sleep in and they also probably have an office," Evan explained.

"How would you think of that?" Carter questioned.

"I spent a summer mowing the lawns of a few cemeteries. Anyway, what do you think? Worth a shot, right?"

"I'm not the biggest fan of staying overnight in a cemetery when our whole life is defined by outlasting the undead. The office, eh maybe. The mausoleum, I don't think so. Dead people are in there," Quinn protested.

"Obviously, sleeping in a cemetery isn't ideal. When push comes to shove, it's about to be dark and it could potentially be shelter for us for the night. Desperate times call for desperate measures." Carter was trying to talk some sense into him.

"Let's not waste anymore daylight and get a move on, then." Quinn changed directions to the left and took off toward the cemetery.

We approached the cemetery from the back. At first, I didn't believe that it was a cemetery—there were hardly any graves. The longer and further we walked, tombstones appeared more frequently and then constantly. We stopped in the middle of the cemetery, searching for a sign displaying the name of the cemetery. I did not want to stay in a mausoleum.

"Does anyone see anything helpful?" Logan asked.

"It's eerily quiet here, making this even creepier. Does anyone have a flashlight?" I asked.

"In the bag that Carter is carrying," Logan answered. Carter turned around and I searched the bag, finding the flashlight. I turned it on and held it close, it helped to ease my nerves.

It was nightfall and we had no place to sleep. We stood in the middle of a cemetery surrounded by tombstones while trying to survive during a zombie apocalypse. It couldn't get any more cliché than that.

"If we think logically about this, we entered the cemetery from the back. Keep going straight to find the entrance with a sign and office." Elana was attempting to quickly solve the pressing issue at hand.

"We came from this way, so we need to go this way. Come on." Logan was off on the task.

We quickly found the entrance to the cemetery along with a sign and a ridiculously small office. Walking up to the sign, Logan shined the flashlight on it, revealing its name: South Lawn. Logan then proceeded to the small office. We could sit cross-legged on the floor and even that would be tight. Given the size of the room, there wasn't much room for furniture. There was a desk with a computer and chair on each side of it and a small table in the corner with two chairs. That was the room. It was not big enough for six people to lay down and sleep.

Once inside the office, we immediately began to search for something with an address on it. Elana searched the desk drawers and quickly exclaimed "Got something!" Logan shined the flashlight onto the envelope she had found, revealing that we were 'in Cambridge City. Quinn brought the map back out and placed it on the desk.

"Here, this is where we are now." Quinn pointed it out on the map. "Here is where the college is."

"Oh my god, we still have so long to go. We barely covered any ground today with walking. It's going to be weeks before we actually get over there." I started to panic.

"It will be okay. We will walk for weeks if that's what it takes to get to her," Logan tried to reassure me.

"Logan, I physically can't walk for weeks. I am exhausted from today. My body and feet can't handle that. A few days, sure, but weeks, I don't know." I felt defeated.

Quinn interjected, "By the looks of the map, it looks like we aren't too far from the main road that runs through town. Maybe we can go there tomorrow and see if we can find any vehicles."

"Great idea, Quinn. That's the next plan. Everyone try to get some rest, we will move out at sunrise," Logan instructed us, sounding like he was back on duty.

I nestled myself in a corner between two walls, hoping that would help me to sleep better. Carter snuggled up next to me, attempting to keep me warm. Logan was right, the temperature had dropped as soon as the sun went away. I closed my eyes, thinking and wishing for warmer places.

chapter forty six

Everyone was exhausted and, despite the incredibly uncomfortable sleeping arrangements, we all slept, even Logan. Since everyone slept that meant no one had kept watch.

The next morning, we slowly began to wake up. "Did we all sleep all night long?" I asked.

"Oh my god, no one kept watch!" Logan instantly leapt up from the floor checking out the window and then dashing for the door. Logan flung the door open and a little pile of snow fell into the office. It snowed last night.

That quickly got everyone's attention. Within seconds everyone was on their feet, making their way toward the door to see with their own eyes.

"Shit!" Logan cursed. I felt the same way. I double blinked my eyes to make sure it was real. The snow had fallen hard and fast, and apparently all night long. There was at least a foot of snow on the ground.

"How did we not hear this?" I questioned.

"We did a lot of walking yesterday. All of our bodies were exhausted, they demanded rest," Carter explained.

"This is going to make traveling impossible," Quinn stated, still staring out at the snow. "I guess we'll just wait this storm out here."

"No, we need to leave. We can't stay here through a snowstorm. This place is basically a closet, nowhere to go to the bathroom, no food, and no running water. This is not an option," Carter argued.

"What's your plan?" Quinn questioned. Carter stayed quiet—he didn't have a plan.

"The chairs. We can pop those backs out and use them as snowshoes," Logan suggested pointing to the chairs we stacked in the corner the night before.

"There are only four chairs, we have six people. Only two people will have them," Elana challenged.

"Each chair can be made into a pair if I do it right. So then four people will have them. Obviously, Evan and Mya, given their current physical status. I figured Elana should get one. I'm fine to not use them, I have my boots on." Logan pointed to them.

"You can use them, Quinn. I'll be fine," Carter offered.

"Then it's settled. Quickly, let's break down the chairs. Quinn and Carter why don't you help with that? Do the rest of you mind looking for something to secure them in place with?" He directed the rest of us.

It didn't take long to break the chairs down and collect paper clips, tape—whatever we could find that might hold them in place. Within minutes, the shoes were rigged and on our feet.

"Where to?" I asked.

"We are right off the main road. I'm sure there's a town. Let's look to see if they have any vehicles. Walking all the way to the college in this is impossible," Quinn suggested.

We prepared ourselves for our long, cold, wet journey. We battled our way through the snowstorm to get back on route and find a town. There was no point in finding another car. The roads were covered in snow, and there were no plow trucks anymore. The snow would hopefully slow down any undead. We quickly found the main road and began to look for anything that would be of use.

"What's that sign say up there?" Elana asked. She squinted her eyes, trying to see through the falling snow.

"ATV!" Logan jumped up and down. No one else was that excited. "It's a place that has four-wheelers and snow mobiles. It's exactly what we need." He began heading towards the ATV shop.

"Don't get ahead of yourself. That place could be empty for all you know," Elana warned.

As we approached the ATV shop, we took notice that the undead were lingering around the shop. I was right, the snow did slow the undead down; they struggled to get their feet out of the snow. We made a plan to divide and conquer, quickly taking them down. Instead of looking for a way in, Logan smashed the window on the door to unlock it from the inside.

We quickly rushed inside, out of the blistering cold, wintery mix that continued to fall from the sky. Surprisingly, the place had been untouched and there were plenty of ATV's available. We frantically began searching for the keys.

"I think I got them!" Elana hollered out from the manager's office. Elana pointed toward a locked display case on the wall.

Logan, wasting no time, grabbed the desk phone and began smashing it against the display case shattering the glass. "Everyone grab some keys and start trying some out. I think we'll only need three ATV's. Look for the ones with the most gas."

All the commotion we caused gained the attention of the undead and they began to throw themselves against the windows, trying to get in. The longer the undead banged on the windows the more undead they attracted. We needed to move fast. We quickly identified three working ATVs with full gas tanks. Logan and Elana shared one, I rode on the back of Carter's and Evan rode on the back of Quinn's. I giggled at Evan awkwardly embracing Quinn to hang on.

"Do you know which way to go, Quinn?" Logan asked. Logan rode on the back of Elana's ATV due to his shoulder injury and was not happy about it. Quinn nodded in response.

"How do we get out of here with these?" Carter asked.

Logan examined the room and identified an exit, "Look at the ceiling, this window opens up like a garage door. I'll lift it up, we just need to go ASAP, or the undead will over run us." Logan took his place, nodded his head, and opened the garage-like door. We instantly stepped on it, rushing out of the shop. Logan hopped onto the back of Elana's ATV with ease. We were back on the right path. We were hours away from Lilianna.

chapter forty-seven

Using the ATVs was much more efficient than walking all the way to the school. We rode for, what I assumed, was two to three hours before we pulled over to re-examine the map. We stayed on the main road the entire drive, hardly passing any undead. The undead that we did see were stuck in the snow. The snow made traveling harder for us, but almost impossible for the undead. It continued to snow outside but lightened as time went on. The bitter cold bit at my cheeks as we drove through the falling snow.

I needed to stretch my legs and warm my cheeks—I needed a break. Carter signaled the others to pull over. We pulled into the parking lot of a breakfast joint and dismounted the ATVs. Approaching the building, we searched for a way inside.

We quickly found an entrance. I yanked on the door handle and to my surprise the door opened. I stepped into the restaurant and the others followed. The floor was littered with dishes, condiments, and trash. The place looked like it had already been picked apart. We each took a seat at a booth. I leaned against the window and put my feet up to rest. No one bothered to look for food, we knew there was none.

Quinn examined the map, "Anyone see anything with an address on it? I think I know what town we're in, but I want to make sure."

Carter got up and went behind the counter, quickly returning with a menu with the address on it. "Here."

"Indianapolis," he murmured, eagerly studying the map in search of our street. "Right here!" He pointed. "We are just on the outskirts of Indianapolis. That's a major city, I don't know about going through it."

"Can I see that?" Logan asked taking the map from Quinn. Logan's facial expression showed he was worried as well. "It looks possible to go around."

"It's still early enough in the day. Do you think we can get to her today?" I asked.

"We still have half a tank of gas, that should be enough, right?" Elana asked.

Logan studied the map a little longer before answering. "I think that we might get to her today. We still have half a day of sunlight and plenty of gas left." Logan hopped up in excitement. "Let's get back on the road."

Out the door and back into the blistering cold, we mounted our snow mobiles and set off on the race to get to our sister.

A few hours had gone by before we saw the pillars that proudly read *Indiana State University*. The snow had let up, but the miserable wind was still lingering. The beautiful fountain that normally boomed with life, was currently frozen over and buried in snow. A campus that normally bustled with students on their way to class, was dead. Not a soul in sight—no one alive or undead. My heart sank. I silently prayed she was still alive and waiting for us to rescue her.

"Mya, do you remember which way to her dorm?" Logan asked.

I tried to remember, looking around at my surroundings. We were by the fountain and welcome center, basically at the heart of the campus. "She didn't directly live on campus but a short walk away. It was the unit 3 apartments."

"Do you remember which way to go to get there?" Logan asked again.

I again studied my surroundings, everything looked different under the snow, "I'm not sure."

"Start looking for a campus map," Logan directed.

"Over here!" Quinn announced. We quickly joined Quinn and studied the map. Within seconds I was able to identify which direction to go.

"Over here. She lives in the Wabash place." I pointed. We sped through the mounds of snow rushing to get to Lilianna—trying to make up for those last few months by saving a few minutes.

When we arrived at the apartment building, I remembered exactly which way to go. I hopped off the ATV and immediately rushed inside to get to her. I wasn't careful and I didn't care, I needed to see her. My pregnancy limited my pace more than I realized. Logan blew by me just as eager to see her. As usual, he was more methodical and scanned the area for the undead. "Second floor!" I yelled after him.

I was so slow that everyone caught up to me and we arrived at her apartment together. The walls in the hallway were coated with dried blood and there were dead bodies rotting against the walls. The college was impacted just the same as the rest of the world. I suddenly developed a knot in my stomach. Logan kicked in the door, revealing an empty apartment. Her belongings were there but it didn't look like she had been for a while. There wasn't any sign of a struggle in there—no blood. It looked like she left in a hurry. She never finished her breakfast. It was moldy and rotting on the plate.

Logan quickly made his way into her bedroom and then into the bathroom. He came back empty handed.

"Look!" Elana pointed to the wall. We were all so busy looking for her that we missed the huge message written across her wall in lipstick. *GOING TO LIBRARY. X.*

"The survivors must have joined together and moved themselves to the library. A large central environment, they probably thought that a search party would look for them there," Elana spoke.

"Let's go to the library then. Mya do you remember where that is?" Logan asked me.

"I think the library is back near the welcome center. I would need to see a map again."

chapter forty-eight

Back in the center of campus, where we started; we examined the map again, searching for the library. All the zipping around campus was drawing attention to us. The ATVs were noisy and the undead began to emerge from wherever they were hiding. The unplowed roads and un-shoveled sidewalks helped to slow them down. If we didn't get a move on, they would catch up to us.

Carter quickly identified the library on the map, which was in the opposite direction of Lilianna's apartment. Hopefully, she made the journey safely and she was sitting there waiting for us to show up.

From the back of the ATV I admired the sign informing us that we had arrived at the library. The ride over from the cemetery was not an easy one. The entire journey wasn't an easy one. The snow hid the dead bodies. Occasionally one of the wheels would hit something and jolt the vehicle, deep down I knew we just ran over someone's head. I quickly learned to stop looking back. One glance at the red stained snow was more than enough.

The building had a traditional over-hang above the main entrance, lined with multiple double doors. Around the building were floor-length windows, allowing you to see straight inside. Logan dismounted the ATV and searched for a way in. The front door was barricaded shut, keeping the undead out. Carter and Quinn joined Logan as they searched for an entry point. I looked over at Evan who was staring off into space.

"You alright?" I asked.

He shook his head and nervously pointed in the direction he was staring.

Nothing was ever easy. Off in the distance the undead lingered. The undead following us had tripled in numbers. The snow had slowed them down, but they were determined to get to us. They were driven by hunger. Nothing could stop them from getting their next meal.

"We need to pick it up, the undead are coming," I informed the others.

Everyone frantically searched for a way inside the library. I leaned against a window searching for any type of movement inside—I saw nothing.

"These kids are smart and came here for a reason. They knew that it would be impossible for the undead to get in here. That's why they picked this place. You can see right in these windows. They wouldn't just hang out here. They have to be somewhere in the center of the building, away from the windows and the doors," I explained.

"She's right. Split up, each half take a side and start banging on the windows and try to get their attention. Make sure they realize that you are alive though and not undead. At this point it doesn't matter if we make noise or not, the undead are coming either way," Logan instructed us. Without wasting another second, we split up. Logan and Elana went right, Carter and Quinn went left, and Evan and I were told to wait at the front and keep watch.

Time felt like it was dragging by and the undead continued to inch closer to us.

After what felt like forever, Carter and Quinn re-emerged after being gone for too long. Carter shook his head, no luck on their side. The four of us sat around and continued to wait for Logan and Elana growing more nervous by the second. The undead were just a couple streets away, they would be here in minutes.

"We need to move. They are getting too close." Quinn stood up and began pacing.

Out of the corner of my eye I saw movement behind me from inside the library, I jumped and turned in defense. I expected to turn around and see an undead, but I was wrong. At first, I thought the entire doorway was blocked off by various items shoved against it. Most of it was, however, the door all the way to the right wasn't. At the doorway was where the figures stood. It was not an undead. It was a girl. Next to that girl was Logan and Elana—they must have found a way in. At first my heart stopped, and I thought that girl was Lilianna. I almost hugged her. I was disappointed when I realized it wasn't Lilianna.

"I was getting worried" I said to Logan as I approached them.

"I know. We found a way in. I explained to Beth who we are and why we are here." Logan pointed to the girl. "She was kind enough to let us in and come let you guys in. She said Lilianna is here!"

"Hurry up and get in, the undead followed you here," Beth snapped.

I turned to see and the undead were there. We rushed into the library and assisted Beth with re-blocking the doorway. As we placed a desk against the doorway, the first undead lunged his body at the door. I looked past him and there were many more that followed.

"This will hold them, right?" I asked Beth.

"It did the first time," She responded and walked away. "We don't stay right here with all the windows, it's not safe. We live within the bookcases where we can hide."

The rest of us quickly followed Beth. I ran to catch up and walk beside her. "Lilianna is here?"

Beth nodded her head and picked up her pace, she was not in the mood to chat. The library was bigger than I expected. After a few turns we arrived at the area they called home.

My eyes scanned the room searching for her face. Finally, they landed on her. She was in the corner lying on her back with her feet against the wall reading a book. *That's my Lilianna.*

295

"Hey Lil. I think your people found you," Beth hollered over. Lilianna shot straight up and turned—her eyes locked with mine.

Lilianna jumped up and raced over to us. I opened my arms wide for her and she leapt into them. "I knew that you guys would find me!" Logan ran over and embraced both of us and the three of us stood there holding each other for a minute. I was so incredibly grateful for that moment.

I pulled myself away and took a good look at her. She looked okay considering the condition of the world. As I examined her, she examined me and realized that I had a growing belly.

"Oh my god! You're pregnant?!" She exclaimed.

"Yeah! It's a girl!" I jumped up and down with excitement. I was excited to finally share the news with my sister.

"Congratulations. I am so happy for you!" Lilianna looked around at our group. "Where is Scott?"

"He didn't make it. We lost him a long time ago, in the very beginning," I said avoiding eye contact with her, trying not to cry.

Lilianna pulled me with her, taking a seat on the floor. "Relax everyone. It sounds like we have a lot to discuss."

We mingled together, learning about each other's group members. I filled Lilianna in on how Scott died, how we met Carter, Evan, and Quinn. We even told her about those we had lost along the way.

During those conversations I learned that Lilianna had pretty much been living inside of the library since the beginning of the cure of doom. They take turns running out to the campus to search for food and supplies. Lilianna had explained that their group was once much bigger, they also lost people. Aside from Lilianna and Beth, there were only four other survivors. They periodically searched the campus for anyone still alive. Rarely would they find people, they usually just found the undead. The other students' names were Donald, Steve, Kim, and Tina. Like Lilianna, they all left notes in the rooms for their loved ones stating where to find them. Other than us, there have only been two other families to make it to them. The rest of the students were still waiting for their families to arrive.

chapter forty-nine

Everyone had been distracted, eager to talk to new people. I knew in the back of my mind that the undead were still outside. We were so caught up in discussion that my mind blocked out the growls and noises that came from the main entrance as the undead continued to try to find a way in.

Beth, who was not a social butterfly, heard a noise and announced she was going to check on things. I had been busy catching up with Lilianna, so I didn't realize she hadn't come back.

"Lilianna, where is your friend Beth at? She went to check on things a while ago." With that, I had panicked the entire group. Everyone was up and searching for Beth. People split up in different directions. The growls were now coming from all over, making it hard to tell where exactly they were coming from.

I stayed with Lilianna holding her hand, not willing to let go of her again. From the far-left corner, came a woman's shriek. "Beth!" Lilianna yelled.

Everyone quickly rushed to where we heard Beth's screams.

The undead had made their way into the library. They captured Beth and were feasting on her innards. We were too late. I held Lilianna as she wept for her friend.

Before anyone realized what was happening, we were quickly surrounded by the undead. They were pouring in from outside. All the exit points lead to more undead. We were trapped. "Oh my God! What are we going to do?" Elana panicked.

"We fight," Logan responded and then stabbed an undead in the head. Each person had to fight for their life. I held the baseball bat and began swinging, making contact after contact, blowing the undead away. I heard screams coming from my left. I turned to see Donald being ripped to shreds by two undead. Inside I panicked more, on the outside I fought harder. I was not going to come all that way and die.

Everyone gave it their all, but there were too many of the undead pouring in from outside. We, inch by inch, moved away from the undead entry point and back into the main part of the library. The further back we moved the more room we allowed for the undead to continue to move in. They were being strategic—they were cornering us.

My arms ached with each swing; I couldn't do that for much longer. "Logan what is the plan?"

He looked at me but said nothing. He had no plan. I turned around and scanned my environment. Our only option was to pick a door and take our chances on the other side. At least we would be out in the open and not cornered.

"Pick a door and take a chance?" I hollered over growls of the undead and screams of the dying. Without hesitation, Carter chose an exit. He tore down the barricade and kicked open the door. Waiting for us on the other side of the door was more undead. There were less of the undead outside than inside. While Carter tried to clear a path for us to get out, we still fought them off from the inside. We were losing the battle.

Tina tripped on an undead, landing on her hands and knees. Within seconds the undead utilized that moment of weakness and jumped her. Tina screamed as they ripped her flesh, consuming her. Instinctively, Lilianna reached for her to help and the undead tried to drag her down.

Quinn had been standing next to Lilianna. He saw what was about to happen, and intervened. Quinn pushed Lilianna back, causing him to fall in the opposite direction. Quinn fell backwards into the undead and the undead devoured him, biting into all his limbs and tore them from his body. Blood sputtered from his arteries as they feasted. "Kill me!" Quinn yelled. My heart sank as I watched another friend die. Logan drew his gun and took aim. He shot Quinn in the forehead, putting him out of his misery.

"Move!" Carter yelled, ushering everyone out of the library. There was no time to grieve. Our group of twelve, their six and our six, had quickly diminished to eight. Everyone pushed their way through the door and continued to run once outside. Carter slammed the door shut behind us, trapping the undead inside.

I scanned the area; Carter had killed all the undead immediately near us. Off in the distance you could see the undead piling into the library. They were looking for us, but trapping themselves in.

"That was a good plan." I kissed Carter, so happy to have made it out of there. Then I thought of Quinn and my stomach did a flip. I stopped celebrating. I went over and hugged Lilianna, so happy that she was alive. She would be dead if it weren't for Quinn. I hugged her long with my eyes closed. I silently prayed to Quinn and thanked him for saving my sister.

"What are we supposed to do now?" Lilianna asked.

"Let the undead continue to pile into the library and we lock them in. We are trapping a huge mob, giving us a great advantage" Carter answered.

"Once the undead are trapped, we can get back to the ATVs. We can go anywhere. Steve and Kim, you are more than welcome to join us," Logan offered.

"But where do we go?" Lilianna asked again.

"We find home," I simply replied, thinking back to that scarlet oak tree.

epilogue
two years later

I stood on the porch and admired Scarlett as she sat playing underneath everyone's favorite scarlet oak tree.

So much had changed over the past two years—and for the better. The journey back from Indiana State, well that's another story. It was filled with its own obstacles and crazy shenanigans. It didn't take us long to decide where to go. Along the way we lost Steve and Kim—for two different reasons—but our core six stuck together. We also gained new friends and lost more along the way.

Once we returned to Pennsylvania, we went back to the church with the scarlet oak tree where Scott's things were buried. Even though we'd experienced so much loss at the church, it was a place we all liked, and the tree had made an impression on all of us.

We turned the place into home. We refurbished the church and lived out of there while we built individual houses. We had our own community. Our community was secluded and had fencing all around to help keep any straggling undead out. The undead were still out running the world. We just co-existed with them, there was no other way. We stayed put and defended our community.

Carter and I were doing well. He proposed right after Scarlett was born. We got married here at the church right under the tree. Scarlett was nearly two. She looked just like me with soft blonde hair. Best of all were her goofy smile and laugh. I watched her play tea party. I rubbed my belly. Carter and I were expecting another baby. We didn't know the gender and I wouldn't risk going to town to find out either. I was predicting a boy though.

Logan and Elana were also married and trying to have kids. Their house was built directly next to ours and we spent all our time together. The same goes for Lilianna, her house was built on the other side of mine. She lives with Evan, they started dating not long after we started our journey back to Pennsylvania. Evan's leg healed completely, and he was healthier than ever.

I joined my daughter under the scarlet tree and told her stories of the journey that we had survived and the people that had helped along the way. I spoke of those that we lost and those that were still a part of our lives. I cherished each one of those people because without them, I wouldn't be able to hold my daughter. Carter had joined us under the scarlet tree, and we watched the sunset as we snuggled Scarlett—thankful to be alive.

UNDER THE
scarlet tree

about the author

D anielle R. Wilson grew up in Bucks County, Pennsylvania. She has a master's degree in Social Work from Temple University and works full-time as a medical social worker. Wilson accepted a dare from her mother to 'write a book' during the time Zombies were all the rage—Under the Scarlet Tree was the result. When Wilson isn't reading and writing, she enjoys spending time with family and friends. Wilson loves lazy weekends at home with her husband, Dan, and two cats, Sadie and Silas. This is Wilson's first novel.